H is disappointment soon turned to feverish excitement, however, as he watched Mademoiselle d'Elbernne sit down on a low wooden bench and begin to unlace her boots.

Mademoiselle d'Elbernne drew off her left boot and began to unlace her right.

Prince Rupert was captivated by her prettily arched bare foot, and the curving swell of her calf and ankle. Her riding trousers terminated just beneath her knees like short knickers.

Prince Rupert settled down to a slow, even rhythm and watched intently, desperate to time his climax with her most mouthwatering exhibition.

CINDERELLA

Titian Beresford

Cinderella
Copyright © 2002 by Titian Beresford
All Rights Reserved

No part of this book may be reproduced, stored in a retrieval system, or transmitted in any form, by any means, including mechanical, electronic, photocopying, recording or otherwise, without prior written permission from the publisher and author.

First Magic Carpet Inc. edition February 2002

Published in 2002

Manufactured in th United States of America
Published by Magic Carpet Books

Magic Carpet Books
PO Box 473
New Milford, CT 06776

cover design: stella by design contact: stellabydesign@aol.com

A Sonnet To The Goddess Circe

(The loveliest of tormentors, the fairest of the cruel)

To view the obsessive weakness in a gaze,
To know that one enthralled is but a toy,
To goad and pout and tease them gently on,
To what more keen torment could they aspire?

Bind them then in fetters at your feet.
Impale them with your laughter soft and cruel.
Enslave them with your chains of fetish dress.
Harness them like beasts in bondage fast.

Watch them fawning at their captors' heels.
Seal their fate with silk and satin bonds.
Giggle while they spurt their worship forth,
In captivated tribute to delight.

Revel in the power of your hold!
Savor all the sweetness of their plight!

—Margravine Godilieva Prumm

Chapter One

Six plumed and prancing horses drew the prince's carriage through the streets of Calauverge. High atop the carriage, liveried guards in the colors of the royal palace accompanied the driver and glanced with narrowed eyes through the milling crowds below. It was imperative that the safety of the heir of the ruling house of Targete be guaranteed, even in the central confines of his own kingdom.

An ornate, braided whip curled and cracked harmlessly high above the broad backs of the splendid horses—inspiring them rather than compelling them to perform their most stylized high steps. The pretty young dressage trainer, Mademoiselle Seline d'Elbernne, was a perfectionist, and it showed even in the gait of the carriage horses from the royal stables.

Prince Steven Targete reclined against the velvet cushions of the carriage and enjoyed the compelling caresses which Lady Jane Broughton so freely bestowed. Bent succulently at the waist, the barebottomed beauty held her skirts up with one hand, and with the other reached back to gently manualize the noble penis.

The pouting girl studied the prince's face for a moment, then dropped her eyes to the blushing crimson head of his sex organ. Allowing herself a brief satisfied smile, the forward beauty began to slowly lower her broad white buttocks, holding the prince's penis just so with her hand, and carefully steering it so that it might be properly engulfed.

The prince gasped as he felt the sliding clench of Lady Jane's circlet slowly swallow his girth and descend. His eyes grew haggard as with her spotlessly gloved hand Lady Jane reached up to check that every hair was impeccably in place—even as she settled herself down to the very base of his penis and began a lewd squirming motion with her hips.

The prince bit his lip as his eyes were drawn through the ivory scrollwork of the carriage's glass window even while his penis pulsed deliciously between the full globes of Lady Broughton's backside. There, below the carriage window, on high tiptoe, stood an exquisite little barefoot beauty. Her back was to the prince's carriage but he found the sight captivating nonetheless. The pretty, feminine curves of her calves did nought but accentuate the trim petite allure of the anonymous girl. The prince's eyes took the time to linger on the perfection of her ankles and the rounded artistry of her bare heels, as the carriage had come to a full stop due to the press of the crowd.

From his private vantage point, then, the prince had ample leisure to admire the anonymous girl, even while Lady Jane was pleasuring his royal person. The barefoot beauty's attention joined that of the rest of the market day crowd, in focusing upon the events unfolding in the central square. Beneath blue and yellow festive pennants, three pastrycook's girls were toying with a pilloried prisoner.

The girls laughed with glee and pulled the naked prisoner's erect penis roughly about in their floured hands and soundly spanked his bared buttocks. The crowd was ecstatic in its admiration of the festive sport and spared no effort in cheering on the lascivious girls. The poor unfortunate in the pillory tried to dance about with a comical twist of his naked hips in hopeful attempt of avoiding their maddening caresses. Of course—severely limited as he was by the stock of the pillory and its clasp about his neck and wrists—he found himself helpless to escape these indignities.

As the crowd roared its approval, the prince's eyes swept down from the scaffold to again find the pretty little feet of the young woman, who stood tiptoed in her eagerness to see such degradation. The barefoot girl's calves tensed lusciously as she stood fetchingly in the highest tiptoed stance it was possible for her to assume. Prince Steven's eyes caressed her highly arched, wrinkled soles, and the faint horizontal creases of her bare heels.

His eyes swept upward occasionally to the scaffold as if to quickly keep abreast of events there, and then swept downward again to adore the feet of the pretty, barefoot girl.

The three pastrycook's girls were shameless, and highly amused by their good fortune in teasing the penis of the hapless pilloried prisoner—as well as in generally showing off for the market day crowd. Two of them clasped the big organ in their hands and began to flog it in earnest, while the third shook the raven locks from her eyes and held forth a basket to catch the inevitable discharge of semen.

The prince's penis, meanwhile, was firmly ensconced

in the delectable posterior of Lady Jane Broughton, who, not content with just the physical exercise inherent in the carnal act, also found a thin volume of sonnets worthy of intellectual occupation as well. The jaded young woman was long a lover of contrasts, and savored the rigidly formalized verses while delighting in the sensation of being probed by Prince Steven Targete's royal organ.

The prince's orgasm, when it came, coincided exactly with the forced ejaculation of the pilloried wretch on the scaffold. As the giggling pastrycook's girls drew the prisoner's strength from him, to the cheers of the watching crowd, the prince's penis jolted and thrust in Lady Jane's backside. Though his seed spurted deeply into the proud young woman, Prince Steven's glazing eyes remained locked on the lovely little foot of the anonymous tiptoed girl in the market day crowd, the smooth-calved little beauty attentively watching the humiliation on the scaffold.

Lady Jane Broughton, who had long prided herself on her ability to accommodate a very large male organ such as Prince Steven's in her backside, was nevertheless annoyed at the discomfort occasioned her when he abruptly withdrew. She wrinkled her nose a bit in refined distaste as the big royal penis spilled the last of its passion across her left globe as it slid from her still-clenching circlet.

The prince apologized as he collected himself and drew up his riding pants, buckling them quickly. "I have seen an old friend in the crowd, my lady," said he. "I shall be but a moment and I crave your pardon."

With that Prince Steven opened the ornate glass-and-filigree door and leapt down from the carriage, closely followed by two startled royal guards—who well knew the penalty if any harm should come to the person of their precious liege.

Cinderella

Lady Jane clutched her cloak and held it to her bare buttocks lest some lad in the crowd outside the carriage soil her noble dishabille with his eyes. She gave vent to an unladylike exclamation of outrage and disgust, then reached outward to slam the carriage door shut.

The prince cut a dashing figure in his long argent coat with gold epaulettes, crimson sash and high riding boots. Many young women in the crowd tried to catch his eye—but his thoughts were only of the barefoot girl, who had by then quite vanished. Many eager young ladies, who moments before had cheered the pastrycook's girls as they masturbated and spanked the pilloried prisoner, now blushed modestly and endeavored to catch the prince's eye with their beauty and innocence.

The prince's question, "Have you seen the pretty young barefoot girl in the green dress?" was met with helpful inquiries, respectful attention and hopeful ideas, but such responses came to no avail. Even the scowling efficiency of some royal dragoons in the crowd could not help the prince find her.

CHAPTER TWO

High on the hillside above the Market Square, higher even than the Madeira vineyards of Challon and Pompere, King Philip, the father of Prince Steven Targete, was in deep conference with his trusted chamberlain, Lord Rodney Fallone. A breeze laden with floral scents gently drifted through the open stained glass window that overlooked the gardens of the palace's south lawn. The sapphire- and diamond-encrusted ring on Lord Rodney's left index finger caught the sunlight as he gestured helplessly:

"I fear it to be a daunting puzzle at best, my lord—truly a Gordian knot—and we haven't a blade sharp enough to cut it asunder."

The king listened quietly to his old and trusted advisor.

"I have devoted the last three years of my life to providing the house of Targete with an heir, but the primary requisite in procuring a suitable bride for Prince Steven has yet to be met. I fear, my lord, that suitable young women are few and far between.

"Our little kingdom is most progressive in insuring that women are not a downtrodden underclass as they are in some of our neighboring nations. But it would seem, my lord, that the pendulum may have swung too far and that we may well be the first nation in Europe to be dominated by the feminine gender. Our women are bold, aggressive and not a few are dangerous, my lord. Young foreign women of noble birth who come to our land are so eager to throw off the shackles of their homelands that they quickly become wild and licentious. I have not seen one to whom I would entrust the future of our nation, as mother of a noble heir. Even pretty young women of more humble birth have strange, twisted appetites—so insistent are they in attending the market day shows in Calauverge, where pilloried prisoners are often fortunate to escape with their manhood intact. I say this not in ingratitude or complaint, my liege, but to convey that my task is difficult at best."

"Don't despair, Rodney," the king said kindly. "There is no other to whom I would entrust this task. I shall place more resources at your disposal. If you need more discreet inspectors from my select palace guard you have but to ask—you may work them day and night in shifts."

The king paused for a moment.

"Tell me, Rodney, what do you think of Lady Jane Broughton? Her family, though English, has had extensive holdings and influence here for some time. Indeed, I rate her uncle, Lord Carlyle, to be one of my truest friends." The king lowered his voice and gave his chamberlain a conspiratorial wink. "Steven has taken Lady Jane on a carriage ride down through the vineyards to Calauverge. Perhaps a romance may yet develop!"

Lord Rodney spoke hesitantly. "I received a packet this morning from my contacts in Britain by way of friends on the French embassy staff. I am afraid, my lord, that Lady Broughton may not be suitable. It seems that she has turned a country house, located in the center of her family holdings in Coventry, into a luxurious den of torture. She and her female friends delight in the infliction of beatings and more intimate punishments on the male household servants and other males without wealth or privilege who are unlucky enough to fall into her grasp. I can only guess at the debaucheries into which she would lead Prince Steven."

"Ah!" The king nodded with regret. "It is a pity, Rodney! And to think when we were introduced she blushed so chastely and curtsied so prettily. One could never guess from her outward appearances her true predilections." The king looked hopefully at Lord Rodney. "What of the Marquise of Rousillion?"

"My liege, do you even wish to hear the sordid tales of her cruelty? She takes delight in making geldings of men!"

CHAPTER THREE

Victoria stood waiting in the tiny shop of the Calauverge harness-maker, savoring the cool Spanish tiles beneath her bare feet. The harness-maker stood at the window looking out into the haggling throngs.

"Is there more market day spectacle on the scaffold?" Victoria asked hopefully.

"No, and for that I am grateful. But Prince Steven's carriage has stopped and he appears to be mingling with the crowd as if looking for someone."

Victoria smiled to herself and imagined what it would be like if the prince were searching for her—a silly, impossible notion, of course—but one delightful to entertain. Victoria's senses had been stimulated by the lewd treatment of the pilloried prisoner and it was easy to imagine the prince sweeping her up in his arms and taking her to his royal chamber high in a palace tower. Her cheeks turned crimson as she thought of clasping the royal member in her hand, and then being slowly and deliciously impaled upon it.

"Three braided dog whips, then, and one Barcelonan pony tawse...." The harness-maker paused when he realized that the lovely barefoot girl in the green dress was lost in revery.

Quickly collecting herself, she apologized with a blushing smile. The harness-maker handed her the narrow paper packet containing the whips, and she paid. She was still thinking of the prince as she walked down the steps and onto the street.

In her vision she lay on her back, legs bent at the knee and toes pointed. The prince knelt, thrusting vigorously inside her, his body bathed in sweat, his motions urgent and fevered. These pleasant fantasies occupied Victoria until she reached the sun-dappled garden wall of her home.

An old pensioner sat on a wooden bench, his wrinkled, pleasant face turned to the sunlight. Victoria smiled and crept up to him, pouncing at the last moment to throw her arms about his neck and kiss his weathered cheek.

"Ah, Victoria!" the old man murmured, delighting in her closeness. "You smell of the Market Square and of leather. For shame, Victoria! The bawdy scenes of market day could end your innocence!"

Victoria blushed and ruffled the old man's white hair. "I did not look."

She continued on to the wrought iron garden gate of her home through which she was quickly escorted by a conspiratorial maid who had been waiting for her.

Victoria's stepmother, Regine, wanted her to always send the houseboy, Lucas, on errands to the harness-maker's in Market Square. She said it was beneath the dignity of a family of nobility to take on such errands themselves.

Cinderella

But Victoria loved to go. She always went clad as a servant in a plain green dress to savor the sights, sounds, and smells of market day. She especially savored the sights on the scaffold when a pilloried prisoner was to be dealt with for the amusement of the crowd.

But now was the time for her and the pretty young housemaid to reward Lucas. He risked a prolonged caning from Victoria's stepsister Marcella if ever he was found to have let the young lady go in his place.

Victoria and the housemaid, Rachel, joined Lucas in a quiet garden nook. Lucas eagerly divested himself of all his clothes until he stood coltlike and naked on the grass.

"Will you suck me today?" he boldly enquired of Rachel, who blushed and rolled her eyes at the effrontery of the lad.

"No, Lucas," Victoria said firmly. "She will pleasure you with her hand, as usual, to reward you for risking a caning on my behalf, and I will show you my legs as she does so!" Victoria added this last with sudden inspiration.

Rachel stood by Lucas' side and, grasping his penis, began to fondle and caress it, even as Victoria sat impudently on a stone bench and raised her green dress until she well bared the smooth allure of her pretty thighs.

She then rested her lovely bare feet on the trunk of a shade tree and watched Rachel masturbate Lucas. Victoria smiled as she watched the young housemaid's hand work Lucas' foreskin back and forth in long, slow, pulling strokes. The young man spread his legs so Rachel would have complete and easy access to his genitals, and he leaned into her strokes. His face was placid with youthful ecstasy.

Victoria noted with amusement that Rachel, for her part, though pretending to be casual and even bored by the proceedings, took a secret delight in her handiwork which her parted lips and flaming cheeks betrayed. Lucas gasped as his scrotum flapped about between his legs, so influenced by the eager force of Rachel's hands. Victoria felt her breath come more rapidly as she watched, fascinated, as the masturbation continued. She knew that her stepmother Regine, and her stepsisters Ana and Marcella, would be revolted by a sight such as she now enjoyed. That realization made Victoria enjoy it all the more.

Lucas gazed worshipfully at the forbidden curves of Victoria's calves and thighs as he strained and finally ejaculated onto the trimmed grass of the garden lawn.

Victoria watched the thick arcs of his seed flip through the air and land with impromptu male conceit upon some flowers nearly a yard before him. The tip of his penis continued to disgorge a torrent of sperm to which Rachel's pistoning hand gave high trajectory.

At last Lucas went down on all fours on the grass, his shaking legs giving way under waves of pleasure, his fogged mind still full of the luscious vision of Victoria's legs. Rachel stood noting the exhaustion of her victim with smug satisfaction, attributing it to the expertise of her handiwork. She bent prettily to wipe her glistening hand on the grass and affectionately chided Lucas for soiling the flowers. Then the trio set themselves aright and went into the house.

Victoria's eldest stepsister, Marcella, awaited them, standing innocently in the kitchen door where she had been amusing herself by bullying the kitchen maids a moment before.

"Victoria, you are wanted upstairs, at once," she cooed, her voice velvet with gloating malice.

Marcella's otherwise lovely mouth had but the slightest petulant downturn at the corners of her lips—the effect of which was further enhanced by the hard, cruel set of her eyes. Many a household servant had learned to rue the day he failed to avoid Marcella when she was bored.

Lucas and Rachel quickly disappeared to attend to their household duties, and Victoria ascended the sweeping stairs to quietly knock on the panelled door of her stepmother Regine's suite.

Victoria's calm poise never left her and long ago she had become adept at steeling herself to face any bizarre tableau that she might find in Regine's chambers.

Regine sat on a velvet upholstered dressing stool, naked save for a short luxurious fur wrap which hung low on her bare shoulders. Her dark hair was piled high in an elegant twist atop her head, giving her delicately lovely face a hint of haughty imperiousness. Victoria had not noticed them as so strikingly beautiful before, but was certain now that Regine had the exotic, almost slanted, eyes of a cat. Regine's legs were bent at the knee, and her bare feet were tiptoed on the rich gold and crimson carpet of the floor. Her fingers, beringed as they were with delicately jewelled bands, rested almost gently on the head of the young upstairs maid, Maria del Castillo.

Maria knelt naked on the floor before Regine and was gently licking her clitoris!

Behind Maria sat Victoria's youngest stepsister, Ana, fully clothed, her buttocks resting on a high-backed chair upholstered in striped satin. Ana smiled as her fingers lewdly caressed the moist shaven mount of Maria's sex.

"Ah, Victoria!" Regine purred smugly, gently chiding Maria for slowing the intimate work of her tongue. "I must inform you that tonight, once again, you have a good deal of work to do in our training rooms. Did Lucas purchase the whips and the tawses from the harness-maker as I desired?"

"Yes, Regine, Lucas has brought them from Market Square. He arrived just a moment ago."

"Splendid!" Regine exclaimed, her breath coming faster as Maria's tongue remained diligently employed and was now stimulating her clitoris with delightful little fluttering sweeps.

"To think, Victoria, that Maria is the daughter of what once was one of the wealthiest families in Lisbon, and would be penniless now but for my generosity in giving her a good situation of employment."

Ana now had the index finger of her left hand worked deeply within Maria's crinkled circlet while the fingers of her other hand teased Maria's genitals with soft butterfly caresses. Victoria could not tear her eyes from her stepsister's violating hands as they gently played with the young maid, delicately turning her to a near fever pitch of helpless and humiliated excitement.

Victoria realized that the caresses provided the young maid inspired her tongue, making it all the more a willing servant of Regine's jaded sexual appetites.

Ana laughed quietly as Maria del Castillo wiggled her curvaceous hips in helpless abandon, pleading with the motions of her body for Ana's teasing fingers to probe her vagina as well.

Regine, for her part, did look beautiful, her face suffused with the glow of sensual enjoyment. She leaned back and gave herself to the lapping, catlike tongue of the kneeling maid, even as Victoria's own sex swelled and moistened at the soft feminine sound of the gentle licking.

Regine presently recovered herself and spoke again to Victoria.

"The Comte de Languedoc will arrive by closed carriage tonight, and wishes to play a new game. He wishes to feel the sting of the Barcelonan pony tawse on his bared buttocks and be ridden about the training room. Then he wishes to be manualized to spending after suitable and lengthy humiliations are carried out upon

Cinderella

him—the duration and type of these, Victoria, I leave as usual to your imagination. Suffice it to say that I require him so pleased when the proceedings are ended that he regards his payment as well directed and even a small price, well worth such heady delight."

"Must I wear the leather hood, Regine?" Victoria asked. "It is stuffy and so confining!"

"Yes, I fear that you must, nor do I want you to ever perform your duties without it. Our clients have often told me how the mystery of their hooded abuser adds delight and intrigue to the games that you play, and several have said that they take pleasure in wondering of every women they meet—is she the one who enslaves me? Why deprive them of their crumbs of enjoyment and profane the mystery on which they have become so dependent?"

As Regine talked of Victoria's clients and male propensities, Ana's mouth curled into a expression of disgust even while she continued to masturbate Maria, now busily employing two of her slim fingers within the maid's vagina. Regine sighed as again the maid's servile tongue swept her to another summit of pleasure.

"You are dismissed, Victoria. Oh, and after the Comte will come the Vicomte Cevenne. He requests his usual game, and sounds so eager for the sport to begin that I do wonder if the vicomtesse has been tending to her husband's intimate requirement."

"May Rachel assist me with the vicomte?" Victoria asked.

"Yes, of course, Victoria, now you are dismissed!"

Victoria paused just outside Regine's door after first gently drawing it closed. Her pretty, full-lipped mouth curled into a smile of satisfaction.

"Profane the mystery indeed!" she said to herself in a lighthearted mimic of Regine's suave tones.

Victoria knew then that Regine insisted on the hood

as a jealous measure to conceal her loveliness. The thought was an angry reminder of her position in this home, and yet it flushed her cheeks with pride.

When Victoria gained the bottom of the stairs she headed for her own chamber. When passing the stillroom door she saw Marcella busy at her typical amusements. Elvert, one of the young household grooms stood naked from the waist down, in a posture of forced and rigid military attention. He watched Marcella use a glazing brush to apply fresh conserves about the cleft of a pretty, blushing, stillroom maid's buttocks.

The stillroom maid, a young apple-cheeked girl named Sonia, knelt on top of the table where the jams and jellies were stirred. Her back was to Elvert and Marcella, though she obediently displayed the saucy bare curves of her bottom by holding her skirts well up. Sonia bit her lip in vexation at the indignity of her predicament. But her glance darted back behind Marcella to note the girth and length of Elvert's penis.

Marcella worked delicately, applying the conserves about Sonia's circlet in unhurried swirling strokes. When occasion necessitated, Marcella brazenly spread Sonia's smooth, broad globes to well apply the conserves to the crack of her bottom. She spread the sweet substance well down until some of it caught in the dark hairs about the pouting mound of Sonia's sex. Sonia gasped, and her cheeks reddened yet more.

Marcella laughed at Sonia's anguish and paid scant attention to Elvert for the moment.

Due to the placement of the doorway in the room, Victoria could watch the game while unseen herself.

Marcella then reversed the brush and dipped its polished wooden handle into the jar of conserves. "Brace yourself, Sonia dear!" she purred. "I'm going to make you sweet!"

With that the bored young woman slowly inserted the

sticky, shining handle of the glazing brush up into Sonia's anus. Sonia squirmed and protested, but knew better than to protest overmuch. Marcella smiled as she twisted the brush about in Sonia's bottom to see that it had left a good quantity of conserves behind, then she abruptly withdrew it.

Victoria held her breath, unable to tear her eyes away from the bizarre sights of the stillroom.

Marcella next turned her attention to the groom and ringed his penis lightly in her soft grasp. "Before you are relieved, Elvert, I do expect you to kindly tend to Sonia's buttocks. She appears to have sat bare-bottomed in sweet plums and oranges!"

Marcella drew Elvert forward by his penis and pressed him down till his mouth was even with Sonia's sticky buttocks.

Elvert resisted having his face pressed forward—he resisted out of shame—but Marcella disdained to spare his dignity. She drew him back by his hair, long enough to slap him soundly across the face. Then she smiled and pressed his face forward, bringing his nose to nestle in the sweet sticky cleavage of Sonia's bare bottom.

"Lick her well, you pathetic boy, and who knows? I may yet reward you despite your insolence."

Elvert trembled, and he began the soft, slow lapping of the conserves from the intimacy of the stillroom maid's bottom. Elvert's testicles hung low and pendant, swaying slightly with his efforts as he set himself to his task.

Marcella viewed the proceedings with her arms folded smugly across her breasts. She was most specific and demeaning in her verbal direction of Elvert's tongue. He started beneath her belly, near the downy bulge of Sonia's sex and slowly worked toward her circlet.

Victoria watched as gradually Sonia's pretenses of outrage and disgust crumbled and Elvert's tongue gently persuaded her body's pretexts of modesty and chastity to give way. Soft sighs of pleasure broke almost unconsciously from Sonia's lips, even though her face still registered dismay at the indignity of her predicament. Elvert's organ thickened and throbbed, shifting slowly parallel to his splayed thighs, helpless to escape this humiliating erotic bondage.

Marcella slipped from her shoes, raising her skirts and exposing her pretty bare legs, and sat back on her heels to enjoy her contrived amusements.

"Yes, Elvert, yes! That's it! Very good, Elvert, and now thrust your tongue within her circlet. No, deeper. Harder! Yes, like that!"

Marcella's right hand found Elvert's penis while her left reached beneath him from behind to capture and squeeze his scrotum. Elvert's mouth was gleaming with the sweet conserves as his penis was ever so gently abused in Marcella's soothing palm. With a low, moaning sob he utterly abandoned himself to Marcella's whims and obeyed her every detailed instruction. He stiffened his tongue and repeatedly thrust it through the resistance of Sonia's circlet into the sweetness of her depths.

A moment later Sonia went rigid and trembled in the throes of a long, satisfying orgasm. Her nipples throbbed, hugely erect beneath her bodice as all her sensation became centered in her bottom. She felt weak as the flames of a base and perverse passion ignited her every sense in a firestorm of delight.

As Sonia's quivering subsided, Marcella turned her attention to Elvert and made him stand once again. Marcella smiled as she brushed her fingers over his lips and then thrust them, one by one, into his mouth, making him suck the sticky jam from each. Marcella held Elvert by the scrotum and used it as a bridle to assure that he cleaned her fingers well.

Victoria took special note that Marcella truly gloated

with every degradation to which she subjected these poor household servants, and smiled despite herself at the thought.

Sonia had stood up, but seemed to be in a quandary as to what she should do next. She still held her skirts high, exposing her bare bottom, which, although Elvert had done his best, was still glistening with conserves. She dared not let her clothes down for fear of soiling them, and bit her lip in dismay.

Marcella noticed: "Turn about, Sonia. That's it. Now bend over well at the waist and hold your buttocks spread apart."

Then Marcella inserted the glazing brush once again, handle first, into the jar of conserves. This accomplished, she slid the handle into Sonia's anus and left it there, "See that it does not slip out, dear girl; tense your buttocks upon it and take care that it remains in place."

Sonia tensed herself and turned about. The brush quivered—but remained inserted. She drew up on tiptoe and strained to hold it in, her expression a reddening mixture of agony of embarrassment. Marcella smirked as she applied a handful of conserves to Elvert's penis. Then she pressed Sonia to her knees before him. Sonia took great care to keep the brush embedded though it nearly slipped from her circlet once she settled on her knees.

"Now, Sonia," Marcella murmured in tones of aggravated sweetness. "It seems that Elvert has also been playing naughtily in a sticky mix of plums and oranges. Clean him well with your tongue!"

The vexed maid had no choice, and soon her lips formed a wet sucking ring that gently drew on Elvert's glistening tool. Sonia's eyes were expressive in their consternation as she felt Elvert's penis twitch and expand on the surface of her tongue. Sonia could not see that Marcella had two fingers of her left hand well embedded in Elvert's anus and was gently twisting them to and fro.

Elvert was excited beyond endurance, and though he did not wish to spend in the pretty maid's mouth, he could do little to stop the course of nature. After being forced to lick her bare bottom, this the very maid that he had adored from afar for so long, and after having his penis stimulated by his mistress, her fingers probing in his bottom, and now after being suckled so deliciously—he surrendered.

Sonia's eyes widened in outrage, but she knew better than to take her mouth away and risk Marcella's wrath. As Elvert's tool jolted and twitched, filling her mouth with thick spurts of warm sperm, Sonia swallowed them all one by one. The tidy maid even kept the seal of her lips tight about his glans to prevent spillage. The tang of the sperm mixed with the sweet stickiness of the conserves Marcella had rubbed on his penis.

Marcella drove her fingers upward then to the depths in Elvert's backside, forcing him upon tiptoe and goading his penis to spurt even more copiously.

Victoria watched the scene to its conclusion, then softly crept to her chamber, her face aflame and her clitoris swollen huge.

Minutes later, on her bed, the vivid erotic scenes of the day coalesced in her mind. The image of the pilloried prisoner squirming as the laughing pastrycook's girls masturbated him, Lucas straining as his penis jolted in Rachel's hand, Maria del Castillo—with Ana's fingers in her bottom—softly lapping Regine, and what Victoria had just seen in the stillroom, all conspired and beckoned her to solitary pleasure. Victoria raised her dress, her fingers found her clitoris, and she gently soothed away its intimate passion.

CHAPTER FOUR

The running lamps at the sides of the Comte de Languedoc's carriage made diamonds of the rainfall in the summer night. The cobbles of the pavement glistened clean, and the streets were empty about Calauverge's Fountain Square.

The driver of the comte's carriage bypassed the front entrance of the house and turned down a narrow side street which descended toward Market Square. He reined in his horses beside a wrought iron garden gate set deep in an ivyed stone wall.

The comte de Languedoc leapt down from the carriage heedless of the rain. His darkly handsome face was set in an expression of anticipation. He rang the bell and waited at the gate in a circle of light cast by a street lamp. His driver drove on as bidden and the comte watched his carriage disappear, the reflection of its lights dancing on the pavement.

A cloaked maid answered the summons of the bell, and the comte followed her down the garden path and into a discreet rear entrance of the large house. She hung his cloak in a stone-flagged corridor and led him down a set of spiral steps. Reaching the bottom, the maid turned about and drew back the hood of her cloak to smile at the comte.

"Ah, Rachel!" he said as if greeting an old friend. "Who will tend me tonight? I do hope it will be the lovely girl who wears the hood."

Rachel laughed. "You are fortunate tonight, comte Yes, the hooded girl will tend you—but pray, how do you know she is lovely?"

The comte answered easily. "A maiden with limbs so surpassingly well-formed as hers must have the face of a youthful goddess! Tell me, am I correct?"

Rachel but smiled in answer and escorted him to a small anteroom where he disrobed. She lingered long enough to feast her eyes on the comte's nakedness, and then withdrew to tend her duties.

The comte waited quietly in the anteroom, his demeanor expectant, savoring the wait for his pleasures to begin.

Ever since his youth he knew that he was of a very different bent than most. Darker pleasures delighted him, the haughtiest and severest beauties captivated him. He thought back to the first time he paid tribute to Venus. He had ejaculated copiously on his young governess' lap during a prolonged spanking. He never forgot the flush of high color on her cheeks, the angry flash of her eyes, but he saw that a trace of delight had mingled with her contempt, that she had excited him so. This vision would impress itself upon him for the remainder of his life.

And now he waited, trembling like a schoolboy, for his lovely disciplinarian to appear. A pity about the hood, but it did add to her mystique. She had the loveliest feet and legs he had ever seen. Even the form of her wrists and dexterous hands made him long to be flogged to spurting by her. And her voice! Soft with an almost fastidious femininity, it made him revel all the more in his grovelling.

Indeed, little did he know that it was Victoria who was his mistress, the possessor of his passions.

The comte thought of Ana and Marcella for a moment. The Hooded Lady lacked, perhaps, a bit of the intensity of their gloating sadism, but nonetheless held a charm that enslaved his nearly every thought. The Lady was the keeper of a pristine, untouched femininity that no dominatrix should be without. And her imagination! The games she played with him! A thousand years at her feet would pass like a summer morning.

Her head encased within the hood, Victoria started with a basic scenario that he communicated to Regine. But Victoria built upon it, and far from showing disgust with his predilections—she gave them life and reality. She clothed his dreams of submission and animated them with a power far beyond even his fantasies.

The door of the anteroom opened and Victoria entered. The comte followed her into one of the three training rooms beneath the house. As Victoria walked ahead of him, his eyes savored her. She was a delightfully formed and perfect beauty from head to foot.

Victoria walked barefoot, stepping lightly, her highly arched, perfect feet with their pert, even toes tempting him to degradation. The curves of her calves and thighs enticed his eyes further upward to her nearly bare buttocks. Victoria wore a snug leather bodice of the most supple tooled leather. A narrow thong ran beneath her from a tiny leather skirt that covered her genitals. But in the back it simply raised, parted, and emphasized the splendid nubile curves of her buttocks.

Victoria walked knowingly, imparting a luscious wiggle to the curves of her hips and bottom. The hood gave her a slightly sinister appearance, so that she looked like some heartless medieval torturer, preparing to perform a cruel sentence. Nevertheless, this severe effect was counterweighted by the lewd, youthful curves of her almost naked body. Victoria's arms were covered from shoulder to fingertip in tight-fitting gloves of the finest and most supple black leather.

The comte's penis stiffened a bit, and lurched to rear from between his legs. He saw that she held a Barcelonan pony tawse. The comte's bared buttocks clenched with an expectation of delicious terror as he followed her into the center of the deeply carpeted training room.

Victoria spun about, pivoting on her bare heels. She noted his eyes were on her bare tiptoed feet and also that he was erect. His penis strained, bold in its salute to her clearly dominant stance. Beneath her hood Victoria smiled. Under the brief leather skirt below the front of her bodice, she felt her vagina moisten. Victoria dearly loved the games she and the comte played. Perhaps even more than he. She was tireless.

Victoria stepped to a small curtained recess in the wall of the low-lighted room. She withdrew a leather affair consisting of a complex set of straps and buckles. Fastening the collar of the device about the comte's neck, she squatted beside him to pass a thick strap down his back and buckle it about the base of his scrotum. Then she placed a hard rubber bit in his mouth and threw the reins to which they were attached across his back. Laughing softly, she withdrew a contrivance of her own creation from the alcove: a thick leather phallus, generously oiled at one end, the other end terminating in a leather curl which cunningly imitated a swine's tail.

"We must hunt for truffles today, piggy!" Victoria giggled in a soft, lilting, playful voice. With that, she knelt behind the comte and slowly inserted the phallus-end of the pigtail into his anus. He grunted in surprise, resisting and tensing his sphincter upon the unexpected intrusion. Victoria took him firmly by the scrotum with her free hand, using her direct purchase on this vital part of his generative anatomy as a bridle to hold him fast. At last the slow insertion was a success, though the comte involuntarily tensed himself upon it, clutching his insides in a pained reaction to the invader. Victoria circumvented his efforts by fastening thin straps from the pigtail phallus to the strap that ringed his scrotum and to the broad strap that ran down his back.

The comte clenched his teeth on the bit and groaned in nearly excruciating discomfort. The eyes he turned to Victoria as she stood above him smugly to survey her handiwork were liquid with debasement and adoration.

Victoria surveyed him with something akin to awe herself. This great, handsome nobleman with his tiny waist, broad chest, huge shoulders, strong arms and the face of a god—desperate to be degraded by a women one third his size. It always amazed Victoria, but it delighted her as well.

Victoria raised the whip, "Lazy piggy!" she exclaimed with mock indignation. "Sniff, you lazy thing! Find a nice succulent truffle!"

The Barcelonan pony tawse snapped abruptly in a well-aimed strike that left a vivid welt across the comte's buttocks. The comte jumped with pain and surprise and began to slowly crawl about the room sniffing the carpet as if its fabric did somehow conceal such a fine rare morsel. The tawse cut him again and then a third time.

"Grunt, piggy, grunt!" Victoria demanded, her bossiness lending greater poise and authority to her lissome form. "A good truffle-seeking piggy always grunts!"

Victoria then pranced about the comte, laughing and

delivering a series of barefoot kicks that pummeled his abdomen, sides, buttocks, and occasionally came very close to menacing the vulnerable dangle of his scrotum.

The comte increased his crawling pace, rooting about in the corners of the training room and thrusting his nose into its every nook and corner. His imaginary search, Victoria was amused to note, was now accompanied by a great deal of grunting and snorting.

Despite his obedience, Victoria continued to lash him with the cruel pony tawse until his buttocks were in a rather sad state.

CHAPTER FIVE

As Victoria and the comte played their private game, her next client, the Vicomte Cevenne, sat in an elegant room at the Chateau Furnald.

The room was filled with well-dressed lordly men, and the haughtiest beauties of the kingdom were also well represented. The costume of the evening consisted of brightly colored styles done in velvets, silks, and satins. All the guests of the Chateau Furnald wore powdered wigs. The women's powdered coiffeurs soared to extravagant heights. Their opulent gowns, however, neglected to cover their bosoms, but rather bared them splendidly, lifting them well in the process.

The guests helped themselves to dainties and the finest claret served by obsequious, endlessly circulating maids.

In one curtained corner of the room several bare-breasted women amused themselves by beating hogtied servants with long, wicked canes in time to the music of a small chamber ensemble.

The naked servants rolled to and fro, desperate to escape the fiery bite of the canes. The laughing women who wielded the supple instruments of cruelty followed their helpless victims about the floor and even among the other guests, applying hard strokes to wherever vulnerable flesh presented a suitable target.

The Vicomte Cevenne was deep in conversation with the host and hostess, the Marquis and Marquise de Besançon. His outwardly calm demeanor belied the lurching heaviness of his heart. A treasonous proposal was outlined in all its ugliness before him, the obscene extent of its rebellion hidden behind patriotic phrases and trite observations of necessity.

The marquise appraised the vicomte, trying to pierce the cloak of his concealed thought. She played it as a seduction. Yes! she must gently lure this pompous loyalist away from his absurd preconceptions.

The Marquise de Besançon shifted in her chair just slightly. She assumed a posture which she knew—by precise experimentations on naked servants—showed her bare bosom to its best advantage. Indeed, the Vicomte Cevenne could scarcely keep his eyes from the deliciously huge nipples of her breasts. And that difficulty from a jaded courtier!

"And so you see, my dear Cevenne. There is really no other choice for a loyal citizen to make. Certainly the Targetes deserve praise for their past efforts, but really, any thinking person can see that their time has come and gone. There are many with us in high places. Of course the turnover will be bloodless. Do lend us your backing, Cevenne!"

The Vicomte Cevenne realized then his peril. He pursed his lips and thought a moment. He must cloak his refusal to join the rebellion in such a way that he would still seem sympathetic to it. Otherwise he was undone.

He fought down the sickening realization that were he to falter now he might well not live through the night.

He was given a moment of grace in an unexpected fashion. One of the bound servants had rolled as far away as he could from his elegantly clad, bare-breasted tormentors.

The poor unfortunate found himself at the Marquise de Besançon's feet. The marquise turned her eyes from the Vicomte Cevenne for a moment and stopped the servant's progress by applying the dainty sole of her high-heeled dancing shoe to his genitals. The marquise's full lips pursed prettily into an elegantly malicious smile. She raised her gloved arm and pointed the servant out to the laughing, cane-wielding women.

They descended upon him with gleeful laughter and subjected his naked body to a veritable deluge of blows. Their breasts bobbed alluringly in time to the motions of their flailing arms.

The Vicomte Cevenne heard his own reply at last as if from far away, "I must have time. The issues you have raised are so vital to our land they require the utmost consideration. I am sympathetic to your cause and will, of course, treat what I have heard tonight as a privileged confidence."

The vicomte did not miss the ire in the marquise's glance that flickered there a moment—cold beyond belief—before it was quickly replaced with a soft, almost fond expression. He rose to take his leave of the Chateau Furnald. Even as the Vicomte Cevenne kissed the Marquise de Besançon's hand, he realized that he might be kissing the hand that signed his death warrant. He exchanged formal goodbyes with the marquis and exited the great room as quickly as was feasible.

As the Vicomte Cevenne's carriage drew away from

the great arched gateway of the Chateau Furnald's receiving door, two lithe assassins flitted across the smooth, rain-soaked lawn.

Clad in black tights and light felt slippers, the two young women raced to the wall that surrounded the chateau and leaped lightly up. There they waited, poised, silent as two shadows, eager and ready for the vicomte's carriage to pass by below them. Their gloved hands held felt-wrapped garotting wire, and their black greasepainted faces were intent and hopeful that the wire would soon be put to its intended use.

The Marquise de Besançon had found their services most valuable in times past and, indeed, enjoyed the retelling of the details of their work after their deeds were complete. Frequently her pampered assassins were so impassioned after a success that the marquise was forced to lend them a well-hung servant or two to soothe their erotic cravings.

However, the assassins were due for a keen disappointment on this particular rain-soaked night. Upon leaving the gate of the Chateau Furnald, the vicomte's carriage turned off into a side street before passing the point on the wall where the assassins waited. The driver of the vicomte's carriage, sitting glumly in the rain and cursing his destiny, never knew that the vicomte's lust for a lovely young Hooded Lady had saved both their lives. As he flicked the reins and indulged in a needless drought of self pity—he owed his life to the fact that the vicomte wasn't returning to his residence, but rather to a discreet house off Fountain Square.

The assassins, deploring this unfortunate turn of events, were quick to return to their mistress, whereupon they were sent out in a dark carriage with hooded lamps. Search as they might, they found no trace of the Vicomte Cevenne or his unhappy, though fortunate, driver.

CHAPTER SIX

As the Vicomte Cevenne was engaged in dangerous conversation with the Marquise de Besançon in the Chateau Furnald, Victoria's games with the comte de Languedoc continued.

She was astride him now, riding him hard, the supple curves of her thighs embracing his sides while her bare heels pummelled his thighs and urged him forward. The Barcelonan pony tawse cracked and snapped about the comte's already well-marked buttocks. Victoria's free hand jerked his reins, slamming the hard rubber bit back into the sensitive corners of his mouth and rolling it under his tongue.

"Naughty piggy!" Victoria pouted, her voice silken and soft in its displeasure. "You have found no truffles again today, you lazy thing!"

Victoria's pony tawse again snapped down across the comte's bare buttocks. Victoria smiled beneath her hood as she added a subtle flick of her wrist to this last blow. The whip thongs flipped upward to smartly flick the defenseless dangle of his scrotum. He gasped and flinched, even as his penis swelled huge with the heat of his arousal, throbbing, potent and urgent between his muscled thighs.

Victoria dismounted and squatted down beside the comte to look him over, "Oh, piggy! You're all in a sweat and lather! You poor pathetic thing!"

Victoria nearly giggled to note that the goaded sweetness her voice had assumed caused the comte's big penis to swell and twitch all the more. She licked her lips beneath her hood as she reached out and slapped the comte's penis up against his abdomen. A string of his arousal flew from the tip of his glans to land across the slim elegance of her leather-gloved hand. Due to her squatting position, Victoria felt the lips of her pussy open, swollen and moist as they were with the longing to have that big penis thrust inside her up to the balls.

Victoria moved to a plush settee, upholstered in purple velvet. She sat sideways upon it, thrusting her buttocks out and arching her back in such a way that she naughtily displayed her most intimate charms. She loosened the thong that ran between her buttocks to expose the sweet pink allure of her most private cleft, between the shapely globes of her bare bottom. Victoria was wet and desperate. Idly flicking the lashes of the Barcelonan pony tawse against the arm of the settee, she wiggled herself wantonly.

"Oh, piggy!" she gasped, her voice low with excitement. "I have found a place for you to sniff for truffles! Hurry, piggy, I am sure that you will find one here."

The comte crawled forward on all fours, his reins dragging behind him, the oiled phallus with the humiliating swine's tail still protruding from his anus. His penis was huge, freely drooling long, clear strings of arousal onto the carpeted floor of the training room. His eyes were consumed with longing as they locked on the pouting well of Victoria's enticingly displayed genital mount.

The settee shook when the comte's shoulders bumped it as he came to a stop. Still upon all fours, the big man pressed his face to Victoria's slit, and gasped his naked longing when he caught the intimate and luscious wild scent of her sex. With a famished, wrenching groan of agonized need, the comte de Languedoc's mouth and tongue took possession of Victoria's most secret parts. He nursed at her fount, licking, probing, sucking and nibbling until she was carried away in a gasping flood of sumptuous delight. She shamelessly churned her hips, wiggling her sex wantonly, grinding herself passionately against his yearning face.

Victoria felt utterly naked, and awash in a flaming heat of lewd pleasure—she gasped her ecstasy, her soft voice sweetly urging the comte on. Her cheeks flamed as nonsense words poured from her parted lips.

"Yes, piggy! Oh, yes! Just like that. Good piggy! You have found my truffle at last! Oh lick, piggy, keep licking. Nice piggy!"

The comte's tongue gently licked the moist pink swell of Victoria's inner lips. He lapped as though starved, greedily sucking up the salty dew of her excitement. His tongue moved to intercept a droplet of her delight that was slowly sliding toward her anus. The comte's tongue continued there, exploring that orifice too and wickedly penetrating the tight, virginal ring of Victoria's sphincter. Victoria pointed her toes and gasped as she shuddered when the intense throes reached a giddy crescendo.

The comte soon returned his attentions to her clitoris, nibbling and tonguing it gently, pressing and licking up under the protective pink hood of flesh that enfolded it. He then applied passionate kisses directly to her flaming clitoris and finally finished his symphony of erotic worship by thrusting his tongue deep into the warm, wet depths of her vagina.

Victoria quivered, her lips a-tremble, until she could bear the sensation no longer. She pointed her toes and pushed the comte away with her pretty feet. He knelt back upon the carpet, supporting himself with his arms thrust out behind, as Victoria squirmed and writhed, mewing on the velvet cushions. The comte's penis beat and twitched indecently against his stomach and his mouth glistened with the liquid of her sex.

At last the maddening tingle between Victoria's legs subsided enough for her to come to her senses. She sat up as if in a daze and extended her pretty pointed toes to the comte's penis. Sometimes she felt as though the man and the penis were two separate entities. She both pitied and adored the pleading gasp of his penile slit and the bloated, strangled purple of its tormented head.

Ever so gently, Victoria took his penis between the big and second toes of her right foot and then she began to skillfully masturbate him in this novel fashion.

The comte was far too excited to hold out for long, and in a moment his heavily muscled body went absolutely rigid. His penis twitched and jolted, squirting out huge jets of sperm that shot up across his stomach and chest.

Victoria smiled as she watched the comte's helpless, slack-jawed expression. She had once heard her stepmother Regine refer to it as the blithering idiocy of the male orgasm. Victoria giggled as she milked the comte de Languedoc's penis dry with her perfect, impertinent toes.

At last the comte fell backward, nearly fainting from the sensation, his penis releasing a few more feeble squirts of his manhood in the process.

"Naughty, messy piggy!" Victoria chided, with a gentle, fond tone to her voice.

Cinderella

Scarcely twenty minutes later the comte paid his compliments to Victoria and bid her goodbye for now. Victoria, still clothed in her leather bodice, hood and gloves, was dwarfed by the tall, cloaked figure of the comte. His eyes were soft with adoration.

Victoria felt small now before this huge man, in his gleaming black boots, long cloak and dashing gloves. Their games in the training room seemed so unreal afterward. Save for her bizarre costume and the still-excited twitching of her swollen clitoris, it could have been all a dream.

He bent to take her hand and gently raise it to his lips. He kissed Victoria's hand and then turned his eyes upon her.

"Adieu, Hooded Lady. You are the sweetest beauty that this kingdom possesses. If there is justice and destiny, then one day you shall reveal yourself and be crowned queen!"

He turned to go, but stopped and spun about for a moment before going out into the rain. "And one day I will see your face, too! I know that you are lovely—like a goddess!"

Chapter Seven

As Victoria summoned Rachel to assist her in preparing another training room for their next guest, her stepsister Ana, and a haughty young friend of hers, Dona Alicia Antigua, were enjoying a lighthearted diversion in an upstairs drawing room. Lucas was unlucky enough to be caught by the duo when they were on the prowl for a male victim upon which to vent their sadism. And now he stood, on tiptoe, with his genitals locked fast in a specially designed pillory that Dona Alicia Antigua's brother had built for breeding slaves.

Poor Lucas was subjected to no little discomfort, as his tiptoed stance was necessitated by the fact that his imprisoned scrotum would receive a terrible wrench if he were to relax his posture but for a moment. Lucas had been in the genital pillory for nearly two hours and by now his calf muscles were painfully knotted.

Ana and Dona Antigua were naked, save for stylish high-heeled dancing shoes fashioned of lace and glitter according to latest court fashion. They amused themselves by applying strokes from cruel little handmade knouts to the anguished tendons of Lucas' calves. In front of Lucas' pendant penis stood a small grinding wheel on a tripod. Ana had amused herself turning the crank to spin the wheel while her dark-eyed companion toyed with Lucas' scrotum most saucily.

The result was that as he achieved full erection, the sensitive head of his penis was chafed and maddened by the spinning surface of the wheel. It was a wheel for fine grinding and, as such, caused Lucas no real harm, although the procedure slowly drew him into a perfect fit of intense discomfort.

Lucas turned imploring eyes to his lovely, naked tormentors—but their mocking smirks assured him that they had yet many long hours to spend at his expense. The poor lad was so tormented and exhausted that their nubile, naked charms—the promising curves of their bare hips and breasts—now held scant allure.

Dona Alicia Antigua put down her knout and began to finger Ana with sly, wanton motions along the pouting lips of her slit.

Lucas' eyes were kept properly straight ahead as they had commanded him, though he could see all that went on behind in a gilt-framed mirror that dominated one wall of the sumptuous room. Lucas had never seen a woman so dark and wild in appearance as Dona Alicia. She was lovely, with a truly beautiful face, and her body was enticing with its stately curves—yet there was something almost savage about her. Perhaps dangerous as well. Her dark eyes sparkled with glee as Ana responded to her coy fingerings.

Dona Alicia stood beside Ana, then, and reached through between her legs from behind to cup her right hand over Ana's mount. Her left hand alternated its play from the erect nipples of Ana's left breast to the moist foliage of her cleft. All the while Ana continued to whip the anguished tension of Lucas' tormented calves, each blow a searing lash of gleefully calculated cruelty.

Dona Alicia slid her fingers slowly into the moist folds of Ana's pussy as she applied her thumb to the tingling bud of her clitoris.

Ana wiggled her hips and gasped in delight—pausing for a moment her punishment of Lucas to enjoy the exquisite sensations. Ana bent her lovely thighs, to bring her vulva down harder on the furtive fingers of her sly companion.

Dona Alicia took up her knout again—this time with a very different object in mind for its employment. She smiled seductively as she gently inserted the polished wooden handle of the knout into the moist tunnel of Ana's sex.

Ana gasped at the slow insertion, suddenly overwhelmed by a powerful orgasm, even while the handle was still sliding into her.

Lucas could see her cheeks redden in the mirror's reflection, and despite his pain and discomfort, his penis jerked to rigidity yet again.

Ana's fingers released her knout, and it fell to the floor unheeded as she leaned back into Dona Alicia's sapphic embrace. In a moment the two companions were a tangle of sighing femininity upon the floor as they each explored the other with indulgent strokes and lewd caresses.

Dona Alicia continued to masturbate Ana while Ana's hungry lips found the large, dark nipple of the Dona's left breast. She sucked the succulent morsel for a long while, then moved her mouth down the Dona's body, kissing and licking as she went, until she came to the tangle of dark hair about the lady's cleft. Ana's small, sophisticated mouth then began the enticing oral delight of her Cartegenan friend.

Dona Alicia moaned and arched her lithe body on the floor, tossing her head so that her long, dark locks spread out in a halo about her. She praised her friend's indiscreet expertise with every writhe and gasping moan.

After a bit, the women retired into a luxuriously appointed bedchamber off the drawing room and closed the door, leaving Lucas in his hopeless predicament. The poor lad's calves were so utterly exhausted from his stance that he knew he would soon be forced to relax—and in so doing would painfully wrench his vulnerable scrotum.

However his salvation appeared in the form of the maid Maria del Castillo. She entered the drawing room, clad in impossibly high heels and a pink-and-lace maid's dress with a minute, flared skirt that left the pouting fig of her sex completely bare. Maria del Castillo carried a feather duster in her delicately laced, white-gloved hand.

"Oh, thank God, Maria! Please help me! Get me out of this infernal pillory, I beg you!"

Maria smiled prettily as she walked about Lucas and surveyed his helplessness. She savored, for once, the helplessness of another and gloated that it was not she, this time, in such a position.

"I will release you, Lucas," Maria said softly, "but first I must soothe my thirst."

With those words the lovely maid knelt in front of Lucas and began to greedily devour his penis, licking and sucking about its crimson head. She applied her gloved hands to his scrotum, kneading it and milking it—as if in an effort to cause him to spurt the biggest load possible into her hungry mouth.

Lucas grunted in shock and surprise as the demanding lips and tongue of the maid drew on him, suckled him, and slowly inflamed him to a passion beyond madness.

From time to time Maria del Castillo raised her eyes from her feast and looked up into Lucas' face to gloat over the helpless, twisted expression of lust stamped on his every feature. Maria knelt, her bare bottom with its broad, flawless globes splayed upon her heels, the pouting fig of her sex freely drooling the moisture of her own excitement. Maria's servitude to Regine and Ana had left her with very little inhibition. Now it would be she who was in control and she was enjoying herself immensely. She slid her lips down the shaft of Lucas' penis to nearly engulf the base, then slowly and lingeringly she drew them back until they popped from the tip with a lewd, wet, sucking sound. Then she busied herself for a time holding the slit of his glans open and licking the clear wettings that his penis vented in tribute to her lovely mouth. At last she began to lick the head of Lucas' penis with bold, firm strokes of her tongue, all the while firmly squeezing and kneading his testicles. Lucas clenched his teeth and murmured her name over and over again, trembling in a paroxysm of crazed pleasure. His penis jolted and twisted, at long last squirting the froth of his excitement into the mouth of the greedy young maid, who swallowed it all with evident relish. When she finally released him, he was so weak for a time that he could not stand.

CHAPTER EIGHT

Once again, Rachel crossed the garden to wait at the gate in the wall, this time for Victoria's second guest to arrive. Dark rags of cloud rolled overhead on a freshening wind to conceal, then reveal the summer moon. The rain had gone, and the dew-wet grass of the garden lawn sparkled like jewels strewn by a careless, over-generous hand.

Rachel did not have long to wait. The Vicomte Cevenne met her at the gate, dismissed his carriage, and kissed her hand. He was more withdrawn than the comte de Languedoc, though perhaps more courtly and sophisticated. His manners were impeccable and his bearing bespoke quiet elegance.

Rachel never understood the Vicomte Cevenne—though Victoria appeared to have her own insight into his character. When the vicomte came to play his intricate game, he did not leave for days. Though Rachel enjoyed assisting Victoria with the vicomte, she could not fathom how anyone could possibly want to be the object of such abuse. Rachel shrugged and smiled as she led him into the anteroom. Such things were not her concern. Besides, helping Victoria with Cevenne was always a delight despite the outlandish dress and happenings. Victoria could make a game of the most bizarre and medieval goings on.

According to the vicomte's wishes, Rachel stood watching him smugly and smiling while he disrobed. He handed her his garments one by one as he removed them. She received them each in turn to lay them across her arm. Then she instructed him to kneel.

Rachel noted with satisfaction that his penis—like the rest of him—was slim and elegant. His balls were large and showed much promise of endurance. Rachel then left him and entered the second training room. The vicomte would wait on his knees in the anteroom while she and Victoria properly costumed themselves for his game.

Victoria's stepmother Regine had many jaded friends—chiefly among women of nobility from northern Europe. One such friend of Regine's, the Margravine Godilieva Prumm, had the strangest taste in fashion that either Rachel or Victoria had ever seen. Indeed, it was rumored that Godilieva had commissioned designers and fabricators to work 'round the clock, turning out strange items of fetishistic apparel. These items were at once unique, and, in their own way, fashionable as well. Regine often visited Godilieva in Antwerp and had acquired a taste for such items of apparel. She was given a good quantity of these garments upon request, knowing with a cunning instinct that such strange garb would captivate male sensibilities and arouse their passions. It was, then, in these garments that Victoria and Rachel now clad themselves.

Victoria was seated in a backless French chair, looking flushed, and laughing. Rachel couldn't help laughing as well. She knelt holding a bizarre, gleaming black boot, while Victoria slowly slid her lovely foot, ankle, and calf into its confines.

The boot was fashioned of gleaming black leather, boasting a row of shining buttons which started from mid-ankle and extended all the way to the top of the boot at mid-thigh. What made the boot unusual, however, was that it had completely upstaged the outrageously tiptoed stance of ladies' court shoes, now in fashion.

These boots were crafted so that the woman's foot inside was subjected to the rigorous bondage of being in a ballerina's point-toed pose. The boots were so affected in their styling as to be useless in any practical sense. Even a court ballerina would find it nearly impossible to take one tottering step in them.

Rachel busied herself buttoning Victoria's boot after her foot had been settled in as comfortably as possible. Next, Rachel assisted her in slipping into and buttoning the other boot. Victoria remained seated, nearly immobile.

As Rachel helped her into the boots, Victoria mused on Godilieva Prumm. She was the only friend of Regine's Victoria liked, and Godilieva seemed to have taken a liking to her. Victoria could easily picture her, hair wild, lithe, slender body all the time clad in the most outlandish apparel Victoria had ever seen. Her eyes had an almost unfocused look. Those who did not know Godilieva well sometimes thought she experimented with drugs. Victoria knew better. Godilieva habitually wore the glazed, lust-absorbed look of an intense sensualist. She often delighted Regine in prescribing the most horrific punishments for wayward servants, and carrying them out with imagination and finesse while clad in her wild custom-made clothing.

Victoria had a vivid memory of one servant—who had

been a lord, but signed away his life and property to Godilieva—grovelling naked at her feet and worshipping her booted calves with his eager, lapping tongue. Godilieva was so taken with him that she took him about with her on her travels in a ventilated trunk. He was no more to her than an amusing toy to be put away when she became bored with him.

The ladies that Godilieva visited loved to fasten the servant in a cumbersome amount of rigid and extreme bondage devices. Then they would practice their slow, sexual cruelties on him while he lay contorted, bound, and utterly helpless. At the same time Godilieva was possessed of yet another sparkling facet. Often, at exclusive parties, in the delicately laced, high-heeled, virtually bare-breasted fashion of the day, she could cause quite a sensation with her ability to suck the penises of the male guests. The same lips that had wickedly derided an agonized servant, mocking him and verbally castigating him, were soft and compelling when tightly ringed about the erect penis of the latest gasping courtier to fall prey to her oral expertise.

Rachel stood back to carefully scrutinize Victoria's appearance. She was smugly satisfied with what she saw, yet strangely excited as well. Rachel would never admit that she was attracted to Victoria—yet the feeling was there nonetheless. It was the basis of Rachel's adoration and perhaps a foundation for their friendship.

Victoria wore—beside the boots—a beige and lavender dress of scandalously short length. It was high-collared with lacy turned-back cuffs. Victoria's thighs were actually more concealed by a short leather apron which covered her lap. The dress was so very brief it would have bared her thighs nearly to the hip, save for the apron and the fact that the boots covered the first six inches above the knee. The dress, feminine as it was, nearly to a fault, served as suitable foil for the almost sinister strangeness of the apron and boots. Victoria's hands were clad in gloves of crisp lace, and she had not yet donned her hood.

"Rachel, I must say that I quite like your costume," said Victoria. "I adore the shoes. At least you can walk in yours! You look lovely!"

Rachel's cheeks flushed with pleasure and she turned about for Victoria. She wore black velvet buttoned shoes with mere five-inch heels—compared to the nine-inch heels of Victoria's immobilizing boots. Rachel was also clad in a briefly cut, flared black dress whose sleeves and gloves were of one piece, fastened together by means of discreetly concealed snaps and buttons. Rachel's hair was atop her head in a bun so precise as to be severe. Victoria's hair was worn down, by contrast soft and free.

"Rachel, I have decided not to wear the hood this time."

Rachel's eyes widened. Well she knew how remorseless Regine could be when disobeyed.

Victoria smiled. "Don't worry, Rachel. The Vicomte Cevenne is our wealthiest client, the one Regine is most anxious to please. He did not specify a desire to have me hooded, so I shall not bother. No one will interrupt us and risk the disturbance of his game."

Rachel looked at her lady doubtfully.

"And besides," Victoria continued in her most persuasive tone, "the hood will not matter when he is completely corseted anyway."

Rachel at last agreed.

Beside Victoria's chair was a dressing rack upon which a strange heavy garment was laid. It appeared to consist of thick fabric, contrived with many straps and laces. Beside the dressing rack was an ornate wooden shelf containing other segments of the strange garment. A brass tube about five inches long also lay on the shelf, gleaming in the warm light of the sumptuously furnished room. Above their heads was an oiled metal rail and a mechanism of finely balanced chains and pulleys. The rail led across the ceiling of the room to a custom-designed closet door having a gap in its top that conformed exactly to the rail.

A chair was placed for Rachel just opposite Victoria. Both women hesitated a moment, appearing in some strange way to be reluctant to go on with the evening's activities.

At last Victoria spoke. "Perhaps you had better go and admit the vicomte," she said softly.

Rachel left the training room and appeared scarcely a moment later with the Vicomte Cevenne in tow. A complex scenario, completely designed in every nuance to play on each specialization of the vicomte's desires, had now begun.

"Now hurry!" Rachel snapped crossly. "You must think we have all night to see to you. Don't be selfish."

"Yes," Victoria purred smoothly from her chair. "We have parties to attend later and guests to entertain. You are obviously much too thoughtless for your own good."

Rachel steered the naked vicomte forward until he stood mute and humble before Victoria. His head was bowed.

Victoria allowed a smile to tease about the corners of her lips. "Have him down, Rachel. See that he knows his place."

Rachel reached beneath the vicomte from behind and firmly gripped his scrotum. Then she carefully used it as a bridle to bring him down so that he was on his knees before Victoria's booted feet.

"Thank her for your punishment and bondage; she is mistress of your torments." Rachel said the words carefully, according to a rehearsed script, almost as though she was enacting some strange ceremony or rite.

The vicomte began to reverently lick the gleaming,

outrageously pointed toes of Victoria's boots. He kept his hands clenched carefully at his bare thighs. He was bent forward at an awkward and painful angle without support. Victoria noted that his penis began to slowly lurch to full erection as he paid oral tribute to her booted feet.

Victoria and Rachel looked at one another. Rachel shook her head in disbelief. Victoria smiled and pursed her lips. At last Victoria commanded him to stop and Rachel made him rise. The vicomte at the moment noticed that Victoria's face was unconcealed. His gaze before had been downcast, his eyes concentrated on her strangely clad legs and feet. Now he gasped in muted surprise.

Rachel did not miss the flash of adoration in his glance: indeed, and surprise, too, that Victoria was so young and lovely. The vicomte's rigid control soon reasserted itself, however, and his face again gave nothing away, save perhaps an expression of hopeless resignation at what was to be done to him.

Rachel pulled a chain, and a sprocket turned above her head. A small cushioned leather seat descended, fixed between two thin steel wires. Rachel assisted the vicomte in standing astride the seat, on tiptoe. Then she pulled his penis and scrotum forward through a brass ring on the front of the seat.

Rachel then took up a segment of the strange, heavy garment from the wooden shelf. She looked at the vicomte.

"Do you know what this is?"

He shook his head as though he did not.

"This is a body corset," Rachel said smugly. "You will experience the bondage of its confines as a suitable punishment for your worthlessness."

She knelt before Cevenne and had him extend his legs forward. She wrapped the garment about his legs so that he was covered from the soles of his feet to his upper thighs just below his genitals. Then Rachel quickly laced the garment up its length with an assured dexterity, and further secured it with thick-banded straps.

According to the carefully orchestrated game, Victoria opened the clasps that secured her lovely dress about her shoulders. Her lace-gloved hands opened the top of her dress like the petals of a beautiful flower and tucked it down on her shoulders to form a low *décolletage*. The vicomte's eyes did not neglect the poignant contrast. The wicked appearance of the boots and apron, combined with the feminine dress revealing Victoria's perfect breasts—and her breathtakingly sweet and freshly revealed face—all conspired to madden his deepest sensibilities. He gasped, his sex organ rearing huge and turgid.

Rachel continued his slow imprisonment with a skill that attested to the fact that she had done such things many times before. She removed the main part of the body corset from the dressing rack and fastened it about Cevenne's torso, starting from just below his navel. She commanded him to lock his arms about the wire that supported the rear of the padded seat behind him. This accomplished, she pinioned his arms behind his back in the secure embrace of another corset section. She fastened the laces and buckled the straps. This then covered the vicomte completely, save for his head and the narrow strip about his bare buttocks and genitals.

Rachel then removed a large, heavy hood from the wooden shelf and, with an impudent smirk, drew it over the vicomte's bowed head. She fastened it to the rest of the body corset with the appropriate straps. Cevenne now hung, seated on the padded leather seat, in absolute bondage, his entire form swathed completely in the corset.

Cinderella

Victoria watched intently as Rachel took the last separate portion of the body corset from the dressing rack and wrapped it about the vicomte's hips and buttocks. It was fastened in place: all that showed of the vicomte were his penis and scrotum projecting through the brass ring.

Rachel smiled as she inserted the five-inch brass tube into a small gap for the vicomte's mouth so that his breathing could never be impeded. He could not move a muscle. Rachel seated herself behind the vicomte and reached up to pull a lever that loosened the apparatus. Then she pushed the vicomte forward with her prettily shod foot to his buttocks.

Victoria smiled as the vicomte swung toward her and, when he was nearly upon her, she grasped his erect penis and casually used it as a handle to send him swinging back toward Rachel. And so it progressed. The bound and swathed vicomte, swinging to and fro between the two pretty women, suspended from the apparatus on the rail that ran across the ceiling.

Rachel and Victoria conversed according to the rigid dictates of the vicomte's script. Though he could not see or move, his hearing was unimpeded.

"As soon as we have this pathetic creature done properly and put away, we can go to a lovely party!" Rachel breathed sweetly.

"Yes!" Victoria cooed. "This one has been so utterly selfish. To think that he cares not a whit if we miss some of the night's entertainment due to the necessity of imprisoning him!"

Their conversation then proceeded to cover items of the latest court fashion rage while the vicomte swung.

The vicomte's penis was huge and hot in Victoria's gloved hand. The sensations he experienced were subtle at first, but grew more exquisite with time. The laced corset effectively sealed most of his body from stimulation, and all sensation was now concentrated in his exposed genitals.

Victoria had just removed her lace glove. He could tell. The feeling that her soft hand gave his genitals was most delightful. Each time she pulled on his penis to swing him back toward Rachel he experience a keen, lascivious tingle. To be utterly helpless, his genitals exposed and vulnerable to two lovely women whom he barely knew, was to the Vicomte Cevenne the ultimate of life's pleasures. It was on such a scale to him that he rationed the heady draughts of it that he allowed himself, lest it become somehow common and less exciting.

And Rachel, the dark-haired one with laughing eyes—each time her brazen, arched foot in its pretty velvet shoe touched him low on the buttocks and kicked him forward, he experienced a strong sensation of pleasure deep in his loins. This further served to enlarge and stimulate his penis until he could hardly control himself a moment longer.

Victoria noticed that her palm was being moistened each time she grasped the vicomte's penis to swing him back toward Rachel, and the dark-haired beauty laughed as she watched her lady's expression of mild distaste over the gleam of the vicomte's arousal on her hand. Rachel sat merrily in her chair, her pretty legs raised, her black dress high on her thighs. Her dress was high enough for Victoria to see the pink pout of her slit. Victoria blushed slightly and turned her eyes once again to the vicomte's penis.

"I daresay he had better not soil your hand," said Rachel, "for if he does, his lewdness will cause his bondage to increase tenfold. We shall imprison him, corseted, in a small closet for the entire night!"

Rachel's menacing tones brought soft laughter from Victoria, and the sound of this haughty glee excited the vicomte. It goaded him, and sent him beyond the brink of no return. Again Rachel's impudent, fashionably clad foot kicked his buttocks, thrusting him forward. Again he felt the all-too-brief, delectable torment of Victoria's bare-handed grasp of his penis. Before her fingers released their hold, the Vicomte Cevenne's penis reared, twitching helplessly. A paroxysm of delight set his body trembling within the confines of the corset even as he swung backward toward Rachel once again. As Rachel's foot kicked his buttocks, propelling him forward, the first spurts of ejaculate squirted from his tortured sex organ, splashing the carpet beneath the path of the swinging seat.

Victoria reached out to grasp the vicomte's spurting organ as he swung toward her yet again. Due to the slippery state of his agonized penis, Victoria's hand quickly slipped from it, yet not before it had imparted to him another bit of heavenly friction to sustain him until he should swing back to her hand again.

Rachel pretended dismay from the moment that the vicomte's orgasm began. "Oh, the disgusting thing!" she cried, as if in the throes of a deep moral outrage. "Do see that you are not soiled in any way by his lewdness!" She imparted this warning to Victoria with a hidden smirk.

Victoria stifled her own laughter, and setting her tone to one of petulant affrontery, she joined in Rachel's righteous tirade, "Oh dear! I fear my hand has been defiled with his seed, Rachel!" she exclaimed in tones reeking with pristine disdain. "We shall have to devise a suitable bondage for his wickedness!"

And so the curious dialog continued as the vicomte swung to and fro. At last there was no sperm left in his loins, but rather it all lay thick and glistening across the carpet, save for that which defiled Victoria's palm and fingers. The women then allowed the vicomte to stop swinging and soon he sat, cocooned and sagging weakly beneath the central pivot of the apparatus. His penis was still extended through the brass ring, but now it merely lolled above his large scrotum. It still maintained the vestiges of its erection and its bulb glistened with the last drops of his passion.

Rachel assisted Victoria in cleansing her hands before pushing Victoria's backless chair forward to where the vicomte hung swaying in his bonds. The chair moved easily across the carpet on silent, frictionless wheels. Then, after Rachel dabbed the last bits of spending from the vicomte's genitals, she gave the final portion of physical bondage to Victoria.

"And now the penile corset, suitable punishment for his foul emission!" Victoria said primly, yet with a conspirational smile for Rachel's benefit.

Victoria's deft fingers fastened the cloth sleeve about the vicomte's still-turgid organ. Then, while Rachel held it across her palm, Victoria began to lace the penile corset, drawing it tight, and crossing the laces carefully from the base of the vicomte's penis to the tip. At last even this final, pathetic piece of his anatomy joined the rest of his body in thralldom to the bondage inflicted by the lovely women.

This accomplished, Rachel moved her own chair aside and reached up to move a lever attached to the trolley from which the vicomte hung. The wheels of the trolley turned in the polished rail that ran along the ceiling, and thus the vicomte was slowly borne toward the small closet. Rachel reached the door well before the vicomte, and opened it so that his muffled form and hanging seat could pass inside. Then, with a turn of a small crank, the vicomte's seat was lowered until his corseted knees rested on the floor of the closet. Rachel shut the door, imprisoning the silent, bound form of the vicomte.

Victoria and Rachel then set about divesting themselves of the bizarre garments that Godilieva Prumm had created. Both young women quickly forgot the vicomte and brightened that their work was finished—at least for this night. Rachel set about removing Victoria's boots and was strangely excited as her hand brushed about Victoria's upper thighs as she unbuttoned them.

Chapter Nine

In the Vicomte Cevenne's bedchamber at his estate of Valbernette, a nocturnal breeze bearing the fragrance of the Pompere vineyards wafted sweetly in through an open crystal-inlaid window. The draperies moved again, slightly this time, and two shadows detached themselves from the wall and moved toward the great canopied bed.

It was well that the Vicomtesse Cevenne was visiting her sister's noble family. The two lithe young assassins had intended to make an example of her as a warning to the vicomte. They knew that Cevenne's carriage had not yet returned home to Valbernette. They hoped to gag the vicomtesse and tie her naked and spreadeagled to her bedposts. They even hoped perhaps to have enough time to gently masturbate her with their smooth poniard handles, and, when finished, leave one inserted to the hilt, blade reversed, for her to writhe upon all night. The assassins were furious when they found themselves deprived of even this consolation and contented themselves with tearing the counterpane to ribbons with their daggers.

A servant passing by in the upstairs hall thought he heard a commotion within, and knowing that his master and mistress were both away, dared himself to enter and investigate. He was a large enough man, but nonetheless no match for the athletic young women in black who met him there. One felt-slippered foot arched through the air to kick him mercilessly in the genitals. As he bent forward, gasping in agony, the second assassin gave him a point-toed kick which impacted his face so hard it caused him to lose consciousness. Upon awakening, the servant found himself tied to his master's bedpost and gagged. Great was his fear and astonishment when one of the assassins approached him, withdrew his penis from his garments and began to rub it slowly. Despite his pain and confusion, the poor fellow erected and began to quietly whimper his fear into the gag as the lithe assassin continued her skillful manipulation. His fear turned to terror as he felt a garotting wire slipped over his head and drawn about his neck by the other assassin. The young women decided that there could be no better warning to the Vicomte Cevenne than a masturbated household servant, found dead, tied to his bedpost.

The assassin who wielded the garotting wire savored her work, tightening it ever so slowly as her companion continued to gently masturbate their intended victim. She knelt behind the bedpost, on the bed, her supple curvaceous body relaxed like a cat as she tightened the wire. The assassins planned to dispatch their victim at the very moment of his ejaculatory ecstasy.

Just as the assassin who masturbated the servant coaxed a gushing load of sperm from his loins, a sudden tumult of footsteps and a thunderous pounding on the door saved the poor wretch's life. As he ejaculated on the floor of the master chamber, the assassins became two shadows once again, shadows that flitted across the floor and escaped by the balustrade of the curtained window.

The door burst open in another moment. Household servants pounced into the room to investigate what had become of their fellow. There they found their friend, penis out, tied to the bedpost. He was still choking and coughing away the effects of the garotte. Of the assassins there was no sign.

A pretty, wide-eyed housemaid squealed in consternation as she stepped barefoot in the still-warm pool of the servant's spendings.

At the very moment that the assassins made their escape from Valbernette, the Marquis and Marquise de Besançon lounged in the receiving hall of the Broughton summer house of Deianeira. They sat with select liveried retainers standing by, beneath a huge portrait of Heracles' young bride kneeling to make a love potion of semen from the dying centaur Nessus.

Lord Carlyle Broughton hadn't intended to keep his guests and co-conspirators waiting, thought their pause was spent in distinctively catered comfort. But Lord Carlyle's lovely niece, Lady Jane—of Prince Steven's acquaintance—had been very persuasive. Now he sat back in his armchair and allowed Lady Jane to bestow her lewd caresses upon a most intimate part of his person.

Lady Jane had his hugely erect penis withdrawn from the unbuttoned vent of his trousers and was suavely agitating it with her practiced fingertips. Already the girl's bold hand had caused his penis to drool its arousal down over the tip. Lady Jane's high-collared blouse was unbuttoned and in a temporary state of flagrant disarray. Her breasts were revealed in all their naked allure to Lord Carlyle's fevered eyes.

He was all too pleased to note that the lush, pale swells of Lady Jane's bare globes were topped most deliciously with large, erect, pink, and perfectly formed nipples.

"My dear!" Lord Carlyle gasped halfheartedly, "My dear, we have guests. Even at this late hour we must go and be a proper host and hostess. It does not do to annoy the de Besançons. I have heard that the cellars beneath the Chateau Furnald fairly brim with those who have angered the marquise."

"In a moment, Uncle," the pouting beauty cooed, her voice as soft as velvet. All the while her cunning hand continued its invasive toying with his rigid sex. "Press them to suggest Lord Rodney advise King Philip to hold a ball. What more perfect way for the house of Targete to find a princess to produce an heir for dear Prince Steven?"

Her hand continued to draw Lord Carlyle's foreskin up and down; her grip was ever so artful and knowing. Lady Jane smiled and continued, "Lord Rodney has scant regard for us, but he still respects the de Besançons. He will listen to them and perhaps be moved by friendship to heed their suggestion."

"But why, Jane?" Lord Carlyle enquired between gasps. "The de Besançons and we have set wheels in motion to overthrow the house of Targete!"

"Uncle, you are so artless at times!" Lady Jane murmured, her eyes on the strangled, purple hue that the head of Lord Carlyle's penis had assumed. "In the whirl of court gaiety that will ensue once the ball is announced, our machinations will be able to proceed unimpeded."

Lady Jane fixed an innocent, liquid look upon her uncle. Her hand urged him, her motions compelled him.

"Please, Uncle! You must see the wisdom of this course."

Lord Carlyle gasped his assent. "Yes Jane. I shall mention it at once."

Cinderella

His last syllable tapered away to a gritting moan as Lady Jane's hand moved more rapidly to induce his orgasm. Even as Lord Carlyle's sperm began jetting from his swollen tool, Lady Jane stood up and fastened her blouse over her breasts again.

"Do hurry, Uncle," she cooed. "I will go down and amuse our guests while you set yourself aright."

Lady Jane descended the steps to the receiving hall to greet the de Besançons. She smiled smugly. Her carefully laid plans were at last bearing fruit. The plot would be masked by the preparations for the ball. Yes, and she would see to it that Prince Steven chose her! And then, when the conspiracy was successful, he would pay for her humiliation in Market Square. Lady Jane almost laughed. Of course, he would pay either way.

Lady Jane embraced the Marquise de Besançon and hugged her warmly. The knowing girl was well cognizant of the fact that she could arouse bisexual passions in the marquise and thus allay any irritation the formidable courtesan might show at being kept waiting. Lady Jane's hands slid artfully down across the marquise's firm buttocks as they at last drew apart from their warm embrace.

Then Lady Jane moved smiling to the marquis, noting all the while the tribute his lingering eyes paid her hips, breasts and bottom. She graciously allowed him to kiss first one hand and then the other. Lady Jane's smile was not for the gallantry of the marquis. Rather it was occasioned by her recalling how her hands had been employed scant moments before and how easily they could—in different circumstances perhaps—work their deft magic on the marquis as well.

"My uncle is momentarily indisposed, but will join us in but a moment," Lady Jane breathed in her most charming fashion. "He, of course, deeply regrets your inconvenience," she added skillfully with an arch look directed toward the marquise and a pat on her knee.

When Lord Carlyle descended the steps, the foursome entered a private chamber, leaving their retainers behind.

The Marquise de Besançon spoke first. "We must move quickly, times are perilous. We attempted to draw the Vicomte Cevenne to our cause and failed. I do not know if he would jeopardize our efforts or not, though I can assure you, Lord Carlyle, that steps have been taken to render him silent."

Lord Carlyle spoke thoughtfully, taking the marquise's hand affectionately as he did so.

"Perhaps you could influence Lord Rodney Fallone to move King Philip to hold a royal ball. All the lovely young women of the kingdom would be invited, of course. What better way for the house of Targete to obtain a perfect royal bride?"

To Lord Carlyle's surprise, the de Besançons seized upon the idea at once.

"I believe we could persuade Lord Rodney," the marquise said thoughtfully. "And in the midst of court preparation we will press on with our redoubled efforts."

Lady Jane poured them all some dry sherry from a gleaming silver and crystal service. They raised their glasses to toast the success of their endeavor.

"And to the other conspirators!" Lord Carlyle said. "To them all!"

Lady Jane smiled like a cat.

CHAPTER TEN

Prince Steven Targete brooded silently, in his chambers, situated within the sacrosanctity of the royal palace's private wing. In but a short time he had become obsessed with the pretty young woman who stood tiptoed in Market Square. If only he had seen her face! A pensive tap sounded on the great panelled door as he sat lost in thought. Prince Steven did not hear it at all. In a few moments the tap sounded again, slightly louder. At the prince's command, the door opened slowly to reveal the face of a trusted retainer. The man bowed, with a dashing sweep of his crimson-clad, elegantly slender frame.

"My deepest apologies for this interruption, sire! However a certain young lady has asked me to inquire as to whether or not there might be anything she could do to increase your royal comfort."

The retainer hesitated, waiting while Prince Steven

almost absentmindedly swirled red wine about in an intricately carved goblet. The dim light of the prince's chamber proved sufficient to set the wine sparkling, an enticing velvet glitter, swirling in the goblet.

"What is her name?" said the prince flatly.

"Giselle, my lord. She is from Lucerne."

"Show her in, if you please, though I may send her back to you in but a moment."

The retainer excused himself and departed; in his place stood a lovely young woman.

She waited a moment by the door, hands folded demurely, then she moved slowly forward. Her face was young, angelic, and posed in a smiling expression of confident sweetness.

"You seem constrained, my lord," she murmured, her voice a low, soothing purr. Her eyes lingered over the prince, noting his deep chest, small waist, and broad shoulders. "I could help you, my lord, and am quite willing to ease your burdens of state in any way that I can." Giselle spoke softly. Her voice was carefully modulated, perhaps even calculated in its subtle blend of innocence and suggestiveness.

The prince looked up and studied her for a moment, "I fear that tonight you may find me but a dull, common clod, Giselle. Certain matters weigh heavily upon me." He paused. "Come forward. Move into the light, if you please."

Giselle stepped forward. She was barefoot, clad in a long white dress trimmed in floral lace. She held the hem of her dress up from the tiled floor as she walked toward the prince's chair. Prince Steven's eyes lingered on her bare knees and the curve of her calves, though soon his eyes travelled lower until his gaze came to rest upon her feet. They were pretty indeed, he had to admit, though they lacked the exquisite perfection of the girl's in Market Square.

Cinderella

Prince Steven got up from his chair and motioned to Giselle, "Sit, if you please, sit and take comfort."

"In your chair, my lord?" she enquired, her voice silken in its delicate hesitation.

"Yes, in my chair. Please sit! Take your ease."

Giselle sat, resting her hips forward at the front of the prince's seat cushion. Her pretty little beringed hands rested on her knees. She licked her lips in slight nervousness, yet she was strangely intrigued with this unusual turn of events. The prince was extraordinary. He did not treat her quite like the other young men of her acquaintance.

Prince Steven sat down on the floor facing Giselle. Her eyes were fixed upon him.

"Raise your skirt a little, if you please. I would see a bit more of your thighs."

Giselle demurely crossed her right leg over her left, supporting herself with her tiptoed left foot on the floor. She drew up her skirts until she exposed to Prince Steven's gaze a generous portion of her curving thighs, "In this fashion, my lord?"

She hesitated. Prince Steven was hard to read. There was no trace of the possessive leer she had so often seen in the male gaze. Rather there was a worshipfulness in his look that amused yet slightly disconcerted Giselle.

The prince lapsed into silence.

"Do you find my legs attractive, my lord?" she found courage to sweetly ask at length.

The prince replied that her legs were indeed lovely, and then began with a series of strange requests:

"Raise your right foot, Giselle, with the sole toward me if you please ... yes! Precisely like that. And now point your bare toes into a rigid, pointed pose."

The prince studied her point-toed foot for a good while. Her cheeks flushed and she bit her lip in perplexity as she maintained her uncomfortable posture.

"Now arch and flex your foot ... no, not that way exactly, more as if it were tiptoed upon the floor as before."

Giselle did so. Suddenly the prince was on the floor at her feet. He knelt quietly, his powerful body poised in a position at once humble yet also a trifle alarming to the pretty young courtesan. At last he reached out and his large, gentle hand careful cupped her heel.

Giselle studied his face as he slowly bent more forward. There was a glisten of perspiration on his royal brow. His chest rose and fell as though he could not find enough air to bring into his lungs. For the first time Giselle noticed the huge bulge of the royal sex organ, tenting its outline in his jodhpur trousers. Her apprehension faded. An intuition dawned gradually in the young beauty's mind. Her .ips curled into a pretty smile. It was a smile of amusement, a reaction which she could not help.

The prince continued to bend slowly forward, as if entranced and captivated with the beauty of Giselle's foot. Soon she felt the cool brush of his lips as he placed a gentle kiss upon the ball of her foot beneath her toes.

Giselle giggled; again she could not help it.

"Do point your toes, please, Giselle," the prince said breathlessly. "Point your toes just as you did a moment ago."

Giselle pointed the toes of her right foot, saucily wrinkling her coy foot-bottom and exaggerating her high arch as she did so. She allowed her skirt to slip yet higher on her thighs.

The prince kissed the big toe of her right foot, then took it in his mouth and began to suck on it gently.

Giselle was struck by a breathless sense that all these events were not really occurring at all. Of course, the crown prince of the kingdom was not kneeling before her, sucking on the big toe of her prettily pointed right foot. Giselle became possessed of a surreal sense of power that made her giddy and bold. A latent instinct, a knowing sense, grew within her by the moment.

The prince's eyes were shut; an expression of ecstasy was stamped upon his every feature. He nursed at her toes with all the urgent need and desperation of an infant.

Giselle could not help herself. She began to laugh at the prince and found that she could not stop. Soon the prince's chamber was filled with the pealing tones of nearly uncontrolled feminine laughter.

The prince did not become enraged or even indignant. Rather, he appeared to become yet more excited. At last he pulled back and drew down his riding trousers, exposing to the still laughing girl the huge truncheon of his royal penis. Then he got down on all fours, his hips swiveling toward her while she remained, legs crossed, toes pointed and laughing. He looked up into her laughing face, his own face possessed of an agony borne of pent-up passion and sexual excitement.

"Touch it, Giselle!" he husked. "Grant me relief with your hand."

Giselle reached down to grip the huge royal sex organ in her left hand, careful all the while to maintain her leg-crossed, point-toed pose. Still laughing, she tightened her persuasive grasp and began to masturbate the prince. The heat of his arousal was so intense it nearly scorched her palm as she tugged his foreskin up and down the rigid length of his organ.

Such was his excitement that the laughing girl had scarce finished her fourth stroke when the prince's penis reared, twitching, in her dainty fist. She continued to laugh softly as the prince shuddered and spilled his seed in wildly squirting spurts upon the tiles and carpet of the floor. The prince sagged forward, weakly pressing himself into the enticing grip of Giselle's shaming hand. At last, when he had fully spent, he sat back upon his heels, trembling and weak. A terrible sense of shame now possessed him and he dismissed his still laughing masturbatrix. When she had gone, he cleaned himself and changed his garments without assistance from any of the many palace servants he could have summoned. He had done it again. He had degraded and shamed himself and shown a lovely, laughing courtesan that he was a slave to abnormal, twisted passions.

He determined never to indulge his fetish again. He sealed this firmly resolved bargain with himself by summoning a lovely royal houseguest to his quarters.

The fair young Princess of Alsace eagerly came. He was determined to enjoy her in the customary manly sense without self-degradation. As she knelt upon his bed, the lush curves of her bare buttocks temptingly exposed to his gaze, he pronounced himself on the mend. As he thrust his again-turgid penis deep into her anus, and felt the grip of her bottom clutch him, and heard the soft gasping murmur of her desire—he declared himself cured.

The following morning, as the Princess of Alsace knelt before him, her lovely large-nippled breasts succulent in their dangling as she wiggled her buttocks and sucked his tool, he knew that the statement of his cure was premature. As his sperm jetted and frothed into the young woman's mouth, his thoughts were on the tiptoed feet of the girl watching the scene of humiliation in Market Square—the girl whose feet were even lovelier than the laughing Giselle's.

CHAPTER ELEVEN

The Vicomte Cevenne knelt in total darkness, in a deprivation of all sensory stimulus that was nearly absolute. He was wrapped and laced in the body corset, his bound knees barely resting on the closet floor. He knelt astride the cushioned seat that hung from the apparatus on the rail. He had scant idea of how much time had passed. He also had no inkling whatever that his present predicament had saved his life. He only knew that his sex organ was desperately swollen and in great need of relief. Sufficient time has passed for the ceaseless factory in his loins to produce a surplus buildup of sperm since his last release in Victoria's hands.

The vicomte's relief was almost at hand. Rachel stood luxuriously stretching on the carpeted floor of the second training room. She had parted the draperies to let in a soft morning breeze laden with the scent of lawns and flower beds. She stood naked. Naked, that was, save for her black velvet buttoned shoes boasting five-inch heels, and a black lace glove on her left hand. She stretched again, indulgently flexing the dimpled curves of her bare buttocks and giggling upon noticing that her nipples were erect. They were erect in anticipation of the task at hand.

The vicomte tensed his bound, contorted body. Did he hear approaching footsteps? His heart thudded with longing. Perhaps his relief was on the way, and his universe would again consist of more than the pathetic throbbing need between his legs. Soon, now, his deprived awareness would explode in overloaded climactic delight as either Victoria, or her smiling assistant Rachel, came to see to him. Every one of his senses was keenly strung, anguished and yet taut with hope.

The closet door opened.

A low giggling voice spoke: "Are you ready for your morning milking? We mustn't allow a bondage slave to split his penile corset in his unfulfilled excitement!"

Rachel always felt a trifle silly when saying the carefully rehearsed words required in the vicomte's complex and bizarre game. Nonetheless, her clitoris was swollen huge and churning at the thought of what she was about to do. She bent over, low at the waist, the curves of her bare bottom and her hips lusciously emphasized, though it was impossible for him to behold her. She held a small silver basin in her right hand as she began to stimulate the tip of the vicomte's penis in her left. The black lace glove provided ample friction as she rubbed and pinched the sensitive head of his penis between her thumb and forefinger. The contrast between the gloved feminine hand and the big imprisoned penis was a stark change, indeed.

The vicomte twisted and shuddered as unaccustomed waves of agonizingly voluptuous sensation swept over him. After so long a sensory deprivation, the sexual pleasure to which Rachel was gently subjecting him had all the force and impetus of an explosion.

Rachel smiled at the sound of his stifled gasps. Her hands never paused in their firm, almost brisk stimulation of the tip of his engorged penis. The bloated crimson swell of the tormented head amused Rachel. It was so exquisitely sensitive! Truly her crisp laced gloved fingertips must provide him with nearly as much excruciating pain as delicious pleasure. It never took him long though. The bare-bottomed girl dutifully thumbed, frisked and rubbed until the vicomte's strangled breaths fairly whistled through his brass breathing tube.

In a moment his manhood spurted in thick tormented gouts from the gasping slit in the head of his penis. He spurted with such force and thickness that the streams slipped end over end in their short trajectory to audibly plop into the bowl Rachel held.

Rachel giggled as she prolonged the torture by scuffing and thumbing the pulsing tip of his penis even after his climax had subsided—in the very moment of its greatest sensitivity. Rachel's cheeks flushed from the intensity of the warm liquid tingle between her pretty legs. Her bare bottom clenched lewdly as if on an imaginary prick as she delicately wiped the last thick drops of the vicomte's passion away. She stood up, holding the silver basin containing the glistening froth of his spend.

"Your efforts were feeble today I'm afraid. See that you do better tomorrow!" With that, the pretty bare-bottomed girl shut the door to the closet, leaving the vicomte to his utter bondage again.

Once back on the carpet of the training room floor, she removed her glove and shoes to recline in languid, comfortable nakedness.

Elvert crept down the steps from the back of the house and waited a moment. Aside from the clamor and clatter of the distant kitchen there was no sound. He moved forward noiselessly. He paused at the door of the second training room for quite some time. At length he summoned his courage and slowly turned the knob to open the door a crack and peep within. He vividly recalled the last time that he had done so, weeks before.

His heart had lurched with an almost sickening excitement as he watched Victoria, bizarrely masked like a mediaeval torturer, riding a hugely fat royal courtier about the room; a pompous courtier that Elvert had once seen at market day, surrounded by aides and bristling with self importance.

Never had Elvert seen boots the like of which Victoria wore then. Black as midnight, gleaming wickedly, with impossibly high heels and decorated with cruel spurs—they captured his fancy. The brief, daring glimpse sent him running for fear of Regine's anger if his voyeurism were discovered. Regine was so terribly imaginative when inventing cruel punishments for her pouting daughters to carry out on servants like himself.

But now he saw Rachel, reclined in the dappled pool of sunlight cast by the partly open drapes. He was captivated by the sight of her naked body. Her lithe, youthful curves excited him, beckoned him and compelled him. The rich dark fur about her mount drew his eyes like a mariner's loadstone. He could just make out the coy peep of the lips of her slit.

Was she asleep? Elvert summoned all his courage and moved forward on silent feet. He stood above her, and then knelt to lovingly study her naked form.

Rachel lay, buttocks on the carpet, one lovely leg drawn up, the other extended. She reclined on her back, though her lithe body was turned a bit to the side in her repose. Her eyes were shut. One hand was out before her, the other pressed to her breast.

Elvert was fascinated with Rachel's unwitting exhibition of nubile charms. His prick hardened, lurching to full excitement within the suddenly too-tight confines of his working trousers. His eyes swept to and fro across the supple curves of her body, to alternatingly linger on the pink nipples of her breasts, thence on the bulging pout of her mysteriously foliated sex.

Elvert's extreme arousal granted him boldness. He moved forward, hardly daring to breathe lest he should startle Rachel and spoil the poignant moment. His knees quietly scuffed the carpet as he moved, then paused, hardly daring to vent the exhalations of his growing excitement. He knelt transfixed for what seemed like hours. At last he extended a trembling fingertip to touch Rachel's thigh. She did not even stir.

Rachel was not asleep at all, though she was nearly so when she heard Elvert's stealthy entrance. At first she did not know that it was he, and in fact the pretty girl feared that it was Marcella or Ana instead. She knew they would punish her for loitering after carrying out her masturbatory duties.

Rachel lay still, waiting with baited breath—then realized that it was not one of her mistresses, but rather a servant, probably Elvert. Only he and Lucas were allowed access to this part of the house, and she knew Lucas was assigned elsewhere for the remainder of the morning. So, as Elvert dared his first tentative touch, Rachel waited to see how far his new-found courage might tempt him to go. Rachel herself was so excited after her masturbation of the Vicomte Cevenne that she was ready and willing for whatever Elvert's emboldened imagination might devise.

Elvert reached out again to gently touch the soft, dark fur about Rachel's slit. He stifled an almost silent gasp at the heat his fingertip encountered there. At that moment something occurred in Elvert's mind that drove him to risk all. He became possessed of an almost desperate hunger. The degradation to which he had been subjected by Marcella—only one of many such incidents, if the truth be known—kept him in a state of intense sexual need. At length he bent down and, heedless of the consequences, wrapped his arms about Rachel's thighs—after first freeing his swollen penis from its trouser prison—and begun to gently nuzzle her slit.

Rachel started, then gasped at the intensity of the unexpected sensation. She turned her upper body and sat up, supporting herself from behind with her extended hands. She looked down across her erect nipples at Elvert and pretended to shake the sleep from her eyes. She squirmed. The wretch certainly knew how to employ his tongue! Rachel bit her lip, then cried, "Oh, my goodness! Elvert! What are you doing! Stop it at once. Stop it!"

She let her head fall back and gave vent to a low whimper of delight—the signal perhaps that persuaded Elvert to go on rather than desist.

Elvert was nibbling her clitoris now, sending hot, darting electric tingles through her deepest parts and fairly taking her breath away. She had but a moment to become accustomed to this treatment and then he turned his attention to the depths of her cleft. Elvert lapped at Rachel's fount, probing her deeply with his tongue. He longingly sucked at the essence of her femininity, lapping her deeply with slow, thirsty motions of his desperate tongue.

Rachel's cheeks flushed like two hot coals. Her bare toes pointed forward, an expression of the delirious ecstasy she felt as she spent. Her unseeing eyes swept across the room, bypassing the basin that still contained the vicomte's long-cooling sperm.

Elvert licked Rachel to climax twice more. The wet, sucking noises that accompanied his services to her intimate parts excited her so that she was nearly beside herself. At last she pushed him away and writhed about on the floor whimpering and gasping with delight. The sheen of her arousal about Elvert's mouth and cheeks complimented perfectly the glistening perspiration about Rachel's own firm buttocks and thighs.

Rachel lay back on the carpet and drew her knees up, nearly to her breasts. She kneaded her nipples as she raised her head and spoke to Elvert in breathless demanding tones. Her eyes caressed his penis, thrilling to its every pleading throb.

"Thrust your penis in me, Elvert. Do it now! I am aflame with passion!"

Elvert was desperate to speedily obey. He kicked his cumbersome clothing away, till, naked below the waist, he knelt over Rachel and, with the help of her guiding hand, steered his penis into the furnace of her sex. Rachel wrapped her legs about his torso as he slowly inserted his agonizingly erect penis, savoring each wicked, sliding inch of delicious pleasure. He held himself upright above her, the heels of his hands resting on the carpet, as he began the slow thrusts of their sexual coupling. Rachel moved her lithe hips to meet his motions, up and down, moving with him, matching his every gyration. Elvert's eyes were fixed on Rachel's face as she writhed below him, their interlocked genitals generating an excruciating blend of lewd sensations. Rachel's lips parted in a pouting surrender to the intensity of his passion.

Both Rachel and Elvert were soon gasping and moaning in the throes of their excitement. In the dark closet, the bound form of the Vicomte Cevenne stirred. His penis twitched to erection. Oh the cruelty of such callous behavior! His heartless masturbatrix was taking her pleasure while he languished!

The vicomte was not the only one to hear them.

Regine stood in the doorway of the second training room, her lovely catlike features both exquisite and taut with indignation. She wore an elegant gown, crafted of black satin and trimmed with the most delicate gold threadwork. The hem was scandalously short, indeed high enough to reveal the graceful curves of her calves. Her feet were fashionably clad in the latest court rage, dainty black kidskin dancing shoes with high heels, pointy toes and velvet bows set prettily to enhance the coy revelation of her toe cleavage. The gown was crafted to reveal Regine's bare breasts, with underpinnings that lifted and compressed them. Her hair was up in a flawless swirl of severe, understated elegance.

Her cheeks flushed with fury as she stepped quickly forward toward the oblivious, writhing couple. Rachel and Elvert were far too engrossed in the lascivious delight of their coupling to hear Regine's footsteps or even to sense her presence.

Another woman stood in the door behind Regine, also lovely, and also dressed for the same exclusive party. She stood still, the amusement in her expression revealing more curiosity than disgust as her eyes locked on the heavy swing of Elvert's scrotum beneath his straining buttocks. The newcomer was the Contessa of Albion, wealthy friend and intimate confidant of Regine.

Regine stood directly behind Elvert, and he and Rachel—both now sweating and moaning with pleasure—were unaware. Regine bent low at the waist, giving the Contessa of Albion a most stimulating view of the trim upside-down heart of her bottom. Regine smiled her cruel self-satisfied smile and took Elvert by the scrotum. Elvert had just thrust yet again into the luscious tightness of Rachel's squirming body. The jolt and twitch of his penis told him that he had just passed the point of no return. He gasped and wiggled his hips.

In a moment, now, he would fill the pretty, breathless girl in his embrace with the thick expenditure of his passion. He gasped for breath as he tensed himself, pressing in most deeply, inflamed with the lascivious sensation. His turgid penis, now deliciously ensconced in the velvet clasp of Rachel's sex, twitched again.

Suddenly Elvert cried out in pain and disbelief. He cried out again as he felt the agonizing grip of a cruel hand compress his testicles in a tightening fist.

Rachel was oblivious at first as, eyes tightly shut and cheeks flushed, she panted beneath him, desperate to feel the hot squirts of his sperm in her deepest parts.

Regine pulled hard on Elvert's scrotum, knowingly tormenting his genitals in an effort to pull him up from Rachel with no regard for pain or dignity. He moaned and thrashed, pulling backward with all his might in immediate obedience to the hand that mastered him.

The course of nature would not be denied, however, and as Elvert's still twitching penis slid to plop from Rachel's sex, his orgasm was upon him. With a slack-jawed expression of horror—for he realized whose hand had him now—he watched the purple head of his penis expand and the first long, thin squirt of sperm shoot from it to bathe the fur of Rachel's mount.

Rachel was in the throes of orgasm herself as, eyes wide with dismay, she sat up and flushed, covering her breasts and closing her legs.

Elvert's penis twitched again and his second squirt splashed across Rachel's shapely thigh. Regine released his testicles and slapped him hard across the side of his face. Stunned and still weak from his ejaculation, Elvert sagged to the side. His penis reared and twitched again, shooting his next gout of sperm through the air to land across Regine's dancing shoe. His fourth spurt soiled the carpet at her feet before he collected himself, blocking the discharge with his own trembling hands.

Elvert gripped his rearing penis, desperately willing his intense orgasm to subside. His penis continued jolting and pulsing, generously soiling his own hands with thick floods of sperm. He found that he could not take his eyes from Regine as she stood over him, the searing and sophisticated tone of her tirade flaying him.

Rachel got to her knees, her dismayed eyes still locked on Elvert's falling member as she tried to wipe the sperm from her legs and mount.

The Contessa of Albion stepped forward to have a better view of Elvert's penis and stood laughing and gloating over his discomfiture.

As Elvert's orgasm subsided, Regine moved to sit on a comfortable settee and extended her leg, raising her lovely shoe with the sperm still glistening across the toe.

"Elvert come forward at once!" she commanded haughtily, as she disdainfully surveyed the mess.

The Contessa of Albion, now giggling, assisted Regine's command by taking Elvert by the curls of his head and dragging him forward on all fours.

Regine, never at a loss to orchestrate an intense humiliation, also ordered Rachel to come forward. She made Rachel kneel by Elvert's hips and slap his bare bottom repeatedly while she commanded Elvert to lick up the sperm that soiled her shoe. Despite the slaps that Rachel delivered most forcefully—knowing well that her only hope lay in complete obedience now—Elvert was most understandably reluctant to lick his own sperm from the toe of Regine's dainty shoe.

Here the Countessa of Albion again proved useful as she reached beneath Elvert to cruelly grasp his still cramping scrotum until the poor youth had no choice. His eyes brimmed with tears of degradation as he extended his tongue to clean his mistress' footwear.

Regine smiled. "Good boy, Elvert! But have no fear. Your punishment has not yet even begun!"

CHAPTER TWELVE

As Elvert quavered under Regine's cooing threat, Prince Steven's rather spoiled younger brother, Prince Rupert, was amusing himself in the royal palace.

Having only just turned eighteen years of age, the lad, at once mischievous and precocious, had familiarized himself with every nook, corner and passage of the royal stables. He was especially knowledgeable of the royal dressage arena and the various dressing rooms and storage chambers about its circumference beneath the judging stands, for Prince Rupert was driven by one passionate obsession—his youthful infatuation with the pretty dressage trainer Mademoiselle Seline d'Elbernne.

Now he lay, cramped in a low crawl space, adjacent to a secret corridor overlooking Mademoiselle d'Elbernne's changing room. The object of his adolescent affection stood—apparently unaware of her admiring voyeur—and prepared to practice the various stylized whip snaps so essential to her craft. The room in which she stood was well illuminated by warm summer sunlight falling through an open latticed window that overlooked the south end of the formal garden. Prince Rupert lay wearing only a rather soiled, loose-cuffed white shirt—now in sad disarray due to his traverse of the dusty crawl space to find his peephole. His boots and trousers were left behind in the corridor.

The lad had a prick that would be the envy of a sergeant-major. It was thick and long, springing upward from a downy forest of golden hair that also generously grew over a pair of large and pendant balls.

Prince Rupert lay stimulating himself in his practiced fist, nearly ready once again to spurt his tribute to the charms of the lovely dressage trainer. He had masturbated to many captivating and highly cherished sightings of his idol from various secret and not-so-secret vantages all about the palace and stables. Indeed, as if his deliberate emissions were not enough, nature conspired also with his obsession to see that he spurted generous nocturnal tributes to Mademoiselle d'Elbernne as well. His experienced fist slid slowly up and down the straining girth of his blushing sex organ, his firm motions regularly revealing and covering the crimson blush of its tip.

Seline d'Elbernne stood prettily, legs together, clad in shining black high-heeled boots that extended upward to cover her from gleaming toe to curving thigh. The heels of her boots were almost excessively high, and graced with the wicked gleam of Spanish spurs with multi-point rowels crafted like silver stars.

Seline's riding pants were a sight to behold, and of sufficient snugness to arouse the passions of a doting pensioner—to say nothing of a bored and randy young prince. The riding trousers clung to every youthful swelling curve of Seline's bottom, hips and thighs—so much so that the bulge of her peach was actually somewhat revealed. The thin material was drum-tight and utterly without wrinkles across the firm yet promising expanse of Seline's backside.

She wore a short-waisted jacket of black velvet embroidered with swirling pink branches and flowers. Her hands were clad in gleaming leather gloves with wide wrist flarings. Seline wore her hair up in an elegantly plain Spanish style, regally topped with a plumed, peaked and visored dragoon's parade cap with a wide chin strap.

Indeed Seline did resemble a cruel yet lovely parade marshal in a circus exhibition of masochistic delight—such as often was found in Prince Rupert's most copious wet dreams. Seline pursed her lips and lashed the whip, its thongs snapping a hair's breadth from a wooden beam, causing dust motes to dance madly in the sunlit air.

Seline practiced several more formalized whip snaps, giving Prince Rupert maddening views of her virtually bare bottom as she did so. Then she turned her attention to a high wooden horse, over whose back was laid a thick, tooled-leather whipping pad. Seline carefully placed the ornate dressage whip in its proper niche within a rosewood rack. Then she uncoiled a long, wicked, black serpent of a whip to use on the practice pad, more as a vent for her own youthful energies than anything else. Certainly she would not dream of using such vicious strokes as she now practiced on an animal.

Seline had attended a convent academy and came to womanhood there. Despite the curves of her body, the young woman was of a rigid disposition and little familiar with the ways of the world. Seline only knew that when she was performing, and her stallions exhibited their unnatural, forced mince-steps for the crowd while her whip snapped above their backs, she always became deliciously aware of the incredible tightness of her riding pants. As she strutted and paraded haughtily before the assembled royal court in the stands, Seline's cheeks would flush with sensations stronger than pride alone. Indeed, returning to her own quarters after a performance, Seline was always a trifle disgusted to find her privates pleasantly moist.

Seline brought the horsewhip down in a vicious, searing cut across the practice pad. She followed it immediately with another and then a third. Perhaps there was some hidden frustration to the severity of her blows. As the whip whistled through the air, coiling its menace to strike again, Seline thought of the gardener at the convent academy who once exhibited his penis to the girls before he was dismissed from service by the outraged sisters.

In her mind's eye he lay naked, bound, legs spread —and it was her duty to geld him with the whip. Perhaps it was the heat of the summer's day, or possibly the vision of the helpless gardener pleading for mercy; at any rate, whatever the cause, Mademoiselle d'Elbernne found her fantasy most delectable.

The whip hissed and whistled through the air to deliver searing cut after searing cut to the practice pad. Her eyes sparkled and her breasts rose and fell with each passionate breath as she practiced her art.

Prince Rupert lay gasping with delight and abusing his big, lurching tool in a revel of long, easy strokes. His worshipful eyes were positively glued to Mademoiselle d'Elbernne's lusciously clad backside.

At last she put the whip down, leaving, in her mind's eye, the hapless gardener quivering and emasculated.

Prince Rupert nearly groaned his disappointment, for being somewhat desensitized with repeat spendings, he was not yet able to attain the solace of ejaculation.

His disappointment soon turned to feverish excitement, however, as he watched Mademoiselle d'Elbernne sit down on a low wooden bench and begin to unlace her boots. Prince Rupert settled down to a slow, even rhythm and watched intently, desperate to time his climax with her most mouthwatering exhibition.

Mademoiselle d'Elbernne drew off her left boot and began to unlace her right.

Prince Rupert was captivated by her prettily arched bare foot, and the curving swell of her calf and ankle. Her riding trousers terminated just beneath her knees like short knickers.

When Mademoiselle d'Elbernne had removed her boots, she stood up and unfastened her riding pants.

Prince Rupert held his breath in anticipation as she drew them down and slipped them off. He was masturbating passionately now, as she stood, backside to him, and surveyed herself in a small wall glass. She still wore the short-waisted Spanish jacket, and her peaked dragoon's cap with the chin strap still properly fastened. Prince Rupert flogged himself with abandon, his eyes glued to the pouting voluptuousness of Mademoiselle d'Elbernnes's bare bottom.

She picked up her whip, raised one leg to place her bare, arched foot in a chair, and then slowly inserted the handle of the horsewhip into her sex. Her cheeks flushed crimson at the sensation, but she did not stop until she had plumbed her depths with the smooth leather handle of the whip. The trainer bent forward, wiggling her hips, and holding the whip handle so that it would not slip from her.

Prince Rupert could plainly hear her soft gasps as she rubbed her clitoris with light circular motions of the fingers of her free hand. As Mademoiselle d'Elbernne flexed her bare buttocks deep within her private revery, Prince Rupert's manual effort bore fruit at last. He pumped his big sex organ frantically, his fist but a flying blur, his eyes absorbed with the charm of the lovely dressage trainer's bare posterior. A moment later, thick gobs of adolescent sperm churned up from the depths of his balls to squirt thickly from the gasping slit of his engorged penis. His buttocks and thighs twitched spasmodically as his eyes glazed from the intensity of the sensation. His penis jolted, rearing and plunging within his working fist, spraying forth the product of his loins in thick gouts to collect in hot puddles across the floor of the crawl space.

Mademoiselle d'Elbernne was approaching the peak of her own passion. She threw herself onto the bench, legs spread and feet in the air. She pointed her bare toes and writhed on the impaling whip handle, gasping and squirming in ecstasy.

The prince's last feeble squirt of sperm accompanied the first quiver of her own delight.

CHAPTER THIRTEEN

As his brother masturbated in the crawl space overlooking the dressage trainer's changing room, Prince Steven slept fitfully.

He was exhausted from his night of reveling with the haughty Princess of Alsace. The lewd beauty had recruited two of her personal maids for her games with Prince Steven, and the quartet's imagination had proved nearly boundless.

Prince Steven passed from one strange dream to the next as if his sleep was orchestrated by a drunken-witless composer of nocturnal surrealism. Prince Steven lay naked on his bed, having kicked the covers down and out of the way with his restless tossing. Whether or not he was awake he could not tell, though he thought himself to be possessed of his full faculties, eyes open and lying quietly.

Then a strange thing occurred. His penis, even

though exhausted by his orgy with the Princess of Alsace and her maids, suddenly reared erect and huge, jutting upward from between his legs like a battle-ram. A warm-scented breeze seemed then to flood his chamber as his stained glass window blew open.

And then, it seemed, two breathtakingly beautiful young women appeared, hovering on gossamer fairy wings above his head. Their angelic faces looked down at him with liquid, condescending expressions of pity. Their hair was long and worn free, though festooned with pink and white flowers. Their skirts were of a strange diaphanous material of the palest blue, and their legs were bared nearly to the full curves of their hips.

The prince tried to sit up, and found that he could not move.

Neither fairy spoke—they hovered above him and extended their lovely little arched bare feet toward his penis. There was almost tenderness now in their limpid soft gazes, though their lips were curved into knowing, archly sweet smiles. Both fairies, then, while maintaining their hovering posture, began to kick his erect penis back and forth between their lovely, arched, barefoot-bottoms. Soft laughter filled the chamber.

Prince Steven's penis was not only rigid and swollen, it was also twitching and tingling with an urgency of arousal, the likes of which he had never felt the half of before. His huge balls hung so pendant beneath his muscular, splayed thighs that they rested heavily on the bedclothes beneath him, full and desperate to be relieved of their fertile load. The two lovely fairies arched and pointed their toes in the most fetching and bewitching manner possible before again repeatedly kicking his tormented organ back and forth. Again the prince tried to move, and found that he could not. He lay paralyzed, though every sense was excited to a fever pitch by the teasing, laughing fairies. Though he tried to speak, no words would come.

Prince Steven turned wide eyes, eloquent in their mute appeal, to his lovely, hovering tormenters. Redoubled fairy laughter filled his chamber, somehow mocking him with sweet, musical tones. One fairy then fluttered about the room, turning and writhing deliciously in her flight. Her gossamer dress flared out, then flew up to give Prince Steven a luscious view of her bare bottom and the supple, beckoning curve of her hips.

Whether he was experiencing a dream, a vision, or if reality itself was set askew, Prince Steven did not know or care. His whole existence became but an awareness of acute sexual need.

The second fairy flew closer to the prince and clasped his pulsing sex organ between her shapely bare thighs. He felt his penis squeezed in a maddening embrace as she wrapped her legs about him, and then fluttered her wings, providing the impetus to work his penis up and down in this fanciful fashion. Tears of mingled sexual anguish and delight rolled unbidden down Prince Steven's cheeks.

The first fairy continued to exhibit her nubile charms directly before his face while the second kept masturbating him with her thighs. The stimulation was prolonged beyond reason and endurance.

At that moment the door to the prince's chamber opened and the lovely young girl from Market Square entered. She was barefoot and wearing the green dress, just as in Prince Steven's cherished memories of market day. Her hair was up, and the upper part of her face was concealed by a black velvet mask. She spoke to the fairies, and Prince Steven realized that she had commanded them to grant him sexual relief. And though a moment later the girl from Market Square was gone, the sound of her pretty voice was forever etched in the prince's memory.

Both fairies, apparently obedient to a fault, now concentrated their efforts on bringing the helpless prince to orgasm. The first joined the second in wrapping her legs about his penis and fluttering to and fro, squirming and writhing. They leaned forward and took each other's hands, rocking fore and aft most compellingly, pointing their toes and fixing him with knowing glances filled with amusement and pity.

At last the prince's paralyzed body shuddered through a long and indescribably intense orgasm. Halfway through the haze of delirious ecstasy the prince became a mindless creature of raw, naked, sensual need and slavery. His paralyzed body was unable to grant him a single voluntary twitch, moan, or gasp, and the suffering of his orgasm was real and excruciating.

At last his penis lurched with such involuntary force that both laughing fairies were thrown from it into the air, where they hovered, toes pointed daintily and eyes wide, to watch the outcome of their efforts. Prince Steven's penis lurched and jumped, shooting copious streams of semen into the air in wild arcs of desperate intensity. He fairly showered himself and the bedclothes about him in torrents of molten sperm. At last his penis flopped weakly back against his abdomen, and he slept. The fairies were gone.

The prince slept all that day and all through the night. When at long last he awoke, refreshed, the memories of the fairies were still vivid, though he attributed them to a spectacular dream brought on by sexual exhaustion. But that did not explain the intensity of the sensation of his dream-orgasm, nor did it explain the amount of sperm that soiled himself and his bedclothes.

Equally mysterious was the bit of pink gossamer cloth that he found on his window balcony.

CHAPTER FOURTEEN

The Vicomte Cevenne was masturbated repeatedly during his stay in the darkened closet of the second training room.

He knew that Rachel stimulated him at least once more and Victoria manualized him two more times all told. He felt another hand on his penis as well, late in the evening after Rachel had extracted his sperm with her black lace glove. He only knew that his third masturbatrix delighted in using her fingernails to give him a painful friction that quickly brought him to crisis, yet made his climax sheer agony as his organ twitched and reared while gripped only by her sharp nails. He, of course, had no way of knowing that his third masturbatrix was Ana, Victoria's pouting, spoiled stepsister.

It was well for him that the allotted time for his game had expired, for Ana had delighted in her discovery of his bound form and had conspired with Dona Alicia

Antigua to see to him as soon as they both might be undetected. In the helplessness of his body-corseted state there would have been no limit to the degradations and cruelties to which they would have gleefully subjected him. Rachel came to release him, dressed in a white high-collared dress and lovely dancing shoes. Her *décolletage* was low enough to expose her breasts but leave her nipples within a hair's breadth of exhibition. She activated the apparatus and watched as his bound form slid along, suspended form the rail, to stop in the center of the room.

As she slowly freed the Vicomte Cevenne from the body corset, Rachel's face exhibited little of her preoccupation and worry. She knew that Regine had just begun punishing Elvert for his presumptuousness. Rachel felt for him and well understood the tension and fearfulness that he was under. Regine had tripled her workload for the next several weeks, but Rachel knew that the ferocity of her vindictiveness would fall upon Elvert.

Rachel also guessed that Regine had some further morsel of humiliation ready to come her own way at the proper time, as well. Rachel gently unlaced and unbuckled the body corset's various segments from about the vicomte's imprisoned form. Her fingers worked with deft surety.

The vicomte's penis was rigid, though the rest of his muscles were slack from the after-effects of his long confinement. Rachel wrapped her arms about the vicomte's naked body when she was finished, and gently drew him off the suspended seat to lay him on the floor so he could recover himself.

Her task was not quite over. She tucked up her dress about her hips, exposing to the vicomte her bare bottom and the alluring downy cleft of her sex. She stood astride him at his shoulders and slowly squatted to sit full upon his face.

In a moment she heard the soft sapping and sucking sounds as he gently worshipped her most private and secret orifices with his lips and tongue. Despite her concern over Regine's coming recompenses, the lovely girl was soon gasping and writhing above the naked vicomte, squirming with wanton abandon to rub her shamelessly throbbing clitoris all over his face. After all she had done to him, mocked him, masturbated him and imprisoned him—the thought that even after all his degradation at her hands, he would want to lay nursing at her sex—this excited her tremendously.

The intricate scenario that the vicomte had devised had not quite come to an end. As Rachel finished climaxing upon his face, generously wetting it in the process, she turned her attention to his genitals. She bent forward lewdly, still gently wiggling herself against his nose and mouth as her orgasm subsided into a warm and pleasant tingle. She ignored the vicomte's penis, but rather extended the thumb and index fingertip of her right hand to pinch the skin of his scrotum. She pulled, raising his low dangling bag high by its own loose skin, and then she used the fingertips of her left hand to tease and knead his testicles as they slid about within his raised scrotum.

Rachel giggled. It was obvious that the vicomte adored this stimulation, for soon his panting breaths were warming her cleft even more delightfully. His penis lay back, twitching its urgency against his abdomen, and generously drooling its excitement from the slit in its purpling tip.

Rachel's nipples grew erect as she maintained the vicomte's stimulation. She spoke, in well-timed accordance to the intricate nuances of his game:

"You are forbidden to soil yourself in any way," she cooed, somehow managing a sullen, pretty pout at the same time.

The vicomte's penis twitched alarmingly in his excitement at her prim words and another string of his arousal dangled, shimmering from its tip.

"You are a wicked man!" Rachel declared. "I most certainly don't wish to see you soil yourself with your own seed. What a disgrace that would be in the presence of a young lady!"

Her fingertips teased his scrotum and testicles until he could bear no more. He went rigid and gasped with a stifled splutter beneath the full bare curves of her broad buttocks. Rachel smiled and pulled his scrotum tight, holding the loose skin fanned out in her dainty fingertips and wiggled her bottom on his face as she watched his orgasm.

As the first squirt of sperm left him, his tongue found Rachel's anus and thrust within, penetrating her circlet of muscle with a desperate, orgasmic urgency. Rachel laughed and watched as his penis reared, spasming strongly several times, to unload the thick warm squirts of his semen all over his waist and stomach.

"What a disgusting sight! Oh, how dare you! Do stop at once!" Rachel exclaimed prudishly, between low, girlish giggles.

At last the vicomte's long slow orgasm subsided and he lay trembling beneath her. She let go of his scrotum with an expression of fastidious distaste and got to her feet, tottering in the unfamiliar high heels of the dainty little dancing shoes that she wore.

Scant minutes later the Vicomte Cevenne was dressed again, in the slender elegance of his fashionable clothes. He stood before her to say goodbye, and bent low to kiss her hand after clasping it affectionately.

"You are lovely Rachel," he said. "Give my regards to Victoria, and I do hope to see you both again quite soon."

CHAPTER FIFTEEN

Upstairs in the house, Elvert's punishment had already begun.

Regine, in her anger, had moved more quickly than even Rachel would have thought. Regine was not present, though Marcella and Ana were. Dona Alicia Antigua joined Ana, for she would not miss an orchestration of humiliation for the world. Regine had conveyed her wishes as to the details of the punishment to the Contessa of Albion.

The three younger women were all most eager to see what refinements their popular and imaginative guest might devise. A youthful, smiling page had also joined the four women. He was a favorite, almost a pet of Regine and her daughters, and had far more freedom and fewer assigned duties than any other household servant. He joined the women at the request of the Contessa of Albion, who herself was quite taken with his smirking good looks. Elvert knelt naked, his hands bound behind him, fastened with three tightly buckled leather straps. There was a collar about his neck, the leash of which was held by Dona Alicia Antigua.

All four women were naked save for elegant, though brief, wraps of the softest fur that covered them from nipple to upper thigh. Regine had a passion for rare furs, and was most generous in making gifts of them for her friends. The page wore a satin short-waisted jacket with red epaulettes, given him as a gift by Marcella. Below that he was nearly naked, his genitals being covered by a brief matching satin pouch attached to a narrow waist belt by a thin strap that ran up between his buttocks.

Ana and Marcella each held long supple canes of the finest bamboo that could be procured from the import houses of the Island Kingdom.

Ana glanced toward the Contessa of Albion, smiling in her eagerness to begin. The Contessa of Albion walked barefoot to Elvert and extended her pretty pointed toes for him to kiss. He did so, desperate at this venture to reduce the severity of his punishment.

The Contessa of Albion addressed the groveling young man: "Elvert, having so wickedly soiled the person of a female servant, by a gross profaning of the female sex, in stark negligence of your household tasks, and in complete disregard for your betters—you are hereby to be given an extreme and humiliating punishment, to be administered at my direction."

"Look, his penis is hard!" Dona Alicia Antigua sneered to her friend Ana, who giggled knowingly, her eyes riveted between Elvert's legs as she fingered her cane.

The page looked at Elvert's penis as well, and managed a casual smile, though his cheeks reddened slightly.

Cinderella

Ana and Marcella were obviously so eager to begin Elvert's chastisement that the Contessa of Albion did not have the heart to make them wait a moment longer.

"Very well!" she purred with a scathing look downward at Elvert's beseeching face. "You may begin his punishment!"

Ana and Marcella stepped forward willingly, their faces betraying the delight they took in their cruel task. Indeed their expressions were but lovely masks of gleefully sadistic anticipation.

They stood, one on each side of Elvert, placing themselves evenly with his buttocks and hips. Marcella drew herself up on barefoot tiptoe, smiling all the while, and reached high with her cane to get the full impetus of the blows about to be delivered to Elvert's backside. Her cane whistled through the air, bending wickedly in the blur of its searing descent to land with a high, thin scorching crack across Elvert's bare bottom. His whole body jolted at the burning sting of the cut and he gasped, biting his lip to stifle an involuntary moan of pain.

Ana giggled, and bent over prettily at the waist, nearly exposing her bare bottom in the process to survey the effects of her sister's strike close up. Then she drew back and delivered her own blistering cut that landed with precise expertise directly across the one Marcella had placed.

Elvert's thighs trembled and his buttocks tensed as his body tried desperately to escape the searing pain.

Then Marcella and Ana took up an even rhythm, taking turns delivering cuts with their canes to precisely mark Elvert's bottom with rows of flaming stripes. Their cheeks flushed with pleasure and pride at every moan, plea and whimper.

Dona Alicia watched the punishment, eyes sparkling, and smiled over at a very amused Contessa of Albion. The contessa was watching the page, whose eyes were glued to the heavy dangle of Elvert's scrotum, swinging in time to the blows of the cane.

Both Dona Alicia Antigua and the Contessa of Albion watched the pouch that covered the page's genitals, as it seemed to bulge the more as he watched the punishment, and smiled.

Elvert's two tormentors redoubled their efforts to quickly flay his backside, and he could stand no more. Despite the tight hold of Dona Alicia upon his leash and collar, he pressed forward, nearly choking himself in the process, and began to crawl about the room in a vain effort to escape his whipmistresses. His doomed efforts only added to their amusement, and they followed him about the room, laughing as they struck blow after blow with smart accuracy to land on his outraged and sensitive flesh. Dona Alicia let him take the lead with the leash to a point, but maintained enough pressure so that he had to gasp for breath as he strained in his agony.

Ana, for her part, was inflamed with passion as she struck and struck again. She stood tiptoed daintily, thighs pressed together as she savored the delicious tingle that spread from the deepest parts of her sex to enlarge her nipples, redden her cheeks, and make her giggle with sadistic enjoyment.

Marcella laughed, partly at her sister's obvious sexual excitement, and partly at Elvert, who now lay prone and pleading, his buttocks twitching and tensing spasmodically under the rain of cruel blows. Tears poured down his cheeks, driven by the searing sting of the cuts to his bare bottom.

The Contessa of Albion spoke softly: "Ana, Marcella, perhaps he has had enough for now. Though if he does not now obey us absolutely, he will find that this was but the beginning."

She walked to where Elvert lay, helped him rise to a crawling position, then squatted down to have him lay his head on her pretty thighs. She smiled and stroked his brow. "Do you want your punishment to end, Elvert? Hmmm?"

Elvert's reply was muffled by her legs, though it most definitely was affirmative.

"Of course you do, Elvert. Of course you do."

The Contessa of Albion stroked his face with her hands and made him kiss her fingertips before she went on.

"Your caning is over Elvert, if you but beg the page to come over and manipulate your penis!"

Elvert's shocked, numbed mind could scarcely grasp the terribly humiliating dilemma of this choice. He was horrified at the thought of the smirking, spoiled page toying with his genitals in front of four laughing, scantily clad women. Yet he knew if his punishment continued he would go mad with pain.

The Contessa of Albion appeared to take his momentary stunned silence as a refusal.

"Oh dear, it seems that Ana and Marcella have then but begun to punish you. I'm afraid we will have to procure a gag from somewhere to quiet you during this second and more severe phase."

Ana and Marcella giggled; they had joined Dona Alicia Antigua in watching the slim page's genital pouch bulge with his excitement at the thought of toying with Elvert's penis while he was bound, helpless and naked.

Elvert's acquiescence was nearly muffled, as it was spoken with his head still cradled on the Contessa of Albion's lovely thighs.

She smiled softly. "Oh isn't that wonderful, girls!" she cooed, her voice high in its dripping sweetness. "You have made the proper choice, Elvert."

The contessa turned her attention to the spoiled page and smiled. "Go ahead. You may come and examine his penis. I will hold him still."

The page eagerly stooped forward and squatted down by Elvert's hips. Dona Alicia, Ana and Marcella gathered close around, not wishing to miss a single detail of the humiliating manipulation. They patted the page on his shoulder and affectionately ruffled his hair, urging him to begin. The page reached beneath Elvert and gripped his penis, holding it lightly in his right hand. Elvert started and gritted his teeth, desperate not to give the page or the women any satisfaction by showing even a single sign of sexual excitement. The page smiled and began to gently knead Elvert's still-soft penis in his hand. After a minute or so of gentle stimulation, the page took Elvert's scrotum in his left hand, flushing in his enjoyment to feel the heavy weight of Elvert's big testicles. The women laughed and encouraged the smiling page to continue.

Elvert tensed his stomach muscles and his thighs, willing himself not to become erect in the page's abusing hand.

The page maintained the gentle stimulation, using knowing, skillful strokes, until the friction proved too enticing.

Elvert's head still rested on the Contessa of Albion's thighs, and she had shifted her position slightly a moment before. He now could see the dark hair between her legs and even glimpse the pink pout of her genital lips. The sight of the contessa's slit, and the friction applied by the page's violating hands, conspired to undo Elvert's valiant efforts at self-control. A moment later his penis was swollen huge and twitching in the page's sliding fist while his scrotum bobbed and swung, dangling low beneath his bare buttocks. The page laughed with lewd glee and fingered Elvert's big sex organ, savoring the hot, smooth throbbing of it in his hands.

Ana patted the page's virtually bare bottom and giggled at the sight of his now obvious erection, tenting the satin pouch. Dona Alicia bent down and briefly rubbed the page's bulge with the palm of her hand. He squirmed away with a turn of his hips from further caresses, intent on savoring the helpless feel of Elvert's penis in his own hands.

Dona Alicia laughed and shook her head, and Marcella shrugged her shoulders, looking at the page with affectionate amusement. The page held Elvert's penis tightly at its base with his fisted right hand while, with his left, he toyed with the swollen tip. He rubbed and fondled the head of Elvert's penis between his thumb and forefinger while his right hand began the slow pumping motion of masturbation.

Elvert was biting his lips, and the women laughed.

"Look! See how he's tensing his shoulders and arms, he's desperate not to have an orgasm!" Marcella purred as she watched, lips parted and eyes wide with interest at the spectacle of Elvert's excruciating embarrassment.

The Contessa of Albion smiled and urged the smirking page to fully enjoy himself. The tip of Elvert's penis was bloated in its helpless condition and freely wetting itself with transparent dribbles of excitement.

Elvert's only faint hope now were his final desperate efforts to avoid ejaculating. The thought of spurting semen helplessly into the page's hands while the women watched was more than he could bear. The page laughed softly, delighting in the defeat of Elvert's dignity as well as basking in the admiration of the pretty women. He abandoned the head of Elvert's penis then, and began to stroke the lower shaft with one hand while the other grasped and squeezed Elvert's balls.

Elvert, thoroughly trapped within this very unique position, gasped in helpless excitement, even while watching the Contessa of Albion's pussy lips swell with her own arousal at his ordeal.

The page pumped him briskly now, confident and eager to show off for the women and pump a big load of sperm from Elvert's tormented penis for all too see. His mouth was dry and his heart pounded over this petty indulgence.

"He can't hold back for long!" Marcella cooed, her glazed eyes gloating over the helpless, vein-popping swell of Elvert's big sex organ as it was casually abused in the page's hands.

Ana now held Elvert's leash taut as if a further reminder of his pathetic state was necessary.

Dona Alicia had abandoned the leash to hold a lace napkin under the tip of Elvert's penis so the rare carpet would not be soiled by his discharge when the page's hands at last defeated him.

Elvert squirmed helplessly, endeavoring to free his bound arms and escape; the only result was the creaking sound of the leather straps that pinioned his arms behind him. His eyes took in the smooth, flawless elegance of the Contessa of Albion's bare heels, calves and knees as he panted now, his head still resting on her shapely thighs. She stroked his fevered brow with a blatant expression of false caring and mock tenderness.

"Oh, you poor boy!" the contessa said sweetly. "Let it happen. It won't do you a bit of harm but perhaps it will humble you in the process. Allow yourself to have your orgasm."

The page's hand pulled and coaxed Elvert's penis until nature could not be denied. Suddenly, as the women oohed and aahed, Elvert stiffened, his body going absolutely rigid. His penis jerked and twitched in the page's hand.

The page was struck by a delightful idea. In that moment he determined to stifle Elvert's orgasm and have more time to enjoy the women's admiration. The page quickly grasped Elvert's penis tightly below the tip, trying to prevent or delay his spend. Elvert's penis jolted again, and a thick gob of sperm fell to plop heavily on the cloth Dona Alicia Antigua held. The page held his penis rigidly, grasping firmly, as every vein stood out with remarkable definition. A bit of sperm lingered at the slit of Elvert's penis but his orgasm was stopped, at least for now. Young Elvert gritted out a long slow moan that was half relief and half humiliated anguish. The hands that had slowly brought him inch by inch and against his will toward the brink of orgasm now denied him in the very moment of his forced obedience. The women laughed and complimented the page on his masturbatory expertise. He let go of Elvert's genitals and settled back to a more comfortable kneeling position.

In a moment the page once again began handling Elvert's scrotum, while slowly and firmly pulling on his penis. Elvert's mouth hung open and his body glistened with sweat. His stifled gasps were still largely muffled by the contessa's flawless thighs. The women watched the masturbation, faces rapt with interest and excitement. The page pumped Elvert's penis for all he was worth now, then stopped a second time as the big tormented organ twitched helplessly on the brink of orgasm.

"He is quite an expert!" Dona Alicia Antigua said with wonder, though she was anxious to see the embarrassing finale. The page flushed with pride and kept smiling as his hands recaptured Elvert's twitching organ to begin the stimulation anew.

The page now rested one hand on his hip, while he pumped Elvert's penis with the other, confident in his ability and showing off for the women.

Elvert's penis began the slow lurching spasm of a full-fledged orgasm. His organ jerked and twitched in the page's fist. The young blond man smirked and the women giggled. He held Elvert's orgasming penis by its base and watched the result of his handling unfold. Hot, burning spurts of Elvert's semen splashed from the tip of his teased penis to plop heavily on the waiting napkin Dona Alicia held ready beneath Elvert's genitals.

The page, now blushing with glee, held Elvert's sex organ throughout his long and copious climax. Puddles of thick molten seed totally drenched the lace napkin as Elvert's penis reared and plunged in the page's hand over and over again. At last Elvert sagged weakly forward, swept by a terrible burning shame at what had just been done to him. He panted, trembling in humiliation, limp against the contessa's thighs. The page reluctantly released Elvert's penis and the women helped him wipe his hands on a cloth.

"There now, you poor boy!" the Contessa of Albion smirked. "I have no doubt that you are feeling less constrained!"

The women exclaimed repeatedly over the quantity of Elvert's sperm and, to his disgust, attributed it to the spoiled page's expertise.

"Oh, Elvert! I wouldn't relax just yet. You see your punishment is not quite over—you still have one duty to perform."

To Elvert's horror the women orchestrated what came next with gleeful sadism and precision. The page was divested of his pouch and waist belt and brought around to stand in front of Elvert. The contessa moved aside and made Elvert remain on all fours, his face even with the page's genitals. The page's penis was perfect, the women cooed, and so very smooth and elegant. His scrotum was tight, gathered high beneath the base of his slowly lengthening penis. Elvert cried out in shock and pain as Ana wielded her cane across his buttocks, searing the still agonized and welted flesh.

"They will give you two dozen each unless you suck the page's penis, Elvert!" the Contessa of Albion said primly.

Cinderella

"Oh! May we not make it three dozen, contessa!" Marcella pouted, pretty in her exaggerated vexation.

"Very well then, three dozen laid on smartly, unless you suck the page!" the contessa added with a girlish giggle.

Moments later Elvert knelt, his cheeks burning with terrible shame, sucking the page's penis. The page smiled and worked his hips shamelessly, fucking Elvert's mouth with no consideration of this horrendous humiliation. Indeed, the spoiled page revelled in the terrible bruising of Elvert's ego and was soon gasping with excitement at the sensation the poor young man's mouth provided him. The contessa now knelt by Elvert's buttocks, sitting back comfortably on her bare heels and applying to his penis an expert and compelling stimulation. Her fur wrap had slipped down about her shoulders to reveal the large nipples of her ample breasts. Her face was sweet, lips parted and eyes liquid with enjoyment as she teased and tormented Elvert's exhausted penis to another erection.

Dona Alicia watched the contessa stimulate Elvert with amazement, and realized that only an accomplished masturbatrix could so tease male genitals, so recently emptied of their seed. Marcella and Ana watched the page with lovely expressions of gloating cruelty. He stood on tiptoe now, slim hips thrust forward, leaning into Elvert's mouth, savoring the sensations as the sucking continued.

"Do what he tells you Elvert," the contessa said softly as her fingers maddened and stimulated Elvert's genitals.

The page smirked and pulled himself nearly out from Elvert's mouth, then had Elvert lick the head of his penis, much to the amusement of Ana and Marcella. Dona Alicia knelt beside the contessa and squeezed Elvert's scrotum in her palm while the contessa concentrated her masturbatory efforts on his penis. Dona Alicia reached out with her free hand, to gently caress the broad bare bottom of the lovely contessa as well. The contessa smiled, kneading, pulling and stroking her humiliated victim's genitals with cool, knowing expertise.

The page laughed as Elvert licked about the swollen head of his penis, then he leaned forward again, imbedding himself deeply in Elvert's mouth before wiggling his hips. At the same time, the Contessa of Albion had Elvert's penis pulled backward now, at an unnatural and straining angle as she fingered and teased it, her caresses ever so gentle yet so terribly cruel as well. Dona Alicia Antigua squeezed Elvert's scrotum in her hand until he gasped and the muscles of his thighs and bottom tightened. He could not beg her to stop as his mouth was full of the page's penis, so she did it again, laughing softly.

At last the contessa's hands briskly took charge of Elvert's penis, flogging it lewdly then coyly teasing it. Dona Alicia pinched and kneaded his testicles to compliment her friend's handiwork and speed him to a second orgasm that the women knew would leave him drained and weak.

As Elvert's penis spasmed thickly in the Contessa of Albion's grasp, the page reached crisis also and pulled back so the head of his penis plopped from Elvert's lips, only to ram forward again, forcing Elvert to take in all his length. The page's buttocks clenched and his eyes shut as a blissful expression transfixed upon his face. Elvert's own orgasm made him gasp so that he did not notice the page's organ flexing and twitching in his mouth at first. Not until the first hot squirts of the page's seed splashed into his mouth did he realize what was happening. Too late—he was forced to swallow every drop as the page greedily pressed forward, intent with the selfish enjoyment he derived out of his cruel actions.

Elvert's own tormented penis spasmed feebly in the contessa's hand as she and Dona Alicia milked his balls of every remaining drop of manhood.

CHAPTER SIXTEEN

Victoria lay sleeping in a splash of warm summer sunshine that pleasantly dappled the coverlet of her rumpled bed.

She slept deeply, on her right side, her left leg bent at the knee and her right leg extended. Her lovely feet were pointed comfortably against the cool, smooth fabric of the counterpane. She wore a white, short-waisted singlet of soft lace that covered her down to a point just above the bare swell of her hips. Below the waist she was naked, her bare bottom flawless and lovely in repose. She was exhausted, having been awake far into the night riding an enormously fat baron about the floor of the fourth training room. This one had bored her—lacking the single-minded obsession of the comte de Languedoc or the graceful, though aberrant, poise of the Vicomte Cevenne.

The Baron Roth-Haupfelds was obsessed with

Victoria's thigh-high boots, with their outrageous heels—and her bare bottom. For a long while he simply had her scold and humiliate him while he slavishly polished the toes of her boots with his tongue. Next he had begged her to place his erect penis flat on a low marble pedestal, and she had spanked it—alternating from her bare hand to a riding quirt—until he ejaculated.

He continued his pleasures by kissing and licking her bare bottom as she tied a vast quantity of pink ribbon about his, by then, drooping sex organ. He then had beseeched her to repeatedly slap his face with all her might and then walk about on his prone, naked body wearing her "succulent boots."

Of course she had been hooded, not daring to again disobey Regine's command to anonymity. When she abused the Baron Roth-Haupfelds, her lips curled in an expression of distaste as he quivered at her feet in an apoplectic fit of masochistic bliss.

As she had masturbated him a final time between the dainty, pointed toes of her gleaming, outrageously high-heeled boots, she thought only of Prince Steven Targete. In her fantasy he kissed her neck, nuzzling her as they lay coupled, thrusting in sexual abandon.

Victoria was not alone as she slept. Regine had stolen into her room, tiptoeing softly over the deep carpet. Behind her, also on tiptoed feet, came the three maids, Rachel, Sonia and Maria del Castillo. Rachel's pretty, dark-eyed face was quite the picture of dismay, for she knew that Regine had planned a private little morsel of delight for her own selfish, gloating pleasure. Rachel realized that she and the other maids would be forced to masturbate Victoria in her sleep while Regine watched. Perhaps Regine would even have Maria perform cunnilingus on her.

Rachel knew Regine often watched Sonia and Maria del Castillo do things to Victoria in her sleep; she knew that Sonia participated in usually indifferent obedience, but Maria del Castillo savored every moment. Rachel realized also that she was included now as punishment for her tryst with Elvert in the second training room.

Rachel was attracted to Victoria—though perhaps she did not even admit it to herself—but it seemed a despicable, beastly thing to take advantage of Victoria's helpless sleeping state, all for the smirking voyeurism of Regine.

Regine wore a dark fur wrap of the softest ermine, while the maids were naked save for thin black thongs that emphasized their supple, youthful charms rather than concealed them. Regine loved watching the bodies of the lithe masturbators as they worked on her sleeping stepdaughter, and would sometimes even caress their own private parts as they carried out her commands.

Rachel only wished that she had told Victoria of Regine's games with her while she slept, but somehow she could never bring herself to do so. She did not wish Victoria to ever know that she had been the innocent, unknowing object of such degrading sport. She once even begged Regine to stop the practice, but was assigned double duty for her efforts.

Regine whispered to Sonia and the maid smiled, moving forward to bend low beside where Victoria slept, lips parted and breathing gently. At some pre-arranged sign, Sonia reached down and, ever so gently, cupped the pouting left mound of Victoria's bare sex. Maria del Castillo licked her lips in anticipation and clasped her hands innocently behind her nearly bare bottom as she watched. Rachel stood uncomfortably, totally unaware of how beautiful her youthful features were, even as they wore an expression of embarrassed dismay.

Regine was very aware of Rachel's exquisite beauty, however, and soon employed her by having her lightly rub Sonia's virtually bare bottom. In this way Regine hoped that Rachel's caresses would arouse Sonia as she masturbated Victoria, thereby sending lewd inspiration to her coy fingers.

Once again, Regine proved to be correct. As Rachel's fingers gently invaded the warm, private place between the cheeks of Sonia's bottom, Sonia gasped and began a light stroking motion of Victoria's pink genital lips with her soft fingertips. Sonia gently, ever so lightly, pinched Victoria's outer lips, slowly sliding her fingertips down their length and deftly kneading them, stimulating the young beauty as she slept.

Victoria breathed deeply and moaned softly. As she slept, she dreamed.

In the first phase of her dream, she was castaway on a verdant tropical island with a lone mariner from her vessel. No others survived. The two of them set about making an adventure of their situation and sought food and water under the tropical sun. Water they found aplenty in a cool cascade that flowed down through a rocky cleft to the sea, but of food there was no sign at all, and their long-term plight looked most grim indeed.

In the sprightly, patternless logic of her dream, Victoria found that the young sailor absolutely adored her, and regarded her with the worshipful awe a young man would possess for a goddess incarnate. In the inhibition-free realm of her dream, it seemed most natural that Victoria and the sailor were both naked, having somehow lost their clothes in the turbulent swim to the tropical island shore.

It also seemed most fitting that Victoria, being hungry and longing for food, should offer to suck the sailor's penis and thus get the sustenance she craved. This was no selfless act, but rather a result of cool, calculated self preservation on the part of the pretty young woman. In a moment, the sailor stood naked beneath the shade of a tall—though fruitless—palm, and Victoria knelt naked before him, sitting comfortably back on her heels, her bare bottom lewdly thrust outward behind to emphasize her lush feminine curves. She held him by the scrotum as she began to gently lick the head of his rapidly hardening penis. The handsome young mariner appeared to become immediately addicted to the pleasures her mouth provided and stood meekly trembling as she licked and sucked his sex organ.

Sonia's fingers were now stimulating Victoria's clitoris with light, feathery caresses while Maria del Castillo was employed to gently stroke her bare bottom and tickle the tight pink bud of her anus.

In Victoria's dream, the young sailor was now begging for relief, and pleading to be allowed to ejaculate while caressed and suckled by the pretty pouting ring of her impudent lips. Victoria relented at last and glanced up at him wickedly from beneath her wild tresses as she redoubled the suction that she gave him, all the while twisting and pulling his testicles. His crisis was immediate, desperately intense, and copious. With a weak, helpless, gritting moan, the young mariner ejaculated into Victoria's lovely, full-lipped mouth. She sucked his thick effusions, swallowing every drop with greedy, gloating relish as she milked his sac to see if perhaps she could stimulate his body to produce more seed, so that she could devour it also.

Regine watched Sonia masturbate Victoria with a beautiful, cruel, catlike smile upon her lips. Rachel still gently fingered Sonia to inspire her to greater efforts and Maria del Castillo, ever so willingly, assisted in the deft, covert handiwork.

Regine had Maria stop her support of Sonia and kneel before her, as she herself reclined in a well-upholstered velvet chair to watch the spectacle. Then she ordered Maria to lick her slit, softly, gently, with trained and disciplined circular strokes of her agile tongue.

Rachel's cheeks flushed at the soft lapping sound from between Regine's legs as she sat, prettily composed, trim bare feet tiptoed upon the carpet, while the maid humbly serviced her in oral degradation.

Victoria's dream continued, the surreal free-form eroticism of its deliciously witless plot unimpeded by the trammels of reality. Day after day, Victoria knelt hungrily to feast on the warm fertile fruit of the adoring sailor's manhood. As time passed upon the paradise isle she flourished and became taller and stronger, more vibrant and carefree. Yet the mariner became weaker and smaller, the spring was gone from his step and he appeared pale and forlorn. However, he did not have the will to forego the delicious pleasure of being brought to orgasm in Victoria's mouth. When she summoned him to her, he still came, frail but willing.

After a time, he realized that she was draining him of all his life-strength, and resisted her summons to come and be sucked by her laughing, bewitching lips. Victoria no longer deigned to accept his refusal but rather sought him out and carried him forcibly to her sun-dappled lair. There she picked him up bodily, effortlessly holding him high by his hips, and sucked him. When he ejaculated, moaning and pleading not to be drained, she prolonged his agony of pleasure and drank him wantonly, afterward carelessly throwing him aside.

Rachel could tell that Victoria was dreaming as Sonia applied light feather caresses to the outer portions of her nest. Victoria's lips parted and she moaned softly, writhing and squirming her hips in her sleep. Rachel's probing fingers found Sonia to be very moist indeed as the lithe masturbator savored the feel of Rachel's feminine fingers in her own private orifices.

The mariner in Victoria's dream was soon too weak to stand, though his goddess had no intention whatever of depriving herself of her source of nourishment. The mariner now lay weakly as Victoria knelt over him, bending low to suck the manhood from his loins and hungrily consume it.

At last, one bright island dawn, a ship appeared anchored in the placid waters of the crescent cove. Victoria and the young mariner were rescued, though the mariner had to be carried bodily aboard the ship by several sailors. On the long voyage home, the poor fellow was gradually nursed back to health and vitality, having come desperately close to death in his drained and weakened state. The sailors all marvelled at the flawless, laughing young woman who seemed so perfectly full of health and vitality, in stark contrast to the trembling, frail mariner they found castaway with her.

Rachel now had her thumb imbedded deeply in Sonia's anus at Regine's command. Sonia stood on tiptoe, bent over prettily at the waist, cheeks crimson with embarrassment and pleasure as she masturbated the sleeping Victoria. Rachel gently parted Sonia's slit with two fingers and slowly slid them into her deepest parts. Sonia began to spend on Rachel's fingers as she bit her lips in an effort to keep silent so as not to wake Victoria.

Sonia's own fingers amused themselves, lending soft butterfly caresses to the pink, hooded bud of Victoria's clitoris.

The vessel that rescued Victoria and the mariner was greeted by a vast throng as it returned to its home port. Prince Steven Targete was there to meet the castaways himself. He led Victoria up a long flight of white marble steps that rose from the quay to the royal summer palace by the sea. The prince then carried her to his chamber and made love to her. She lay atop him on his great canopied bed, softly urging him on as he slid his huge sex organ slowly into the moist, welcoming velvet of her cleft.

Victoria felt as though she would split asunder as the sensations of pleasure and fullness mingled and intensified. In that moment, it seemed to Victoria that the prince's palace chamber dissolved away, though the prince kept thrusting beneath her. A moment later, a breathtakingly beautiful young Goddess sat by their bed, weaving on a huge and indescribably intricate ivory loom. About her feet fawned naked men, down on all fours, and male animals too, all excited and swollen with adoration. The Goddess barely deigned to notice them.

Victoria had received enough classical education before her own father's passing to realize that the young Goddess was Circe, the enchantress who enslaved the crew of Odysseus when they fell into her clutches whilst on their voyage home to Ithaca from the Trojan wars.

Circe smiled at Victoria and showed her the vivid scene she was weaving on the intricate tapestry taking shape on her loom.

Victoria still writhed upon the penis of the dream prince, who seemed oblivious to the presence of Circe in the room.

The tapestry depicted exquisitely detailed scenes of sexual slavery and humiliation. Many people were woven that Victoria knew personally, and others that she did not. The Goddess laughed and extended her bare point-toed foot for a naked slave to humbly lick. Victoria arrived at orgasm on the prince's penis as the lowly slave ejaculated in his bliss at being allowed to perform his own humiliating service for the young Goddess.

Two fairies flew toward Circe, their pretty legs and buttocks revealed beneath flared skirts of the lightest and most gossamer fabric. When they reached her, they became Circe's own handmaidens and their wings melted away. They spoke to Circe, and Circe looked to Victoria.

"Prince Steven is yours, Victoria!" Circe cooed, smiling. "I have given him to you for a gift, and not just in your dreams!"

Regine looked down at Victoria as she slept. Victoria gasped softly, the nipples of her breasts were obviously erect, and the dew of her spendings glistened on Sonia's hands.

"Sonia you are giving her a most delicious dream I am sure!" Regine exclaimed.

Maria del Castillo looked up from her intimate oral task between Regine's legs and nodded her assent. Her mouth glistened with Regine's excitement. Regine's eyes narrowed and her smile, though beautiful, boded ill for Rachel.

"Rachel, lick Victoria! Sonia will move aside," she said softly.

Rachel trembled, but knew better than disobey or argue.

Regine commanded Sonia to kneel beside Rachel as Rachel herself knelt to lick Victoria. Regine ordered Sonia to caress Rachel's genitals as she began to softly lap Victoria's folds, the desperate pleading in her expressive eyes unheeded. Rachel's tongue probed and explored the intricate depths and crevices of Victoria's salt-dewed cleft with a shy resignation.

Victoria drew up her legs and mewed in her sleep. Regine watched, fascinated, as Maria del Castillo's tongue worked busily between her own lovely thighs. Rachel could not quell the growing excitement she felt as she licked her dearest friend's bare genitals and savored the feminine scent of her arousal.

Sonia knelt, her lewd fingers gently teasing Rachel's anus and clitoris. Rachel continued licking Victoria, terribly ashamed at her liquid, passionate response to Sonia's gentle fingerings as she did so. Victoria squirmed, arching her back as her erotic dream and the lewd sensations

Rachel's tonguing gave her conspired to raise her excitement to a fever pitch.

Rachel's lips and tongue were soon generously sprinkled with the nectar of Victoria's excitement and, dutiful friend that she was, Rachel made certain her tongue intercepted the wayward flow that slowly slid downward from Victoria's wet pink slit toward her anus.

It was then that the intimate tickling of Rachel's tongue awakened Victoria. Her eyes fluttered as she lay gasping in her sleepy and disoriented state. Still, she wiggled her curving hips unconsciously in time to the luscious caresses received from Rachel's tongue.

Regine noticed that Victoria had awakened at once. She had Sonia and Maria del Castillo jump up quickly and hold her down, helpless on the bed. Maria laughed at the idea, and licked the last glistening dew of Regine's passion from her pouting lips.

"Do not stop, Rachel!" commanded Regine. "I shall make your very existence a mystery if you cease now!"

Rachel, to her horror, had just realized that Victoria was awake, but she did not dare disobey the velvet smooth menace of Regine's imperious voice. A tear started down Rachel's left cheek as she, ever so gently, almost apologetically, licked Victoria's secret and most private recesses.

Victoria squirmed in her disorientation, but the nearly-naked, smiling maids held her fast. Her bleary eyes cleared to see Regine standing over her. Regine was smiling, clutching her dark, elegant ermine wrap in a way that lifted and emphasized her nearly-bare breasts without exposing them entirely.

Victoria's eyes grew less bleary, then finally cleared altogether as she awakened. She raised her head, her cheeks flaming with shame and rage.

"Traitorous Rachel! And I thought you were my friend!"

CHAPTER SEVENTEEN

A *lovely summer evening*, but two weeks later, found Victoria sitting forlorn on the dew-jewelled lawn of the garden off Fountain Square.

Lucas and Elvert sat miserably with her, eyes downcast, desperate to help yet knowing they could do little to ease their lovely friend's sadness. A warm wind from the vineyards softly ruffled Victoria's uncombed hair as she stared thoughtfully at some flowers by her feet.

"She can't prevent you from attending Prince Steven's ball!" Lucas said, his tones harsh with disbelief and bitterness.

"Even Regine couldn't be so cruel and wicked could she?" Elvert wondered. His recent treatment by Regine's friend the Contessa of Albion, however, left scant doubt in his mind.

Lucas spoke again. "It's against the royal decree not to permit you to go, Victoria! Have we no recourse?"

Victoria smiled sadly at her friends. "Regine's declaration was crystal clear, I'm afraid. She, the Contessa of Albion, Dona Alicia Antigua, and, of course, her two wicked daughters have been powdering, perfuming and dressing for hours. A king's ransom has been spent on clothes of the latest fashion for Ana and Marcella, and they do look ever so lovely—though I fancy they would look much lovelier if they were not so vile and cruel! At any rate, Regine says there are no more funds to purchase apparel for me, and beside, an enormously important foreign noble, Lord San Sebastian, I think, has scheduled me for tonight—months in advance, even before the issuance of the royal proclamation!"

Victoria's thoughts were interrupted by the appearance of Rachel as she walked slowly forward from the flagged paths that circled the formal flower beds. Her eyes spoke volumes of apology and sadness. Victoria looked away from Rachel to the ground. Lucas and Elvert shifted about, miserable in their discomfort for both young women who had so recently been friends and companions. Both knew that Regine had planned from the beginning to drive a wedge between Victoria and her only close female friend. They were helpless and burned with fury at the extent of the cruel though lovely woman's success.

"Victoria!" Rachel blurted, desperate not to be interrupted and sent away. "You must go! I shall wear the hood and discipline Lord San Sebastian! No one shall ever know the difference! A carriage has come for Regine and the others, and they have already left for the palace. Please, Victoria!"

Victoria remained, face averted. In a moment Rachel's eyes filled with tears and she turned away and went back into the house. Victoria's eyes were moist too, when she turned back toward Lucas and Elvert, though her mouth was set in firm resignation. Lucas and Elvert shifted uncomfortably, longing to comfort both Rachel and Victoria.

At that moment a crash resounded, there was a brilliant flash of light, and the part of the garden wall beside the postern gate collapsed inward, only to vanish before the stones hit the grass of the lawn.

Rachel heard the noise and ran back, terribly afraid that harm had befallen her three friends. Lucas and Elvert leapt to their feet, braced and trembling, ready to defend Victoria with their lives. Victoria knelt, poised in a posture of ready flight, her pretty lips parted, her lovely wide eyes flashing with alarm.

Rachel halted abruptly at the scene that met her gaze, and stood stock-still, riveted to the spot, with an expression poignantly balanced between fascination and terror.

The air filled with the soft sweet notes of an erotic, wild and sweet music. Rachel stood aghast, silent as were her friends. All were caught utterly by surprise at the sudden, explosive disintegration of a segment of the garden wall.

And then a strange procession swept into the garden through the newly created gap. First came fawning dogs, grunting pigs, and prancing stallions. Then came graceful leaping gazelles, many pointed stags with great racks of horns, and huge snow-white bulls. Next in the procession came exotic creatures of the tropics, animals strange and unheard of in the European Island Kingdom; tigers, ocelots and leopards stalked into the garden, tawny eyes gleaming with menace. All the animals were obviously male.

Victoria, Rachel, Lucas and Elvert had now drawn into a tight group, clasping each other's hands, gaping at the strangeness of the procession of beasts before them.

Following the animals came naked male slaves, crawling on all fours with studded iron collars about their necks. All were erect, their impossibly huge and turgid penises nearly brushing the ground in the vibrant heat of their sensual excitement.

Behind the male slaves minced lovely naked young women, their hair long and free, garlanded with pink, white and blue flowers. The young women held long, supple whips in their left hands and used them to chastise the bare genitals of the slaves who crawled before them. In their right hands the young maidens held golden cups from which they sprinkled cascades of flower petals back over their bare shoulders. The flower petals were sprinkled in deference to she who came behind the pretty young maidens.

The four friends gasped as a lovely young golden-haired Goddess appeared, astride the penis of a massively muscled, and monstrously erect giant. The Goddess was laughing and pulling at a leash attached to the giant's great scrotum as he walked upon the petals strewn by the maidens.

The laughing Goddess was naked, save for point-toed shoes with heels so high and sharply tapered that her lovely feet were in the stylized toe-pose of a ballerina inside them. They were fashionably made, dainty shoes, cut low at the tops of the Goddess' feet so that the intimate little clefts between her toes were erotically highlighted. The shoes were crafted of black onyx, of the darkest and purest jet. Their menacing heels and gleaming allure gave the Goddess a captivating, though wicked and outrageously cruel, appearance.

The Goddess directed her beasts and slaves to fan out about the garden and grounds of the house on Fountain Square. The animals and male slaves did so, instantly obedient, setting up positions of guard and protection everywhere. The Goddess' maidens formed a half-circle upon an expanse of velvet lawn, with the giant standing in the center facing Victoria and her friends. The Goddess sitting astride the giant's huge sex organ smiled and began to squirm, stimulating the giant as she lusciously flexed her lovely thighs and wiggled the lewd curves of her bare hips.

She jerked at his testicle leash so that his fat balls bounced and churned about inside the heavy dangle of his scrotum. And then she spoke, her voice so soft, feminine and sweet that Lucas' and Elvert's penises immediately tented their clothing in helpless tribute to her form and purring tones. She addressed Victoria almost exclusively, with some attention to Rachel as well. The two male servants went virtually ignored.

"Victoria! Don't you know that you must attend the royal banquet and ball at the Targete palace this very night! Your fortune and the fate of the entire kingdom rests upon your attendance—for you are destined to be queen!"

Victoria stared, her lovely eyes wide with surprise, awe, and perhaps delight as well, under the Goddess' words.

Victoria blurted, "You are the enchantress Circe! I saw you working at your loom in my dream ... in my erotic dream! I ..."

Here Victoria's own words stumbled, and she looked toward Rachel uncomfortably. Rachel's cheeks flushed and she bit the pouting swell of her lower lip as she stood, eyes downcast, prodding at the grass with her bare toes.

Circe laughed, the tones of her amusement soft and musical.

"Yes, Victoria, and I told you in your dream that Prince Steven was yours, and so he shall soon be—but we must make haste for my enchantments have power only until the tolling of the midnight hour!"

The Goddess' expression softened and she spoke

again. "Come, Rachel and Victoria! Let not the designs of others despoil a friendship meant to last a lifetime. Embrace and forget Regine's artifices!"

Victoria extended her open arms to Rachel and the friends rushed together to embrace warmly. Lucas and Elvert watched, expressions transfixed with happiness and relief.

The Goddess gave the giant's penis one last lewd compress between her thighs and then leapt down from his sex organ, to walk effortlessly and lightly with a wickedly strutting stride in her outrageous jet and black onyx shoes.

A string of gleaming arousal now hung from the giant's penis. Circe reached up and grasped it, and it became a long, cruel whip in her lovely hand. She drew back, and, with an abrupt forward motion that lusciously bounced her bare breasts, the Goddess curled the whip through the air and snapped it expertly, barely six inches above the ground. She snapped it again a moment later and Victoria gasped to see a pair of dazzlingly translucent dancing slippers of the purest crystal appear amidst a myriad sparkle of fairy light.

The dancing shoes were cut of jewelled glass, and scintillated with the understated echoes of all colors of the rainbow. The dancing slippers were fashionably tip-toed, set upon outrageously high heels of transparent elegance.

Circe walked to stand beside Victoria and placed an arm gently about her shoulders.

"Do you like them?" she cooed with a soft smile. "I, for one, believe the most important part of a woman's costume to be the shoes, and certainly you must have proper ones for dancing at the royal ball!"

Victoria hastened forward to put the shoes on, her eyes wide and face expressive with delight, but the Goddess asked her to wait. The Goddess stepped over to stand before the giant once again. She beat his penis with the cruel snapping whip, but that seemed only to increase his arousal and another long string of excitement soon hung, scintillating from the tip of his sex organ. The Goddess scooped up a bit of the giant's excitement and walked to Victoria who stood prettily aghast.

The Goddess applied a bit of the giant's arousal to Victoria's hips, and, in a flash of radiant light, her simple dress was transformed into a gown of pristine and priceless court fashion. The gown was wrought of creme satin and pink velvet, its allure set off deliciously with shoulder-gloves of black kidskin.

Victoria stood, pirouetting on delighted tiptoe, as the Goddess bade her maidens gather about and do her hair. In but moments Victoria's hair swept high in a haughty yet lovely swirl that would enslave the eye of even the most jaded notable.

Circe gave Victoria a black velvet mask and said, "Tonight Victoria, you shall be the Princesse de la Masquerade!"

Then as Victoria still stood on tiptoe, flushing with pleasure and smoothing her upswept hair with her gloved hands, the Goddess led the giant forward by the leash about his testicles. At the Goddess' command he was soon levering his gargantuan, heavily muscled bulk into a kneeling position before the smiling girl.

"Kiss Victoria's feet!" Circe commanded with a lighthearted giggle. Her imperious order was given emphasis by two of her handmaids who stepped forward to give his buttocks a sound taste of their whips.

The giant bowed his head and bent forward, his face stamped with an expression of nearly worshipful deference. As the maiden's whips chastised his bare buttocks, and even occasionally curled between his legs to deliver smart stinging cuts to the back of his impressive scrotum—the giant gently grasped Victoria's left heel and raised her lovely, arched bare foot to his lips. Victoria pointed her toes with a smile and licked her lips, her eyes on the heavy, bobbing throb of the giant's vastly swollen male organ. The giant trembled with restrained desire as he—ever so gently and lightly— kissed Victoria's bare foot.

Victoria gasped, for in that moment she was covered from toe to thigh in a stocking of the sheerest and smoothest silk. The giant placed a gentle, humble kiss upon the toes of her other foot as well, and it too was instantly and magically covered in a lovely stocking— far finer than any available at the most exclusive corsetier and hosiery shop in the entire kingdom.

At the Goddess' bidding the giant rose back to his feet and gently carried Victoria in his arms to where her fairy shoes glittered in the moonlight on the grass. He lowered her until she could effortlessly slip her point-toed, stockinged feet into the shoes. She found the fit to be exquisitely perfect.

"You may put her down, now, and please stand straight, arms at your sides, and don't move a muscle. I am not through with you just yet!" the Goddess commanded the giant, who meekly obeyed.

Circe smiled at Victoria, her expression showing genuine warmth and regard. "These shoes were made for you, Victoria, and no other. On your lovely feet and no others' they will sparkle. Were another woman to seize them from you and put them on, they would become a terrible embarrassment to her, I fear."

Victoria and her three friends looked so questioningly at the Goddess then that she laughed.

"Victoria, any woman but yourself who draws your dancing slippers upon her feet will become possessed of a sensual longing for pleasure and release so intense as to unseat all her normal sensibilities and inhibitions!"

Cinderella

Victoria stepped lightly forward and, daring all, embraced the Goddess and thanked her for her kindness and generosity. Circe returned her embrace and reached out an arm to include Rachel as well.

"I hear that you cannot go to the ball as you must discipline the Lord San Sebastian tonight, Victoria! Rachel has offered to perform those services in your stead, but I have other plans for her, so I shall just have to be mistress of the house this night. I trust Regine will not mind!"

Victoria and her friends laughed at the Goddess' mischievous reference to Regine.

"I'm sure that you shall dazzle Lord San Sebastian!" Rachel ventured with a nervous giggle.

Circe smiled thoughtfully. "I think perhaps I shall, and in ways he never dreamed! But now we must send you off to the ball in style, Victoria, and for that you shall need a fine carriage!"

The Goddess stepped forward to the giant and again took up her cruel whip. As he stood motionless, her whip snaked through the air to wrap about the huge shaft of his penis. The Goddess then stood prettily bent forward at the waist, her bare buttocks flexing lewdly, as she briskly pulled upon the whip, thus stimulating the giant's teased penis to an unbearable degree.

Circe's handmaids escorted Victoria and her friends backward a bit so they would not be inundated by the giant's orgasm. The Goddess was an avid and expert masturbatrix, and Victoria's and Rachel's eyes turned glassy in excitement to see the way that she teased and tormented the giant's huge penis with her cruel whip. He stood gasping, the great muscles of his chest and shoulders tensed to the hardness of living rock. His stomach muscles knotted, his thighs flexed and sweat stood out upon his brow.

Even under the agonizing delight of his masturbation

he obeyed his mistress, his huge hands remained locked to his thighs.

The Goddess smirked prettily as the giant's penis lurched and jolted in the coiled merciless embrace of the whip.

Victoria and Rachel stood, flushed and fascinated, as the giant ejaculated the hugest and most copious load of sperm they had ever seen.

Elvert and Lucas stood, eyes riveted to the sight, slack-jawed in the presence of a male so vastly huge, who bore a phallus beyond all boasting.

Great, heavy jets of thick sperm splashed down upon the grass of the garden, followed by a veritable torrent of yet thicker volleys of manhood. The giant's seed did not lie on the grass to slowly thin and liquefy, however, for something seemed to be foaming and churning in the very depths of the puddles. A radiant scintillating light rose about the pools of the giant's sperm and suddenly, in the moment he finished ejaculating, there stood a huge fairy carriage of silver and glass. The carriage was clearly fashioned by a craftsman beyond all mortal ability. Interlocked scenes of goddesses and nymphs, coupled with centaurs and giants in spectacles of erotic delight upon backdrops of sylvan glades, made up the sides of the carriage. Inside, the seats were of the deepest and softest beige velvet and satin, with warm blue hangings of plush, brocaded embroidery. Victoria's heart pounded with astonishment and delight.

The giant sagged forward, exhausted and weak.

"And any properly equipped carriage would be, I fear, of little use without horses!" Circe exclaimed, turning her attention to Lucas and Elvert who stood dumfounded.

The Goddess commanded them to remove all their clothing and, to Rachel's and Victoria's amusement and surprise, they obeyed instantaneously, apparently unable to stop their trembling hands from carrying out the lovely Goddess' desires. In a moment both stood naked and defenseless before the Goddess, her maidens, Rachel and Victoria.

Two of the Goddess' handmaids stepped up behind the chagrined servants. Circe commanded them to bend over and grasp their ankles with their hands. The handmaids reached through between their legs to suavely grasp and fondle their scrotums. Soon they were panting, their genitals swollen with sensual excitement in the knowing, teasing hands of the naked maidens.

Then Circe cracked her whip but an inch before their noses, and Victoria and Rachel were startled from their appreciative ogling of the genital fondling. Lucas' thighs began to thicken and turn white, as fresh sinew and muscle roiled beneath his changing flesh. He cried out in alarm more than pain, as did Elvert who found the same changes happening to him.

The Goddess' maidens stepped lightly back on barefoot tiptoe, giggling and obviously amused at the transformation befalling the two young servants. Both men appeared nearly as centaurs then, their hindquarters those of powerful horses, their tails swishing desperately with alarm and consternation. Then their bodies whitened and enlarged, their arms convulsively straightening to reach the grass of the garden lawn, their hands suddenly lacking all dexterity and forming into great black hooves. Their necks lengthened and became muscular, their dismayed faces elongated, and flowing manes were soon running up their necks.

As Rachel and Victoria stood stock still in disbelief, the transformation was quickly completed. Before them stood two huge white horses, stomping and neighing with wide-eyed surprise. They were truly lovely, possessing the power and stature of quarter horses, combined with the beauty and form of the finest Arabians.

"Will they ever be men again?" Victoria asked with concern and no small alarm at what had befallen her loyal friends.

"Of course, Victoria, at the twelfth stroke of midnight they shall be mere men again!" the Goddess' eyes flashed as she continued. "But think of the sport they shall have until then, the drama, the sensation, the flowing wind in their manes, raw animal power! They will look back on this night with longing, years hence."

As the Goddess spoke, several of her other handmaidens backed Lucas and Elvert up to the carriage and fastened them in its elaborately jewelled harnesses and bridles. Their penises hung, immense with newfound pride, as other naked maidens set blue and silver plumes upon their heads.

"And now a driver. You must have a driver, Victoria!" with these words Circe took Rachel's hand and pulled her forward to stand beside the carriage.

"Touch the carriage, Rachel and you shall be clad only as in your wildest dreams!"

Rachel put forth a tentative hand and touched the carriage. In a flash, her apparel was changed. Rachel stepped back, exclaiming with delight over her magically fabricated clothing. Her feet were clad in gleaming boots with high heels, set with dazzlingly polished silver spurs. The boots extended up her leg to mid-thigh where they flared out and terminated in a style both bold and elegant. Rachel's legs were bare, though a silver and blue epauletted dragoon's coat with a flared waist only barely covered her buttocks. White gloves graced her hands and wrists, and an ornate parade cap was set upon her head, affixed with a wide chin strap, and a deep blue plume. At Rachel's hip, hanging coiled by her belt, was a long and intricately cross-braided Spanish riding whip.

Cinderella

Rachel stood flushed with an excitement that bordered closely on the erotic as she surveyed the spectacle she presented.

"And lastly, we must have a footman, mustn't we!" the smiling Goddess purred with a knowing glance toward two menacing jaguars who were approaching the carriage.

Victoria's friend, the old pensioner, walked nervously between them, gaping at the strange tableau in his neighbor's garden. He surveyed Victoria's and Rachel's costumes, the two huge horses, the naked maidens, the giant, the slaves, and, of course, the naked blonde Goddess, tiptoed in her shoes of purest jet and onyx. At last he stopped, and mindless of the menacing presence of the jaguars, he leaned upon his cane to stiffly kneel before his friend Victoria and her Goddess benefactor.

"I always knew there to be greatness in you, Victoria," he murmured, his voice trembling with the mix of a dozen emotions.

The Goddess herself seemed touched by his devotion to Victoria and his apparent fearlessness.

"Faithful friendship such as this should never go unrewarded!" Circe said with a smile.

She bent prettily to take his gnarled hand and help him up. The old man was gone, and in his place stood a young man, as proud as the day he marched to the war that enfeebled him. His chest was broad and his arms and shoulders were strong. He was clad in a livery identical to Rachel's—save for it being the masculine counterpart. He was so young and strong that even the handmaidens stared at him.

The old pensioner walked forward and threw himself prone on the ground at the feet of Victoria and the Goddess. Streams of gratitude flowed down his now youthful cheeks. The Goddess extended the elegant pointed toe of one of her onyx pumps and he covered it with kisses. When he again got to his feet, Victoria embraced him warmly and kissed him.

"And now we must add a liveried carriage guard, or perhaps two, for these are perilous times," the Goddess said as she beckoned two of her naked male slaves forward.

They obeyed her summons without a moment's hesitation and were soon clad by her in magically contrived garments of prestigious splendor, befitting those who served the Princesse de la Masquerade.

"Remember, Victoria," the Goddess cautioned. "My power here on these shores becomes void at midnight, so do take care to return before then—else my transformations shall all be undone."

One huge-shouldered carriage guard held the door open for Victoria to step into the plush, comfortable opulence of the carriage's interior. The other released an intricate silver catch at the side of the carriage to deploy a swinging, velvet-covered footstool for Victoria to use to climb inside. Victoria spun about and embraced the Goddess in a selfless gesture of gratitude, before finally allowing her footman to gallantly assist her in stepping up into the carriage. The footman carefully shut the door after she had set her skirts aright, and the guard retracted the velvet-cushioned footstool into its recessed storage place.

The first guard assisted Rachel in climbing up onto her high driver's seat at the top of the carriage and then went up himself to sit beside her. The second guard joined the footman in mounting up to their high seat at the back of the carriage.

At a nod from the Goddess, Rachel uncoiled her whip and cracked it across the broad white backs of Lucas and Elvert.

She giggled, "Though friends, I will not spare you if you lag! So step lively then!"

Cinderella

Rachel delivered an expert cut to their hindquarters and skillfully managed the reins as well. The big silver-and-glass carriage wheeled about the lawn, leaving soft, deep ruts in the wake of its turning passage. Rachel steered it expertly through the gap in the garden wall and onto the street.

The Goddess, her slaves, her maidens, and her beasts watched the running lights of the carriage dwindle, even as its polished beauty sparkled in the moonlight. A moment later they heard its heavy, jewelled heels rumble across the wooden span that connected onto the high road and thence led up past the vineyards of Challon and Pompere to the palace. The Goddess kept her beasts and the giant posted as guards about the grounds of the house on Fountain Square. She motioned to her maidens and her naked slaves.

"Come! Let's enter the house. I shall be Mistress tonight!" Her slaves followed her, and her smirking maids walked at her sides. "It seems I have some tasks to perform here and things to set aright!"

CHAPTER EIGHTEEN

High above Calauverge, colored lights twinkled from the windows of the grand ballroom in the royal palace. A thousand elegant guests, along with their consorts, courtesans and cavaliers had assembled together in the opulence of the cavernous vaulted room.

Towering, intricate chandeliers of priceless jewelled crystal hung from the high ceiling, bathing the room in dancing, festive lights. The royal architect and his journeymen had so fashioned the ballroom that it was the core and center of the palace, surrounded as it was by private and semi-private drawing rooms, all furnished in sumptuous and exquisite comfort. Curtained doorways along the south side of the room gave access to balconies overlooking moonlit gardens and fountains. Ivyed trellises lent each separate balustrade the secluded atmosphere of an isolated alcove.

Royal servants, both male and female, skillfully navigated the bustle of the ballroom floor, carrying golden trays of delicacies from land and sea and glass decanters of the finest claret and Madeira.

Godilieva Prumm held sway in one corner of the ballroom, observing the introduction of an unending parade of guests by court heralds with a sweet smile. Only her intimates knew that her garments were so contrived as to admit the penis of a boyish young cavalier who stood behind her into the lush recess of her clenching anus. A bevy of wealthy, jaded friends gathered about her, engaging in conversation both explicit and scandalous.

Godilieva stood, the picture of flawless and primly feminine propriety, her bustled dress of the richest burgundy satin cut just low enough to expose the succulent nipples of her bare breasts. Ever so slowly she moved her hips, gently and subtly back and forth, savoring the slow secretive slide of the well-endowed cavalier's penis in the tight clench of her bottom.

A worldly-wise friend bent to whisper in her ear, "Good God! This one is the youngest you have had yet, isn't he? I don't think he'll last five more strokes, and, when he comes, you'll be lucky if he doesn't cry out and start thrusting madly!"

Godilieva laughed and kissed her friend's cheek, maintaining her lewd covert motion while asking another friend to obtain a glass of dry sherry for her. As she waited, she joined in a conversation two young women were engaged in as to whether or not the health of a male slave could be endangered by being excessively and slowly masturbated while contorted and bound.

Godilieva observed that the health of a male slave was of little or no consequence, and her friends laughed at her cleverness.

The young cavalier knew that the lascivious sensations he was experiencing were going to force his ejaculation very soon. He was obsessed with Godilieva

Prumm; he adored the ground she walked on and was maddened by her wicked beauty. Until now he had considered himself lucky to be one of her playthings and sometimes to be allowed to kiss her bewitching feet. He was overcome with gratitude and pleasure at the liberty she allowed him now.

Both the Marquis de Besançon and Lord Rodney marvelled at how the chief herald, the Baronet d'Aubercharet, seemed to have no difficulty in remembering the names of each and every pretty, perfumed guest as they arrived.

The marquise pointed out the exquisite form of Lady Jane Broughton, who entered clad in a gold and white gown of breathtaking expense and complexity. She was escorted on the arm of her uncle, Lord Carlyle, and did indeed look ravishing. In this, King Philip readily agreed with the complimentary assertions of the marquise.

The Vicomte Cevenne stood at the broad steps that led down onto the sunken polished dance floor from all sides of the ballroom. He had sent a courier with a note warning King Philip of the plot to unseat him, but had received no answer or acknowledgment. He had no way of knowing that his courier had been waylaid and was now imprisoned in the cellars beneath the Chateau Furnald. His life was spared for now, as the two assassins considered him handsome, and found it amusing to play humiliating sexual games with him.

The Vicomte Cevenne had spent the last two weeks in hiding, after having sent his wife to the country estate of a cousin, far from the capital. At least he would be safe here in the crowd at the royal ball. He looked up at the royal gallery to see the de Besançons sitting with the king and despaired of ever having his warning taken seriously.

The Baron Roth-Haupfelds engaged an obviously bored Contessa of Albion in a deep conversation from which she sought every opportunity to escape. Indeed, she silently cursed her friend Regine, who walked past with a knowing smirk at her misfortune, making no effort to interrupt the conversation at all. The Contessa of Albion's pretty eyes flashed with both amusement and annoyance when Regine was recognized and greeted by the dashing figure of the comte de Languedoc, and he bent to gallantly kiss her hand.

Dona Alicia Antigua accompanied Ana and Marcella about the crowded ballroom, and, indeed, the striking women attracted their own flocks of young, eager male admirers.

Prince Steven Targete stood at the great entry doors of the ballroom at the bottom of the wide marble steps and bowed politely to all the young women the Baronet d'Aubercharet introduced. His cheeks reddened ever so slightly as Giselle descended the steps in a simple gown of blue and white, sown with sapphire stones. Her briefly-cut dancing shoes flirted with Prince Steven's deepest weakness as he bent to kiss her hand. Her soft laughter made him bite his lip in chagrin and turn his attention to his next arriving guest as Giselle swept past.

The Baronet d'Aubercharet next introduced the Marquise of Rousillion and the Princess of Alsace, who arrived together. The Marquise of Rousillion was a petite laughing girl, whose sweet and pretty face would never lead one to believe the debaucheries of which she was capable. As the Princess of Alsace curtsied to the prince, and he bent to kiss her hand, she smiled knowingly at the recollection of the carnal delights they had shared.

As the musicians readied themselves to begin playing dance pieces, expressly composed by the music master for the occasion, the Princeling Rupert followed his idol Mademoiselle Seline d'Elbernne. He watched her as she passed the ornate scrolled screen that secluded the royal musicians from the guests but did nothing to shut out their music.

Prince Rupert's heart thudded heavily in his breast. Mademoiselle d'Elbernne wore a tight gown of the palest green that fell away from her breasts and shoulders to form a scandalously low *décolletage*. Her firm breasts sported large, lusciously pink, conical nipples, and she moved easily in the extravagant height of her high-fashion dancing shoes.

Prince Rupert chafed in a silent, impotent jealousy each time Mademoiselle d'Elbernne lingered to talk to a handsome young lord. Such interludes were all too frequent, it seemed to Prince Rupert, as his idolized beauty was often accosted by guests involved in the mirth and merriment of the occasion. He nodded politely to the many female guests who greeted him as he passed, they being ever hopeful of a royal liaison or dalliance. However, he soon excused himself to continue following the wavering course of the lovely dressage trainer about the pillared room.

He pondered what to say to her: ever it seemed when he addressed her or she him, his words would be but crudely formed and stick in his throat. She must think him a dreadful boor and, horrible thought, perhaps she was deliberately avoiding him. He was many paces behind her and though his course through the crowd appeared as haphazard as her own, he was ever worried that she sensed his obsession. Indeed, the bare-breasted beauty had starred so extravagantly in his copiously erotic dreams since the masturbation in the royal stables that he was certain his heartbeat was audible to the entire assembly as he drew a bit nearer.

Princeling Rupert's eyes caressed the delightfully narrow waist and flaring sensuous hips of his idol, then swept upward to linger over the firm bare curves of her stylishly exposed breasts. He vividly imagined himself lying across her lap, one succulent nipple offered to his lips, the dressage trainer smiling as she gently reached for his pleading young erection.

Little did Prince Rupert know that he was being followed himself. The assassins from Chateau Furnald had cast aside the black and felt trappings of their secretive profession. The pretty young women had gleefully planned the slow torments to which they would subject both Prince Steven and young Prince Rupert when the rebellion was successful. Lady Jane Broughton and the Marquise de Besançon had promised them the reward of disposing of the royal brothers. The assassins had secret artisans contrive instruments of cruelty they designed themselves and were most anxious to use them in the cellars beneath the Chateau Furnald.

Now, however, less delicious and more immediate concerns occupied their keen and practical minds. Both were clad in ivory gowns of a snugness that prohibited even the slightest formation of wrinkles. Their pert breasts, like Seline d'Elbernne's, were prettily bared, and supported by rigid underpinnings designed into the gowns that they wore. Both cruel beauties realized that in following his idol, Prince Rupert was approaching a drawing room set off the main ballroom.

Within that room, de Besançon couriers were finalizing arrangements with the Contessa of Albion's representative concerning properties to be given in exchange for her support of the rebellion. The assassins could not be absolutely certain that even in his star-struck state Prince Rupert would not notice the exchange, placing the shadow of royal suspicions over their treacherous designs.

Rudely ignoring the overtures of the many young lords who tried to engage them in conversation, the assassins strutted purposefully in their exquisitely high-heeled court dancing shoes to catch up to the prince, before Seline reached the drawing room where the exchange was taking place. They succeeded in their efforts and drew up on both sides of the prince, taking his arm in a gesture of familiar affection.

The lovely assassins easily escorted the bewildered young man into a small retiring room just opposite the one that Seline had entered and in which the conspirators conferred.

They laughed and chatted pleasantly as they steered him through a knot of guests and into another more intimate chamber beyond. One assassin locked the door, while the other embraced the prince and kissed him on the lips, pressing her lithe curves most lewdly against him as she did so. She pulled back and looked at him with laughing eyes, noting his own gaze lingering on the exposed nipples of her breasts.

The assassins counted on bold, sensual and even outrageous behavior on their part to totally fluster and distract Prince Rupert.

The blonde assassin who kissed him purred, "I do beg your forgiveness, prince, but you are so young and handsome that I could perhaps be pardoned my insolence?"

Her brunette companion occupied herself by reclining on her back upon an elegant settee and raising her lovely legs in the air. She pulled up her dress, and beneath she was naked. The blonde assassin in Prince Rupert's arms drew him forward to have him captivated by the naked charms her companion so wantonly exposed.

Prince Rupert was as a helpless lamb in their hands and they revelled in his blushing uncertainty and inexperience.

The assassin who kissed the prince rubbed his erection through his trousers gently, and chided her friend for her lewd behavior, "Goodness! Do put your dress down at once! Have you no idea how you effect the sensibilities of a handsome young man!"

The brunette assassin writhed in a motion of supple languid allure and cooed, "Oh but it feels so delightful to relax and give my feet a rest from those dreadful shoes with their impossible heels!"

She kicked one of her pretty shoes from her coyly arched silk-stockinged foot and raised it to prod the velvet cords of Prince Rupert's epaulette.

"Be a sweet prince and rub my pretty foot!" she pouted in a voice silken in its sexual inflections.

Prince Rupert stood stock-still, his eyes riveted to the luscious shaved morsel of the brunette's slit as she lay cooing and teasing before him. The blonde assassin soon freed his penis from his clothes and began teasing it bare as he gently and sheepishly rubbed the brunette's pretty tiptoed foot.

Prince Rupert trembled and tried half-heartedly to twist away from the masturbating hand of the blonde assassin who smiled invitingly as she gazed up into his face, her pouting lips parted in an open invitation to lustful pleasures. His gaze dropped to the strangled bloat of the head of his penis as it protruded helplessly from her sliding fist.

Prince Rupert was very well acquainted with his own penis, and with masturbatory exercises in general, but had never before felt a hand other than his own caress his sex organ. He stared down with unbelieving eyes at the assassin's little hand as it gently coaxed and abused the tingling, rigid flesh of his shaft. He had never felt so swollen: his sex organ was so inflamed with passion that it literally hurt. Prince Rupert felt that the pretty young woman who so readily manipulated him was teasing and tormenting his very soul. He looked past the strangled tip of his own throbbing sex organ to the pouting, lithe brunette who lay below him, back arched, with a luscious smile on her full lips. His excitement amused her. He not only could see the lush, shaved mound

Cinderella

about her pale pink cleft, but the crinkled opening of the brunette assassin's anus was exposed to his glance too, between the full, broad curves of her buttocks.

The assassin masturbating Prince Rupert, knowing that the couriers and representatives had by now ample time to make their exchange, decided to put him out of his misery. Using quick, firm motions of her hand, she brought the prince to crisis in but a matter of moments. She laughed in soft triumph as he leaned into her abusing hand, and pleaded with the motions of his body for release.

The brunette giggled and made sure to continue holding her dress well flared so their victim could see the exposed delights of her femininity as he was drawn of his sperm. The brunette assassin's stockinged foot, now rested—dainty little toes prettily pointed—on Prince Rupert's shoulder. Her other foot, still clad in the high fashion of her court dancing shoe, was raised enough to gently prod the prince's chin with the thin spike of her heel.

The prince, in his disorientation and desperate lust for release in his laughing masturbator's hand, scarcely knew what he was doing or saying—or even where he was, for that matter. As his penis submitted to the assassin's ever-so-insistent hand, he moaned softly, trembled, and unconsciously licked the spiked heel of the brunette's pretty shoe, which she had so impudently raised to his face. His penis reared, twitching with orgasmic desperation, held fast in the blonde assassin's deft little fist.

A strangled cry erupted from deep in Prince Rupert's throat as his penis jolted again, then poured forth mad splashing arcs of sperm. His seed flipped through the air to soil the broad bare bottom and bare shaved slit of the assassin who writhed smirking beneath him. She oohed and aahed at the heat of his thick passion as it generously squirted upon the most priv... e parts of her person, one thick spurt even landing just below her cleft to slowly slide downward and come to rest in the tight private bud of her anus.

As they watched Prince Rupert's humiliating orgasm, both cruel young women thought only of the games they would soon be allowed to play with him deep in the cellars beneath the Chateau Furnald.

They smiled.

CHAPTER NINETEEN

The page lay on his stomach across his bed, naked from the waist down. He wore only the white silk shirt that Regine had given him on his birthday the year before. He lay, chin in hand, slowly rubbing his genitals on a fluffed pillow placed beneath his hips. The sensations were by now quite exquisite and his bottom clenched repeatedly with private joy.

The page had determined to ask Regine for permission to play more humiliating games with Elvert. He would have to wait until the time was right and her mood was favorable toward his wishes. He loved savoring the thought of what he had done to Elvert under the supervision of the Contessa of Albion. Perhaps some of Regine's, Ana's, or Marcella's, lovely fashionable friends would enjoy seeing a repeat performance. The page's slender penis rubbed the soft snow-white cover of the pillow most deliciously. Already he could feel the stirrings of impending orgasm. His balls had drawn up tight, ready for the release of a copious ejaculation.

In his mind's eye the page was standing beside a chair in which Elvert sat, securely bound. The page was naked below the waist, clad in but an ornate jacket. Elvert, of course, was naked and virtually helpless. Several noble women, beautiful pampered favorites of the royal court, had gathered to watch him perform for their enjoyment. Their eyes widened and lewd smiles formed on their pretty lips as he reached down to grasp and rub Elvert's erection. The page rubbed and teased Elvert's swollen penis ever so gently, ever so slowly.

In his fantasy, Elvert pleaded, begging for the humiliation to end, for the page to stop before the terrible embarrassment of orgasm occurred. The page then abandoned Elvert's drooling penis to grip the heavy wrinkled purse that hung full and rounded below.

The page gasped as his penis twitched and tingled against the pillow. He had not intended to orgasm so quickly, and rolled sideways to remove himself from the stimulating friction. He clenched his bottom, desperate not to ejaculate until it was timed with the proper moment in his fantasy. His penis reared, poised precariously on the very brink of orgasm, the tiniest stimulation being all that was needed to send it over the edge.

He was caught absolutely by surprise when the door to his room was flung abruptly open and two naked, smiling young women entered.

The page's chamber was situated at the front of the house, high under the broad eaves, and its window overlooked Fountain Square, not the garden. He was therefore utterly unaware of the commotion that began with the disintegration of a segment of the garden wall.

The young maidens carried long, wicked-looking whips and they smiled at the gasping naked page. They walked on tiptoe, and, as soon as they entered his room, they stopped, one on each side of the doorway as if preparing the way for some more important personage coming along behind. The maiden closest to the page uncoiled her whip and swung it, its lash searing the air to curl over his cringing bare hip and lay a smart welt across his clenched bottom. The cruel whips in the maidens' hands were in stark contrast to the lush, enticing curves of their bare breasts, and to the delicate flowers in their golden hair. The page jumped at the smart of the whip and rolled over as a reflex action to the sting and surprise. His rolling motion brought his penis into sudden contact with the coverlet beneath him. The resulting friction was enough. With an expression of horror and embarrassment, the page realized that his orgasm was not to be denied. As his penis twitched and tingled lewdly beneath him, the Goddess entered his chamber. She appeared as a youthful, laughing beauty, her golden hair up in a regal swirl, utterly naked save for her onyx shoes with their wickedly high, strutting heels.

The page stared open-mouthed, gasping with awe and sudden passion for the luscious young Goddess—even as he helplessly continued to spend over his bedclothes.

The Goddess smirked and fixed him with an arch glance of mocking pity. To his surprise, the page then saw that a naked male stood behind her, hugely erect, his low, dangling scrotum flopping between his legs even as he too entered the chamber. The naked male seemed to be the Goddess' slave—his neck was imprisoned in a tight collar and there were whip scars on his thighs and buttocks.

The Goddess spoke to the page in a voice as smooth as satin. "Show us your orgasm. Exhibit yourself!" she cooed.

The page found that he could not help but obey. He turned his body, exposing his jolting, spurting penis to his four visitors as they watched, mocking smiles upon their intent faces. Six arcing squirts leapt from the tip of the page's penis to spatter at the cruelly clad dainty feet of the laughing Goddess. At her command, her pretty maidens descended on him with their whips and chastised him throughout his long and abundant orgasm, until at last he lay exhausted, his penis limp and soft between his trembling legs.

The Goddess then gave the maidens another command and they took the page by his arms and dragged him from the bed, placing him on the floor and ripping his shirt entirely from his body in the process. The page struggled feebly, too awed and intimidated by the breathtaking Goddess who towered sternly over him to do anything else; notwithstanding, Circe's maidens were far stronger than they appeared.

The page lay on his back, one maiden holding him down so that his knees nearly rested on his heaving chest. The other maiden knelt beside him and smiled down at him while the Goddess stepped closer to stand at his head. The page squirmed uncomfortably as the naked slave knelt down, hugely erect, at his bare and vulnerable buttocks. The maiden who was not holding the page down moved to kneel beside the slave and reached through under his buttocks from behind to grip his testicles.

The Goddess smiled at the slave and nodded her head.

The page squirmed his desperation, his eyes wide with dismay as he realized what was to befall him. He lay, his small penis still weak and oozing from his masturbation, gasping and desperate to squirm away as he felt the tip of the slave's huge penis prod at his tight anus.

The slave reached down to grip the page's hips in his powerful hands.

Squirm as he might, the page realized then that his helplessness was absolute.

The collared slave gasped as the lewd beauty who knelt beside him fondled him and goaded his nakedness into a flaming pitch of sexual excitement. He thrust his hips forward in a slow, forceful motion that could not be resisted or denied. The page grunted as he felt the huge purple tip of the slave's throbbing penis stretch his anus and begin its firm, sliding entry.

The maiden who held the page down looked at him from above the bare erect nipples of her breasts and smiled, gloating over his terrible humiliation and reveling in their utter disregard for his dignity and person. She realized that he was quite immobile, so she then applied one of her hands to his flaccid genitals, tugging and handling his moist, cringing flesh with motions that only added to his degradation. The other maiden maintained her grip on the slave's scrotum, urging him to penetrate the page's backside yet deeper, and smirked as she inserted a finger in his anus.

A moment later, the page lay writhing, gasping for breath, every muscle at maximum tension, as the slave's penis was fully embedded in his tight bottom. He looked to the Goddess with adoring yet beseeching eyes, hoping that she would stop his torment, but she laughed down at him, the soft tones of her feminine voice ridiculing him, sending hot tears down his cheeks.

Her eyes widened in an expression of sweet mockery then, and she extended the pointed toe of one of her black onyx pumps to the page's lips.

Two stories below the page's chamber, Sonia and Maria del Castillo were themselves most pleasantly occupied. Both wiggled wantonly, glazed in a glow of perspiration, as they squirmed, impaled on the rigid pricks of two other naked slaves. The Goddess was in firm control of the house off Fountain Square, and every occupant felt full the weight of her erotic presence.

Two of Circe's huge enthralled males, scarcely more than wanton beasts, had entered their chamber. Sonia lay, legs spread, upon her bed while Maria del Castillo stood beside her, bent lusciously at the hips and giggling. After much pleading, the wanton heiress had persuaded the ever modest Sonia to allow herself to be masturbated. Such was the state of the two lovely young women when they were surprised by the slaves.

Both had remained still, eyes wide, gazes locked on the unbelievably ponderous male equipment that hung between the collared slaves' legs. Their faces were suffused with the crimson blush of appraising feminine approval as they virtually gawked at the big men in their doorway.

The slaves entered and, in a trice, scooped up the naked young women, holding them up like trophies before their flat, muscled bellies and impaling them from behind on their gigantic erect pricks. The young women gasped, giggled and mewed the ecstasies of their pleasure as the slaves began to work in unison, thrusting their great cocks to the hilt in the moist pussies so eager to admit them.

The slaves stood facing each other, and, in their lewd abandon, the young women embraced, naked breast to naked breast, and kissed one another passionately, as the slaves slid their penises nearly from their slits, only to slowly run them in again, enjoying sensations at once compelling and delightful. The room was filled with the low throaty moans of the young women, the grunts of the perspiring slaves, and the moist slap of sexual union.

Sonia's lips blindly sought Maria del Castillo's as she whimpered her delight, lost and disoriented in the throes of her passion. As their erect nipples rubbed together, both women began to have powerful orgasms, even as their tongues met in a lewd, lingering kiss. The writhing motions of their embrace proved more than sufficient to send the naked slaves themselves over the brink of crisis.

Sonia and Maria cried out in unison, clutching each other, their lovely, lithe bodies bathed in sweat as the jolting organs of their steeds flexed and jumped within their deepest feminine parts. The buttocks of the male slaves clenched to rigid tension as the great muscles of their upper arms and shoulders knotted in the extremity of their pleasure.

Both young women nearly fainted as they then received the thick, pulsing spurts of the Goddess' slaves. The slaves stood, eyes tightly shut, and ejaculated the essence of their manhood into the eager young clefts of the women they so deliciously invaded. Two pairs of bare heels pummeled the muscled thighs of these thrusting, grunting steeds as the couples locked in a universal clutch of sexual delight.

Sonia gasped, virtually in a daze, as, with lips parted and cheeks, flushed she kicked her legs in the air and pointed her toes, savoring the molten overflow of the slave's passion as it drooled abundantly from her madly throbbing sex.

Maria del Castillo twisted about, causing the slave's penis that skewered her to unseat itself from her slit with a lewd plop. She wrapped her thighs about his waist and kissed him wantonly, probing his mouth, her body trembling, reaching heights of renewed desire.

Soon both slaves sprawled on the floor, with the pretty young women seated full on their faces. From beneath the broad bare bottoms of the eager women came the sounds of intimate licking. Maria hung her head, her hair wild and falling into her eyes. She was nearly fainting with pleasure.

Upstairs, the page was discovering new depths of

stark humiliation. The slave who penetrated him was being goaded on by the smirking maiden who fondled his scrotum. The other maiden had succeeded, after no small exertion, to bring the page to another, and dreadfully humiliating, erection. His penis now throbbed helplessly in her hand, its slit gasping the proof of his excitement in a clear string that soiled her fingers and palm. The maiden's low giggles mocked him, even as her hand enslaved his helpless male organ.

The page gritted and moaned, feeling as though he was to be torn asunder by the big penis that slowly pistoned to and fro in his cringing backside. He felt that his sanity hung only on the fact that the generous laughing Goddess let him slake his infantile need by allowing him to lick her onyx pumps in his terrible degradation.

The Goddess fixed him with a knowing gaze, a look that left him naked, defenseless, and desperate to please her. Her face exuded so much sweetness, pity and innocence that it drove him mad. The page cried out, tensing his helpless, contorted body as the slave lunged forward, gritting his teeth and groaning as he began to orgasm.

The maid who held the slave's testicles squeezed them hard to cause him the most copious ejaculation possible.

The Goddess laughed, the sweetly musical tones of her amusement exciting the page beyond endurance even in his agony. His own penis jolted in the hand of the gloating maiden who abused him. The page moaned and shuddered as the slave's huge penis filled him with squirt after squirt of searing sperm. His own slender penis helplessly surrendered to the laughing maiden's hand and spurted a surprisingly copious load of its own up across his tensing stomach.

The Goddess laughed again, noting the page's tongue never paused in its oral worship of the toe of her onyx dancing shoe.

Lord San Sebastian knelt in the near total darkness of

training room four. The thick stone walls of the basement room kept him in isolated and deaf to the commotions elsewhere in the mansion and he, like Maria del Castillo and Sonia four floors above, had no idea that the house had fallen into the Goddess' hands. His knees had begun to throb as he knelt, beginning his third hour now, waiting for the capricious young woman with the beautiful little feet to come and enslave him.

His head was bowed and his eyes were shut: they would remain so until his sweet tormentor entered and told him to open them.

The door to the fourth training room opened. Footsteps clicked across the flagstone floor and drew nearer—mincing feminine footsteps. Well Lord San Sebastian knew the sound of elegantly clad female feet.

"Open your eyes!"

The command startled him, because it was not the slightly muffled though sweet voice of his hooded abuser. This voice was just as sweet, and bespoke of a young woman just as lovely, but the accent was slightly foreign, as if the speaker was from a place unknown to Lord San Sebastian and far away. He opened his eyes and immediately his penis twitched to a full erection, rearing desperately between his legs. Before him stood a youthful golden-haired Goddess, haughty and beautiful beyond compare and comprehension. She was naked, save for wearing the most wickedly captivating shoes that Lord San Sebastian had ever laid eyes on. Her hair was up in a regal swirl, save for one lock that fell across her eyes in a way that made her appear at once wanton and invincible. He quivered when he saw the coiled whip in her left hand.

The Goddess strode to him, bent prettily, her bare bottom flexing, and took his chin in her hand.

"I am a dear friend of Victoria's and I shall see to you tonight!"

Lord San Sebastian trembled, sensitive to the authority and power that fairly radiated from the Goddess. At last he found courage enough to quaver, "Who are you?"

His question simply amused Circe, who answered with a soft cryptic purr, "Suffice it to say that I have long experience enslaving men, turning them into rutting beasts and then tormenting them!"

The Goddess took Lord San Sebastian by his hair and forced him to a standing position. Then her fingers began to gently toy with his privates, slowly stroking them and titillating them. He felt as though he would ejaculate already as he stood trembling and astounded at the Goddess' expertise. He looked down at his penis, throbbing its desperation in the Goddess' soft, alluring hand.

Lord San Sebastian then felt as though something were terribly wrong. The Goddess was finding it necessary to bend succulently at the waist to maintain her hold on his genitals. To his absolute horror, he realized then that he was shrinking!

Bit by bit, inch by inch he was growing smaller. Somehow the smirking Goddess was doing it to him. In a few moments his head came level with her hip. Soon she squatted beside him, still masturbating him, and he stood scarcely as tall as her knees. She was laughing now, relishing his dwindling body and his proportionate weakness.

He twisted his genitals from her cruel, toying grasp and, sobbing for mercy, he threw himself at her lusciously clad feet, kneeling to embrace the rounded strength of her calf. He begged the Goddess to stop diminishing him, his face streaked with desperate tears. He feared he would disappear altogether.

Not since his early childhood had the wealthy and powerful Lord San Sebastian felt such a totality of helplessness, such an abject realization of his own smallness and insignificance. His erection still throbbed lewdly against the Goddess' pretty ankle. Strangely, he felt his penis was proportionally much larger than the rest of him.

Finally, Lord San Sebastian also noticed that the shrinking process had apparently stopped, at least for now, and he clung to the Goddess' pretty, curving calf, gasping out the tearful sobbings of his relief. The Goddess was unmoved and looked down at him, laughing softly:

"You poor thing!" she cooed, her velvet voice mocking him in his anguish. "Perhaps you do not like my game. We shall see if it can be made more enjoyable for you then!"

With these words the Goddess bent and picked Lord San Sebastian up by his hips. He was but one foot tall now and she held him playfully in one lovely hand. Her other hand grasped his penis and pulled on it for a few moments, gently abusing its helpless, twitching shaft. With a giggle, the Goddess released her hold on Lord San Sebastian's hips so that she held him dangling by his proportionally huge sex organ.

He bit his lip, kicking his arms and legs in mingled fear and ecstasy. He was horribly afraid she would drop him and let him fall onto the cruel, hard flagstone floor far below. Yet the sensation of her grip on his sex organ gave him the most compellingly sensual feeling he had ever experienced.

The Goddess began to prance about the training room, strutting naked in her outrageous onyx shoes as he dangled from her careless hand, held fast by her firm grip on his rigid penis. He swung helplessly at her hip, moaning and crying out in his delight and desperation, even as his back arched and his muscles contorted with both pleasure and shame.

At that moment the Goddess' hand unmanned Lord

San Sebastian and he began the most intense orgasm of his life.

The Goddess opened the door of the fourth training room and carried Lord San Sebastian by his orgasming penis up the steps toward the central part of the house beyond the kitchen wing. Lord San Sebastian, in the throes of his pleasure and humiliation, pleaded not to be taken into the public parts of the house. He swung to and fro from her fingertips, his body as tense as an iron bar, as his penis jolted and reared in the Goddess' hand. Waves of orgasmic pleasure assaulted his very mind and soul, soon reducing him to a drooling, trembling thing, hanging limp and still spending from the smirking Goddess' grip on his genitals.

The pleasure that possessed him left him soaking in sweat, gasping for breath, too weak to utter a sound or to plead for the agonizing orgasm to end. Over and over again his penis reared in the Goddess' hand, squirting foaming jets of manhood in high, haphazard arcs to soil the floor at her lovely feet.

Something was horribly wrong! Somehow the Goddess was forcing him to orgasm without pause. He tried to scream as a desperate outlet for the insane pleasure but only gritted out an incoherent mumble instead. His penis jolted and jumped, pulsing endlessly in the Goddess' firm hand as he hung wracked in erotic torment and swinging at her bare hip as she walked.

Semen continued to pour from his tortured sex organ, almost as though in the presence of the Goddess there was no limit as to how much his body could produce and ejaculate. He hung, insensible, aware only of the pulsing of his penis in the Goddess' hand as she laughed and carried him like a toy through the house off Fountain Square. They passed servants, who knelt or shrank back before the imperious beauty of the haughty Goddess and the helpless gasping thing that hung by its penis from her hand, shooting semen everywhere. They passed other groups of the Goddess' own maidens and slaves, who led the remaining household servants in various debaucheries.

At last the Goddess reached the door of the room where Maria del Castillo and Sonia lay naked, oozing sperm from their slits in the sodden aftermath of their pleasure. Their consorts had left the room to be about other aspects of the Goddess' business in the house.

As the Goddess entered, holding the helpless squirming thing that was Lord San Sebastian, Sonia sat up, her nipples erect, her face flushed with her slowly subsiding pleasure. Both she and Maria del Castillo were in awe of this naked beauty in her fetishistic onyx shoes with their impossible heels.

Circe only stayed a moment. She laughed and tossed the still-ejaculating lord through the air so that he landed softly on the rumpled coverlet of Sonia's bed, beside her primly tiptoed feet.

"Enjoy him!" the Goddess commanded generously. "He only thinks himself exhausted. I am sure his lips could impart many lascivious delights to your clefts and bottoms."

As the pretty young women stared, eyes wide and lips parted in astonishment, the Goddess turned about on her stylish heels and was gone.

From rooms nearby and from downstairs came the moans and giggles of groups and couples engaged in a sexual frenzy.

Sonia ran on tiptoe to the door and closed it firmly. Maria del Castillo was already kneeling by the gasping form of Lord San Sebastian as he lay dribbling on Sonia's bed, his orgasm at last subsiding.

"Oh, he's adorable isn't he, Sonia!" Maria del Castillo purred. "We can have fun with him!"

Sonia giggled and climbed onto her bed beside Maria.

They both began to fondle Lord San Sebastian's still miraculously erect penis. His stuttered pleadings were of no avail. Sonia had a perfectly splendid idea. She lay back, bringing her bare knees up to her breasts, exposing the luscious, rounded orbs of her broad bare bottom along with the wet pink pout of her slit.

"Make him lick me, Maria!" she purred. Sonia wiggled her hips with lewd abandon. "Do it, Maria! I want his mouth at my slit!"

Maria giggled and gently picked up the pleading lord, caressing him as one would caress a helpless pet. Then she held him against Sonia's privates and bossily ordered him to pleasure her. With one hand, Maria del Castillo gently stimulated Lord San Sabastian's sex organ, while with the other she moved him to and fro, so that his little face scuffed and rubbed Sonia's swollen clitoris.

Sonia bit her lip and squirmed wantonly at the pleasure Lord San Sebastian's face provided her. She mewed and whimpered as Maria lewdly used the helpless shrunken lord to begin an orgy of gloating pleasures.

Lord San Sebastian knew he was at the mercy of the two naked beauties, now five times his size. His nostrils filled with the lush scent of Sonia's sex as he resigned himself to his fate and began to worshipfully lick her hooded pink clitoris. As he licked, he moaned and squirmed helplessly, for Maria del Castillo's fingers proved most knowing in their explorations between his legs.

Lord San Sebastian was carelessly used for hours as a plaything for the pair's lewd pleasures. His begging for release simply amused his cruel tormentors, who despised him and taunted him in this helpless state.

Chapter Twenty

High on the hillside above Calauverge, in the ballroom of the royal palace, the sonorously nasal voice of the Baronet d'Aubercharet was announcing the arrival of the latest powdered and perfumed delicacy to grace the occasion.

The young Contessa of Aragon swept in with her courtesan and gelded cavaliers, assuming an air of icy boredom. Prince Steven turned for a moment as he danced with the Marquise of Tuscany. His gaze met that of the Contessa of Aragon, and for but a moment their eyes held. Then hers dropped almost tentatively as she swept purposefully toward the side colonnade of the west amphitheatre to find the denizens of viscouncy, over whom she held haughty court.

Prince Steven was bored. Absolutely, terribly and unforgivably bored. Perhaps the Princess of Alsace, who had proved most generous in discreetly lending her private bodily orifices to him for his carnal gratification, had ought to do with his boredom.

The Marquise of Tuscany blurred before the prince's jaded eyes as they swept through the crowded dance floor, now thronged with elegant couples. Still, the prince was oblivious to the dark-eyed beauty in his arms.

And then d'Aubercharet announced her! The one! The laughing beauty from nowhere! The Princesse de la Masquerade! Prince Steven fancied even effeminate d'Aubercharet—whose interests hadn't run to women for a dozen years—was startled at this one's form, face and flair.

The chief herald was not the only one entranced. The crowd of guests, servants and courtiers slowly parted as the smiling young princess descended the wide marble steps and swept down toward the polished sunken dance floor.

"Scandalous! She's quite unattended!"

"Magnificent gown nonetheless, you must agree!"

"My God! What a delicious young beauty this one is!"

Such exclamations broke unconsciously from the lips of those near to the prince and his now forgotten dance partner. Closer to the Princesse de la Masquerade, however, there was but a hush of admiration that followed her, quieting all tongues as she swept down the steps.

The prince stood dazed, the dark mysterious beauty of the Marquise of Tuscany long forgotten.

High above the throng, in the royal gallery of the king, Prince Steven's father leaned forward and asked his chamberlain, Lord Rodney Fallone, as to the lovely new guest's identity. To King Philip's surprise, and the amazement of the de Besançons as well, the venerable expert of protocol and lineage did not know.

The comte de Languedoc had paused with the others as he danced with Giselle held close in his arms. He stared at the Princesse de la Masquerade with a worshipful half-smile upon his ruggedly chiselled face.

He wondered. Could it be the lovely girl who wore the hood to abuse him in the house off Fountain Square? He studied her admiringly, pondering long and hard. The comte truly hoped that this lovely masked new arrival was the same young woman who administered his discipline, rode him about the training room, allowed him to lick at her sex, and then granted him sweet relief with her flawless feet.

There was no leering in his gaze, but rather an awe and a questioning. Were she to become queen tomorrow, the secrets of her past would remain locked forever in the comte de Languedoc's breast and eternally stay untold.

The Vicomte Cevenne knew beyond a shadow of doubt who the masked beauty who descended the steps was. He last had glimpsed her lovely face as Rachel sealed his form in the laced head-segment of the body corset. His gaze, like the comte de Languedoc's, was worshipful and admiring. He had paused while dancing with Regine and released his hold on her hands as he realized that the sight of Victoria had erected his male organ almost instantly and against his present wishes.

He flushed and excused himself, moving quickly to the broad steps that led to the marble-pillared lower gallery about the ballroom floor.

He gave two young women in extravagantly tight ivory gowns a wide berth as they smiled at him invitingly, though even the de Besançon assassins looked with envy on the loveliness of the masked beauty.

The Vicomte Cevenne, suspicious of the assassins, moved into the safety of the clique of confidantes gathered about the Marquise of Rousillion. His heart rejoiced for Victoria. He had always known there to be greatness in her.

Prince Steven found himself thunderstruck at the sight of the luscious vision that descended the grand stairs. His poise and self assurance were both shaken to the core by the laughing young beauty. A single question burned in his mind, absorbing all his thoughts. Was she the tiptoed girl from Market Square? Her hair was long and swept up in a style simple yet regal. Her pretty mouth smiled coquettishly just below her black velvet mask. Her gown was composed of creme satin and pink velvet. Her slender arms were graced with close-fitting shoulder gloves of the most supple black kidskin. But it was her loveliness below the knee that swept the prince away. She descended the steps gracefully, her left hand at her thigh to draw her hem up from the floor. Her ankles were beautiful! Trim and perfectly turned, formed at once to tempt the gaze upward toward further delights and infatuate the eye with its own perfection. Her stockings were of the sheerest and most gossamer silk. And her shoes! Dainty little high-heeled dancing slippers expertly crafted of jewelled glass and crystal. The heels were so high, and the dancing slippers so transparent, that the Princesse de la Masquerade seemed to be moving down the steps, barefoot, on high tiptoe. Indeed the prince would have thought so himself had it not been for the jewelled scintillations of color cast by the fairy shoes across the broad marble steps.

Prince Steven found himself walking toward her, as in the beginning of a vividly erotic dream. The crowd between them parted.

The Princesse de la Masquerade reached the bottom of the steps and likewise moved toward the prince. The crowd released its muted exaltation and something like a drawn-out gasp swept the room. His heart thudded in his breast. Emotions surged within him, awakened like fire by the vision of graceful loveliness. Her beauty captivated Prince Steven so that he found himself childlike and breathless in his adoration. Slow seconds ticked by, and then she stood smiling before him.

He bent low in a graceful bow that would have done justice to the pomp of any court. Prince Steven took her kidskin-gloved hand and gently drew it to his lips. The prince's kiss was ever so gentle and lingered almost longingly, as if to sense beneath the black glove, the warmth of the feminine hand.

The prince raised his gaze to drink in the beauty of the Princesse de la Masquerade. Her eyes met his. Her expression surprised him. Interest there was aplenty, but no awe; rather, an almost impudent smile flirted at the corners of her pretty lips—a smile made the more beautiful because of the subtle impertinence which it conveyed.

And then they were dancing. A great open circle had been cleared about them as other couples moved back away from the center of the polished dance floor. An understanding deeper than words swept the huge room. The prince was smitten by the mysterious masked young beauty in the fairy shoes.

The music master launched into a series of new compositions especially reserved for such an occasion of high court romance. Prince Steven and the Princesse de la Masquerade swept across the ballroom floor in exquisitely matched, gracefully measured rhythms. In due course, other couples followed their lead and joined in, one by one.

Regine and her daughters were utterly mystified and did not recognize the Princesse de la Masquerade at all.

The Princeling Rupert stared unashamedly, obvious in his worshipfulness. The Princesse de la Masquerade had achieved an ascendancy over Seline d'Elbernne in his pantheon of goddesses. He sought out the de Besançon assassins, hoping they would relieve the sexual tension the masked beauty had caused between his legs. He was mortified when they coolly turned their backs on him, smirking at his discomfiture.

The Contessa of Aragon stared at the sweet beauty in the prince's arms, realizing that her icy style had been effortlessly upstaged.

Lady Jane Broughton realized the same, as she stood in a circle of her own admirers and saw that their eyes were no longer upon her.

The prince felt himself a commoner in the arms of the dainty little Princesse de la Masquerade. His title was born of political and national reality, but hers sprang effortlessly from the fountainhead of her flawless feminine loveliness. In short order his being and his very senses were enslaved by the laughing, masked beauty. Prince Steven danced enchanted, bewildered and overcome.

The music master's baton swept precisely over his orchestra, as if by motion alone it could inspire them and exactly control the timing and pitch of their every note.

Justine de Besançon stood prettily, her pert breasts barely covered by her emerald gown as she waited, pouting and bored in the private carpeted passage that led to the royal gallery overlooking the grand ballroom. She was eager, hoping that her aunt the marquise was correct in saying that there might be a chance for her to toy with King Philip. Justine did so love to toy with men. Her innocent, youthful wide-eyed beauty—combined with her slender, girlish frame—gave her great power over male sensibilities, power that she relished and savored.

In some fashion, perhaps, Justine de Besançon lived a sheltered life. Her uncle Maximillian and the contessa rigidly structured most of her time with foreign language and music lessons. She was trained and drilled regularly in every social grace and skill until she effortlessly blended at the most formal social occasions with those twice her age. Yet, at other times, her aunt and uncle overlooked her little predilections.

Sometimes Justine was allowed to descend the long flights of steps to the cellars and amuse herself for hours tormenting the genitals of spread-eagled prisoners. Justine was a virgin; indeed, for the present, she disdained the thought of allowing any young man to touch her. Yet she truly loved playing with males' genitals. She was an expert and consummate masturbatrix. Her specialty was slow manipulation.

She turned a bored gaze on a gulping young royal guardsman who stood at the door that led onto the royal gallery of the grand ballroom. Justine had been teasing him, smiling and flirting, then pouting and ignoring him altogether. Her little feet were fashionably clad in the daintiest dancing shoes with the narrowest and highest heels that could be procured in all the kingdom. Money was no object to the de Besançons.

Justine had also, in apparent innocence, toyed with the skirts of her lovely gown with her little silken-gloved hand. The result was that its folds at one side were raised far enough for the blushing guardsman to see a good deal of Justine's leg. Indeed, all of her calf, her knee, and much of her thigh were visible to the guardsman, alluringly clad in the sheerest and most expensive stockings.

Justine liked the guardsman. He reminded her of a prisoner she had teased in the cellars beneath Chateau Furnald but two days before. He had been fastened to the wall, naked and helpless. One of the assassins had brought her a comfortable chair and set it beneath the prisoner. The assassins were always giving her lovely ideas. She adored them and they her.

Justine licked her lips, causing the young guardsman to gulp, as she thought of the games she played.

She had toyed with the prisoner ever so slowly. Despite his agitation on the night before his execution, Justine de Besançon coaxed four loads of sperm from his penis. She savored the memory of every hot squirt in her hand, and the picture of the prisoner's crumpled and defeated face.

Justine de Besançon giggled.

The door leading from the royal gallery opened and her uncle Maximillian and the royal chamberlain Lord Rodney Fallone entered the passage and passed her, headed for the spiral steps that led down to the main ballroom floor. As they passed, Justine heard them speak of the Princesse de la Masquerade and speculate on her identity.

Justine was too overjoyed at the prospect of toying with the king to pay much attention.

The door to the royal gallery opened again and the Marquise de Besançon beckoned Justine to come in.

As soon as she entered, the marquise locked the door. Lord Rodney and Maximillian could tap on the door and wait a bit when they returned, for all she cared. The marquise delighted in even the most trivial humiliation of the house of Targete.

Far below the royal gallery, on the polished dance floor, the smiling Princesse de la Masquerade pressed closed to Prince Steven. Her lithe hips and legs moved as one with his, and the scent of her maddened him. In short order the prince's erect penis surged against her thighs as they flexed and moved beneath the pink velvet of her gown. She did not pull back or exclaim in outrage or surprise. Rather she laughed and shielded his arousal from the gaze of others on the dance floor by artfully positioning herself, pressing her body against him all the more.

Up in the royal gallery, King Philip was more than a bit distracted, though not so much as to dilute his plea-

Cinderella

sure in seeing his son's mysterious consort. He was pleasantly occupied while awaiting the return of his chamberlain with news as to the Princesse de la Masquerade's identity. It was good that he was so poignantly distracted, for Lord Rodney's venture down onto the dance floor was to prove fruitless.

Justine de Besançon sat on one plush, padded arm of King Philip's high-backed chair. Her pretty little right hand, above his head, traced the outline of the Targete signet, etched in the rosewood and ebony grain of the wood portion of the chair's ornate back.

The Marquise de Besançon chatted cozily with the king, her mind ever weighing, assessing moods, and analyzing possibilities.

"Justine is a lovely girl!" the king murmured, glancing up at her and nodding his head.

The marquise cooed, "She is not only lovely, my liege, she is also most skilled! There are arts in which a young and well-bred girl may truly excel."

The king was startled, astonished to feel the butterfly fingers of a sweet, smiling Justine de Besançon sliding toward his genitals from a low caress that began at his abdomen. The king held his breath, eager to see what the luscious young girl was up to.

Justine's aunt, the Marquise de Besançon, watched with an encouraging smile on her wickedly pretty lips.

King Philip grunted despite his considerable efforts to maintain a courtly air of propriety. The bold little bitch smiled sweetly as she grasped and squeezed his convulsively hardening penis through his royal garments. King Philip cleared his throat, preparing to order the forward little beauty, who now practically sat in his lap, to stop. The Marquise de Besançon distracted him by pointing out the clique about Godilieva Prumm, down on the steps that led to the polished dance floor. As the king turned to the marquise, Justine's practiced fingers undid his fastenings and bared his big penis. It throbbed in her hand, its nakedness all the more compelling when contrasted with the pretty little hand that held and enslaved it.

Justine de Besançon fondled the king's penis in her left hand, as her right moved about him to rest impertinently on his shoulder. The king tore his gaze from the marquise's, and turned to look up to Justine's face as if silently imploring her to unhand him and restore his royal dignity. Her lips parted, and she fixed him with eyes so wide, flawless and innocent that he was overcome.

As King Philip turned back toward the now-smirking Marquise de Besançon to maintain the illusion of casual conversation, the corners of Justine de Besançon's mouth curved upward ever so slightly in a smug, self-satisfied smile. Her hand began slow, subtle kneading motions, pulling the loose skin of King Philip's penis up and down the rigid stalk of his tingling shaft.

King Philip looked down upon the dance floor, spread out in a panoply of crowded elegance far below. In the center of the swirling couples danced his son, Prince Steven, and his mysterious new consort, the Princesse de la Masquerade. King Philip Targete had excellent eyes, and they lingered on the legs of the masked beauty who was held close in his son's arms. As she swirled about the dance floor in accordance to the measured rhythms of the music master's current composition, the skirts of her elegant gown flared up and away from her lovely feet, calves and flawless ankles.

His organ pleaded its sensual torment, in the domineering little fist of his youthful, though accomplished, masturbatrix.

"Oh, I fear I am thoughtless!" the Marquise de Besançon purred with exaggerated concern, her eyes drinking in the helpless, bloated hue of the head of King

Philip's penis all the while. "Justine, dear! We cannot allow our king to soil himself or the royal gallery in his passion! This at least—we as two of his royal subjects—and I like also to think, close friends— can do for our liege."

Justine pouted, though dutifully halting her manipulations until the Marquise de Besançon had tucked a scented lace handkerchief about the royal penis. She smiled at her pretty niece, "And now you may resume, Justine! Do see that you grant King Philip a generous release from the heavy burdens of state that he bears. Why should this ball be a festive occasion for all but him?"

Justine looked down at the king, her eyes soft with assumed pity. The tempo of her stroking hand increased between his legs as his rigid organ was deliciously abused and fondled ever nearer to climactic release.

Justine's nipples swelled beneath the low lace *décolletage* of her emerald gown. Tonight she would lie naked, writhing upon her bed, her fingers caressing her shaved slit as she squirmed and relived the joy of abusing the penis of King Philip Targete.

As Justine de Besançon breathed more rapidly, and as her cheeks slowly flushed with secret enjoyment, King Philip turned his eyes once again to the masked beauty that seemed in so many ways to be the center of all intrigue and attention. She laughed, youthful and at ease in his son's arms. Once again the king's eyes swept to her calves and ankles. The royal glance lingered also on her lovely high-heeled dancing slippers, a most bewitching fashion, that both revealed and emphasized the flawless beauty of the Princesse de la Masquerade's feet.

In that moment Justine de Besançon imparted a lewd little twist of her wrist to the manipulations she gave the king's now desperate and drooling sex organ. She giggled softly, savoring the first rearing flex of the king's orgasm as his penis leaped in her hand. Justine slid her hand to the base of the king's penis, grasping it tightly so the sensitive skin was stretched and taut. Then she sat, pretty in her lewd complacency, to watch the king's ejaculation.

King Philip felt paralyzed: all the strength of his body was centered in his maddeningly twitching organ, imprisoned in Justine de Besançon's hand. His eyes widened, he leaned forward a bit, trembling and gasping as he began to ejaculate. Thick volleys of royal sperm squirted from King Philip Targete's abused sex organ, splashed high in the air, and plopped back earthward to almost magically land on the confines of the scented lace handkerchief tucked about him.

His glassy eyes were feverishly locked on the pretty calves and feet of the beautiful Princesse de la Masquerade throughout his long and copious orgasm. Each time his penis throbbed in his smirking little masturbatrix's hand, the sensations were a mingling of pain and pleasure. The bold little beauty was holding the skin of his penis so very tightly within her warm fingers, and she cruelly giggled at the anguish that consumed him.

Far below the royal gallery where the king's orgasm left him shaken, the prince and his mysterious young consort trod the measured steps of the latest intricate court dance, amid the elegant, laughing couples that swirled about them.

They danced a long while, the masked beauty artfully concealing his anguished erection. At last he gently steered her to a curtained doorway which led to the privacy of a columned outdoor portico. An understanding court well recognized his need for a private moment and the ball continued on without them.

The prince and the Princesse de la Masquerade stood at the marble balustrade, under the silvery, velvet sparkle of summer moonlight, looking downward at pristine lawns and shimmering fountains in the garden below. Their lips met in a scorchingly passionate kiss of such intensity that it seemed to last forever, even as the music and gaiety provided a festive backdrop for their private tryst. Not fully understanding what he would next do, the prince—as if under the influence of some powerful enchantment—found himself on his knees at the feet of the masked beauty.

Her gloved hands went to her thighs and slowly drew the hem of her gown upward to once again expose the loveliness of her flawless calves and ankles. Her perfect little feet, highly arched in the high-heeled dancing slippers, beckoned him. The tiptoed pose of her feet, enforced by the jewelled heels of her dancing slippers, captivated him.

From rounded heel to high arch and on to her perfect, even toes, the Princesse de la Masquerade's feet enslaved the kneeling prince. With a low, moaning gasp, venting an emotion he had never felt so keenly before and did not still understand, Prince Steven reverently removed the glass high-heeled slipper that graced the masked beauty's right foot. In a gesture of unutterable gentleness, the prince set the gleaming jewelled shoe carefully down on the cool flagstone. His hands trembled as they reached for her foot. With his right hand cupped beneath her heel, and the fingers of his left hand held below her perfect toes, the prince raised his gaze to hers.

The masked beauty smiled at the look of naked longing that pleaded for her understanding and her permission. Slowly he raised the Princesse de la Masquerade's pretty foot to his adoring lips and kissed her perfect toes. The sheer gossamer silk of her stockings teased his lips, as the subtle, understated scent of her burned like fire in the core of his very being.

Prince Steven covered her foot with kisses as sobs of a longing too deep for words or comprehension wracked him. At last, with a strangled groan, he released his purchase on her lovely foot and, with both hands, clawed at his trouser buttons in a frantic effort to free his penis with the utmost speed. The prince was not content with the pace of these proceedings and nearly tore his clothing in his haste. At last he drew his trousers open and tucked them hastily down about his knees.

The Princesse de la Masquerade gasped at the sight of the high sex organ that throbbed and twitched between the prince's legs.

The prince looked up at her, his eyes liquid with pleading. "He is your slave too, sweet princess, as am I. We are your bondservants, your serfs. My God, but what a sweet beauty you are!"

The Princesse de la Masquerade's lips were parted in a gesture of pleasure or surprise—it was difficult for the prince to read as the expression of her eyes was concealed by the black velvet mask.

Her velvet gloved hands found his hair. Her fingers entwined themselves in his curls as she raised her right foot and gently caressed the head of his penis with her impertinent, perfect toes. The masked beauty pursed her lips and thoughtfully studied the prince's turgid sex organ and its dramatic response to her obliging foot. Her gossamer-stockinged toes worked the great penis up and down, pulling at his foreskin and exposing the crimson blush of his glans.

The Princesse de la Masquerade noted the visible swelling of the tip of Prince Steven's penis, and the pleading heat of its throbs and twitches beneath her prettily arched foot. There was nothing out of place at all in the scene they were enacting, she determined with a secret smile that made her lips all the more beautiful. She did have lovely feet, and it was but natural that the prince would want to adore them, to be slowly drawn to the gasping edge of delight by them, to pour forth his tribute of manhood in vulnerable homage to their prettiness.

Oh—but perhaps she was hurting him! His organ was abnormally large, and his handsome face with its haunted pleading eyes conspired with his sweat-streamed brow to make the masked beauty wonder if he was perhaps very ill. Her foot stopped, poised just above his pleading organ, the delicious stimulation momentarily suspended.

"No!" he cried out in apparent agony. "Please, sweet beauty, do not abandon me now!" The prince gasped for breath and seemed seized with a fit of trembling. "For the love of heaven, princess! Do not stop now, I implore you!"

The masked temptress realized then his need and began again the gentle torment of his manhood under the coy impudence of her silk-stockinged toes. His hands became fists that kneaded the knotting muscles of his bare thighs as her foot worked between his legs. The Princesse de la Masquerade's dainty gloved fingers played about the locks of his hair as she gently prodded his swollen, purpling manhood, and, in sudden curious inspiration, pressed it back against his abdomen to work it with the ball of her foot. The lovely little princess savored the power she felt as she watched the prince's great shoulders tremble and his noble head bow. His broad chest rose and fell with the frantic need to fill his desperate lungs with an adequate air supply.

The masked beauty had a sudden liquid urge to see his crisis, to make his crisis come upon him. With a soft, musical laugh, she worked the more busily. His hugely inflamed, lurching penis was exercised the more by the prettily arched, determined little gossamer-stockinged toes that ever-so-slowly enslaved it. Prince Steven watched the merciless, beautiful little toes as they gently kicked his penis back and forth. His mind, numbed by the mixture of agony and pleasure, noted the Princesse de la Masquerade's low giggle as her toes prodded his organ backward to slap against his abdomen.

In that moment the prince was undone. His penis began a long slow series of jolts and spasms against the compelling bottom of the masked beauty's little foot.

Prince Steven bit his lip, childlike in his helplessness to stop the tide of orgasm that surged within his loins. His fevered, haggard eyes were fixed on the prettily arched foot with its perfect toes that still worked his tortured sex organ.

The Princesse de la Masquerade licked her cherry lips, eager to see the liquid tribute and the fervor of his surrender.

High above, the bell in the illuminated clock tower of the royal parliament began to toll the midnight hour.

The first peal of the great bell coincided exactly with the first thick squirt of the prince's seed. It spurted up across the satin sash of his jacket to dangle from the velvet cords of the epaulette on his right shoulder. The relentless little toes of the masked beauty extracted two more spurts with her maintenance of the deliciously intimate gossamer friction.

Above the prince's tousled head, the pretty lips of the Princesse de la Masquerade parted once again, this time in an expression of surprise, and perhaps a bit of alarm as well.

Prince Steven gave forth a low sob of despair as the delightful little foot abandoned his ejaculating penis. The little gloved hands disentangled themselves from his hair and quickly pushed him away.

As the clock in the high, illuminated bell tower continued its slow tolling of the midnight hour, the prince fell backward to collapse against the marble balustrade, still in the throes of his intense orgasmic weakness.

Cinderella

Between his legs, the huge royal penis continued to pour forth its thick, twitching volleys of fertile tribute to the cruel little toes that had abandoned him. His sperm glistened on the cool flags under the silver shafts of moonlight.

The Princesse de la Masquerade's gloved hands tucked up her pink velvet gown as she ran lightly down the broad marble steps and onto the dew-jewelled lawn of the royal garden. In a moment she was gone.

The prince finally came to his senses, lying beside a cooling pool of his sperm and softly calling for her over and over again. He sat up and shook the haze of his intense orgasm from his mind. He got to his feet at last, shaking mightily with the effort. And then he saw it! The abandoned high-heeled glass dancing slipper, sparkling in the night at the head of the flight of marble steps leading down into the garden

CHAPTER TWENTY-ONE

While the Princesse de la Masquerade lingered with Prince Steven on the outdoor gallery high above the garden, her friend Rachel had been erotically occupied as well.

Rachel stood, locked in the lewd embrace of a royal dragoon, beneath the fantastic shadow of the silver-and-glass fairy carriage. The footman and the two carriage guardsmen sent as escorts waited some distance away, accompanied by two other royal dragoons.

There were many elegant carriages waiting with the liveried attendants of many royal houses in the moonlight.

The night was laden with a wind fresh from the nearby vineyards, and the tall trees above the carriages sighed in the fragrant air.

The carriages waited in orderly rows between a formal flower garden terraced into a hillside and the shadowed stone wing of the royal stables.

Beside the glass and silver carriage that had conveyed the Princesse de la Masquerade, a paved path rose high, set with gradual stairs and lit by hanging lamps. It led all the way up, across a moat-spanning footbridge, to the inner citadel and the main ballroom doors.

Rachel and the tall dragoon were locked in a kiss that was lingering and anything but chaste. Her wickedly booted thighs were wrapped about his waist and she pressed her breasts tightly to him as their tongues met with passion. The powerful dragoon held the lewd, raven-haired beauty in his arms with ease, grinding himself excitedly against her. Though Rachel's coat barely concealed her bottom and her privates, she was naked beneath it and she was very excited as well.

Lucas and Elvert stood stamping in their traces, for the first time smelling with all the keenness of an animal's sense the luscious scent of a pretty young woman's moist excitement. Their huge penises dangled hoselike and nearly dragged the ground in a helpless response to the sweet and pungent odor of Rachel's slit. Lucas neighed and tossed his head, raising his nostrils into the air to catch more of the scent that drove him mad. He rolled his bit in his mouth as he thought of Rachel, and how her hands had worked his penis time after time in the garden, while Victoria watched, fascinated. Elvert was occupied with memories of his own interlude with Rachel in the second training room. The smell of her brought back the memory of thrusting his penis deep into the intimate heat of her sex while she squirmed beneath him. Both horses neighed their mute and helpless torment.

The hem of Rachel's ornate coat had ridden up past the curves of her broad bottom to nestle wickedly in the small of her back.

The royal dragoon who kissed her somehow succeed-

Cinderella

ed in freeing his penis, with a little giggling assistance from Rachel to hasten the proceedings.

A short while later, Lucas' and Elvert's torment was greatly increased as they smelled the scent of Rachel's furtive sexual joining with the tall, panting dragoon. The dragoon stood rigidly, almost as if at attention or on parade. He held the smooth, bare curves of Rachel's hips, and with strong arms literally slid her back and forth, sweetly impaled on the huge shaft of his penis. Rachel's hands clutched the epaulets on the dragoon's shoulders as she bit her lip and mewed in the lascivious pleasure of the moment.

The dragoon looked down at the young woman so eager to sample sensual pleasures with him. He could not see her eyes at all, for her gaze was downward upon the sliding girth of his prick, and the rakish visor of her plumed parade cap concealed them from him. Her gloved hands and the wide chin-strap of her peaked cap gave the sweet squirming beauty a most proper and authoritative air, causing the dragoon's penis to flex and twitch dangerously in her tight, clenching slit. In his dreams she was a wickedly demanding parade drill adjutant, desperate to slake the selfish desires of her body before beginning once again to bossily order him about the parade grounds, and perhaps even beat him if he proved slothful.

Rachel turned her head and squirmed, then she giggled—the delightful sound of her merriment, soft and low, mingling with the wicked intimate noises of their coupling. Her flashing eyes were fixed on the huge penises of Lucas and Elvert while her cheeks flushed with lascivious glee. "You nasty things! How indecent your dangling penises are. How indecent indeed! I shall have you smartly whipped for this rude affront to morality!"

Rachel would have gone on with her prudish tirade, even while being lusciously skewered on the big prick of the royal dragoon, but the sensations peaked and soon took her breath away. She writhed against the dragoon, her lithe body flexing and moving with his thrusts as her gloating eyes locked onto the helpless and tormented pricks of Lucas and Elvert.

Lucas and Elvert, for their part, now well understood the torment of the slaves Circe transformed from men into animals in Homeric legend. To grovel, helpless and speechless, newly dullwitted at the feet of the laughing Goddess and her lewd, impudent maids, was torment enough. Yet even that subjugation was terribly compounded by the fact that their keen animal senses could smell every luscious scent from the intimate parts of their giggling feminine tormentors, a smell to drive them mad and tease them with what they could never hope to have.

Rachel and her lover were concealed in shadow beside the sparkling fairy carriage so beautifully crafted of silver and glass.

Below the formal garden, viewing the opposite side of Victoria's carriage, stood two Prumm footmen in the gold and lavender livery that Godilieva favored for her servants.

Two pretty royal maids—on their way to check with a wine steward as to the whereabouts of a fine old vintage, ideal for the celebration—paused agreeably to masturbate the Prumm footmen with but scant persuasion and set themselves readily to their task. In a trice, the pretty maids freed the two throbbing pricks and set about rapidly skinning them up and down in their lewd bare hands. As the footmen gasped and strained, eyes clenching shut in furtive pleasure, one maid caught sight of Lucas' and Elvert's dangling pricks. She laughed and nudged her companion with her free hand.

"Look there! See those big horses harnessed to that lovely huge carriage of silver and glass? They must wish that they were getting a little of this themselves!"

Both pretty young women giggled between exclamations of amused outrage at the carnal sight of animal excitement—even as they masturbated the now-panting Prumm footmen with wicked hands. As the footmen leaned into the briskly rubbing hands of the smirking maids, and as their sperm splashed from their organs to glisten on the stone pavement—their masturbatrices indignantly agreed that the offending beasts should be gelded.

Rachel savored the sight of the two huge dangling pricks. She was excited beyond endurance, and she felt safe to relish her wanton pleasures with the tall dragoon to the fullest. Victoria's carriage guards and footman were nearby, along with the two other dragoons, so she felt protected and invulnerable. As her lover once again grasped the smooth bare curves of her broad hips and pulled her forward so his swollen sex organ could plumb her depths, Rachel gasped and the keen liquid tingle of her orgasm began. At the same time she felt the dragoon's big tool flex and expand lusciously inside her and she gasped in lewd delight, savoring the sensations.

The dragoon gave vent to a low gritting moan as his penis jolted repeatedly and he began to ejaculate profusely into the wicked, goading beauty who had her booted legs so tightly wrapped about his waist.

Rachel felt each spurt of the dragoon's passion and, rather than cooling her, his manhood served but to further inflame the burning center of her sex. Throughout her climax, her head was turned so her eyes could feast on the desperate, longing pricks of Lucas and Elvert.

Rachel did not hear or notice the first two tollings of the great bell in the illuminated tower of the royal parliament. At the third tolling of the bell, she remembered the words of the Goddess and, despite her orgasmic pleasure, quickly drew herself from the embrace of the still-ejaculating dragoon. The two last squirts of the dragoon's sperm splashed obscenely onto Rachel's trim, booted thighs as he reeled in surprise from her abrupt departure from his arms.

The dragoon gripped his big prick, substituting the desperate friction of his own hands for the luscious tightness of Rachel's slit.

The events of the following moments seemed to blur in Rachel's mind, and looking backward on them after, she was never quite sure if her memories were reality or part of a vivid dream or hallucination. She shouted for Victoria's footman and the two carriage guards to prepare to leave at once, desperate that the carriage should not vanish before conveying Victoria back to the house on Fountain Square.

Rachel looked up the long steps that led down from the upper terraced garden levels to the main ballroom doors and on down to the carriage courtyard where she stood. Her heart leaped! Victoria came running swiftly down the steps, skipping two at a time in her haste, her gown tucked up above her knees, and but one glass slipper clutched in her hand. The resonances of the fifth toll of the parliament bell had just subsided when Victoria breathlessly joined Rachel, her eyes flashing and her cheeks flushed in a kind of wild excitement.

"He was delightful! I had a perfectly splendid time, Rachel!" the tiptoed beauty gasped, her nearly bare breasts rapidly rising and falling.

"We haven't time, Victoria! There are but seven tollings to go and we shall have no coach!"

Victoria's footman sensed the urgency of the situation and scooped his breathless mistress up in his arms while one of the carriage guards held the door. Victoria giggled, looking back over her shoulder at the still-huge, though now shrinking, penises of Lucas and Elvert. She also noted the last feeble spurts of the dragoon's tribute to Rachel's beauty as they fell to plop on the pavement.

The footman placed Victoria in her seat, and kissed her hand. He then shut the door and sprang up in the high seat at the rear of the immense carriage along with one of the carriage guards. The other guard lifted Rachel bodily and placed her in the driver's seat, leaping up beside her but one second later.

"Run as you have never run before!" Rachel commanded Lucas and Elvert as her whip snaked out across their backs and curled about to snap wickedly along their heaving flanks.

The huge carriage's wheels rumbled across the stones of the pavement as its wheeled about, nearly running down the two maids, the royal wine steward who had just found them, and the two—now satiated—Prumm footmen.

The dragoon stood with his two companions, having tucked his male organ away once again, looking wistfully as the carriage disappeared through the arched gateway that led from the royal stableyard to the road that descended down to Calauverge.

The parliament bell had just completed its eighth tolling.

CHAPTER TWENTY-TWO

High above the royal palace, in the ringers' chambers, six levels below the great cast iron bells that tolled the hours for the island kingdom, the chief bellringer was otherwise occupied.

He stood naked between two likewise naked female guests of the royal ball. One sat wantonly, her broad bare bottom planted firmly on his velvet-cushioned official chair, her bare feet tiptoed against its ivory legs—as she giggled and suavely licked the head of his swollen penis, holding his foreskin pulled back and out of the way.

The other young woman was also naked, and stood behind the royal bellringer, one lewd finger inserted up into his anus to the knuckle. The bellringer's face and lips glistened with the dew of passion from between their legs, and now they were repaying him in kind.

"Now I want to suck him a bit!" the seated girl told

her naked companion with a smug giggle. She stopped licking the bellringer's penis and began to sweetly suck it instead. Her eyes showed amusement as she looked up at the intense features of his face as he grimaced in his pleasure.

The other girl removed her finger from the royal bellringer's anus and began to slap his bare bottom smartly with the palm of her hand, driving him up on tiptoe and wickedly embedding him in the sweet mouth that lusciously sucked him.

The two guests who amused themselves with the bellringer were lewd and pretty young members of the Marquise of Rousillion's entourage. They were more accustomed to applying the rod to naked chateau servants than engaging in these more simple and innocent pleasures.

One level above where the bellringer was sucked, two blue satin knicker-clad parliament squires stood together in the bell-rope loops to ring the great bells. Occasionally, the chief royal bellringer disconnected the automatic mechanism of the bells and allowed the two squires to ring it manually—especially if he had persuaded them to masturbate him as he sat naked from the waist down on his blue-cushioned official chair while they stood on each side, reaching down between his legs to handle him deftly until ejaculation occurred. So once again they had earned the privilege to toll the midnight hour, but their master was too otherwise occupied to see that they were not interrupted.

Before they could apply their combined weight to the looped ropes and toll the ninth toll, they were startled and shocked to see a most delicious and outrageous vision. Suddenly there was a flash of rainbowed light that brightly illuminated the dim but sumptuous chamber. There appeared a pretty woman, with the form and perfection of a youthful Goddess, standing before them—divinely naked, save for stylish dancing shoes of the purest jet and black onyx with wickedly high heels.

She laughed and wiggled her bare hips, exposing the golden down about her slit with wanton abandon. Her face was set in an expression at once both impudent and domineering. The parliament squires stepped down from the loops of the bell ropes as if in a daze, standing on legs gone suddenly wooden as their cheeks flushed burning hot at the sight of the young Goddess. The blue satin of their knickers tightened about their crotches as they helplessly erected, their penises larger and harder than they had ever been before. Harder even than when they masturbated their master, harder even than when they found their own release in furtive dalliances with royal maids.

The Goddess spun about in her high-heeled dancing shoes until the luscious curves of her bare bottom faced the squires. She looked back over her bare shoulder to them—still laughing—and wickedly wiggled her bare hips, flexing the smooth muscles of her broad buttocks as she did so.

The parliament squires could bear the sight no more. They gave vent to strangled cries of shame and surprise as their huge penises began to lurch and jolt, distending the blue satin fabric of their breeches most indecently. They cried out as the twitching of their penises soon brought forth thick spurts and gouts of sperm that shot out to soil their clothing in repeat dousings of fertile seed. Their orgasms seemed endless, and in moments the squires were on their knees before the teasing Goddess till ejaculating in copious intensity, reeling and faint from their unbearably prolonged climaxes.

The chief royal bellringer at last realized that something was wrong. The bells overhead had stopped ringing with the eighth toll. He wasn't sure how much time had elapsed and a sense of urgency possessed his pleasure-crazed mind. He tried desperately to squirm away from the mouth that sucked his penis and from the hands of the other young lady that held his balls and continued to slap his buttocks.

The young lady spanking him simply giggled and clutched his balls more tightly, virtually holding him prisoner by his manhood. The tightened grip of her hand on his scrotum, coupled with a particularly luscious suck given by the beauty who had so expertly captured his prick in her mouth was his undoing. In a moment the royal bellringer was gasping in climactic frenzy as his organ jolted in the skilled suckling mouth of the lovely, cheekily naked Rousillion courtesan.

He rammed his hips forward, trembling with pleasure as he ejaculated. The sound of sperm being swallowed and the sound of a hand spanking a bare bottom filled the tower room.

The presence of the teasing, laughing Goddess lay heavily upon the entire royal palace.

Godilieva Prumm now enjoyed an openly lewd orgy with her friends and retainers.

All throughout the great ballroom, dancers lay sexually coupled on the dance floor, on the steps leading down to the dance floor, and in the intimate drawing rooms and plush nooks that surrounded the ballroom.

The comte de Languedoc knelt behind Giselle's bare bottom, helping her tuck her skirts up, while thrusting his huge penis to and fro in the pouting fig of her sex.

High in the royal gallery, King Philip Targete's noble penis was buried to the hilt in the Marquise de Besançon's anus, while Justine tantalized him by squeezing his scrotum.

Lady Jane Broughton masturbated Prince Rupert Targete, who leaned into the smirking blonde's caresses with a wide-eyed, youthful expression of delight.

The Marquise of Tuscany sat upon the face of the

Baronet d'Aubercharet, writhing to rub her sex all about his mouth and nostrils, while the Contessa of Aragon impaled herself wantonly on his prick. Indeed, the jaded baronet was the most surprised when he ejaculated into the haughty contessa.

The Princess of Alsace and the Marquise of Rousillion accosted Lord Rodney Fallone as he tried to return to the royal gallery—and admit that he couldn't discover the identity of the Princesse de la Masquerade. The two women virtually raped the venerable chamberlain, pushing him back against two columns that bore the weight of the vaulted ceiling and took turns skewering themselves upon his large prick.

Mademoiselle Seline d'Elbernne held the penis of Lord Carlyle Broughton in her hand and masturbated it gently until he ejaculated on the polished floor, his eyes lingering on the luscious supple curves of her breasts. She did not even know why she did it, but, like the others, she was firmly under the influence of the laughing Goddess. Seline's lips curled in distaste as the last bits of Lord Carlyle's seed spurted into her bare hand.

The Baron Roth-Haupfelds was being sucked by one of the de Besançon assassins, while the other gyrated naked on the floor of a drawing room, her sex filled with the Contessa of Albion's consort's penis.

The Contessa of Albion and the Chatelaine of the Penrith Duchy amused themselves with royal winebearers and servant boys.

Regine and her daughters, Ana and Marcella, were shocked to find how much they delighted in the pricks of some royal guardsmen, drawn into the ballroom by the commotion.

Dona Alicia Antigua allowed herself to be pulled down to the floor and have her slit licked by three pretty serving girls.

In all levels of the royal palace the Goddess' influence was felt and it is certain none gave a thought to the bells overhead.

The only exception was Prince Steven, who had entered the ballroom from the balcony where he had lingered with the Princesse de la Masquerade. He had intended to summon the captain of dragoons and an entire troop to find his lovely, mysterious consort. Instead he stood bewildered, looking down upon the polished dance floor now filled with the orgiastically gyrating and interlocked forms of his subjects.

Eager, fresh-faced serving boys plunged their cocks into the most haughty noblewomen, who writhed and gasped beneath them in delicious abandon. Sweet young contessas and haughty margravanes squirmed on the pricks of stuffy old lords and barons, their extravagantly expensive ball gowns tucked up about their hips and their dainty, wickedly high-heeled dancing slipper clad feet wantonly raised in the air. Youthful soldiers and royal guards sucked the fashionably bared breasts of suddenly willing and eager courtesans and court favorites, ever before content to but treat them with disdain.

Prince Steven Targete stood, utterly befuddled—by the Goddess' own design—as he surveyed the scene, his thoughts absorbed with the laughing, masked temptress.

The royal bellringer at last found the strength to disentangle himself from the two pretty guests who had amused themselves with him. He staggered up the deeply carpeted spiral steps to the bell-ringing chamber. There before him squirmed the squires, rolling on the floor, their eyes locked on a beautiful, laughing, naked blonde who stood wiggling over them in wicked jet and black onyx shoes. The chief bellringer halted as though electrified. Between his own legs, his so-recently emptied penis jerked to convulsive stiffness and began ejaculating once again. He stood gasping as his penis pumped and twitched its helpless tribute to the Goddess.

In a flash she was gone.

CHAPTER TWENTY-THREE

While the royal bellringer joined his squires on the floor, rolling and gasping in helpless ejaculatory tribute to the vanished Goddess—whose wild scent and presence still seemed to linger throughout the palace— Victoria, Rachel, the footman and the carriage guards enjoyed a wild ride indeed!

The great silver and glass carriage rumbled down the steep paved road leading from the high hill upon which the royal palace stood. The high jewelled wheels were but a whirling blur as the heavy carriage fairly careened about sharp corners in its mad, nearly uncontrolled descent. Atop the carriage, in the high seats at the front and back, the hulking guards and the white-faced footman hung on for dear life.

Rachel sat, the reins that controlled Lucas and Elvert in one hand, and her Spanish riding whip in the other. The powerful guard beside her—one of the

Goddess' own slaves—reached about her waist with his massive right arm to keep her from flying from her high, precarious seat. Rachel looked wild, lovely and cruel, with her steeply visored and chin-strapped dragoon's cap with its proud plume upon her head. Her silver and blue coat along with her wickedly fetishistic boots conspired with her flashing eyes and laughing mouth to lend her a look at once both fetching and untamed. She lashed Lucas' and Elvert's hindquarters and their flanks mercilessly and without pause.

Lucas and Elvert ran as they had never run before, their minds fairly drunken with the raw, unaccustomed sensations of their animal power. The great muscles of their legs flexed and contracted as their manes streamed out in the wind of their rapid passage. Their hoofbeats thundered on the stones of the road. Under the setting orb of the full moon the carriage sped between vineyards fragrant with lush summer fruit.

It was good that the fairy carriage was equipped with sparkling running lamps at the front and rear of both sides. Otherwise, those disturbed in the hillside cottages and tiny villages would have thought a thunderstorm occurred in the clear and moonlit night.

The carriage rounded an especially abrupt corner and swept through the center of a tiny vineyard village, narrowly missing a freight cart full of wine casks of a fresh Challon vintage of Madeira. The carriage rumbled around another corner and nearly ran down a group of drunken revelers who had just enjoyed the first fruits of a fine Pompere harvest.

Two gendarmes groggily eyed the blurring passage of the huge carriage, pulled by the most massive and powerful horses they had ever seen. They turned to gaze at their own inferior, tethered beasts, shrugged their shoulders, and went back to their wine cups, first turning their gazes to the twinkling lights of the royal palace on the bluff high above them, shaking their hands at the irresponsible antics of the nobility.

Victoria leaned back in her seat, her cheeks flushed, her unhooded clitoris aquiver with the memory of Prince Steven Targete kneeling servilely before her, his penis nearly scorching the gossamer-stockinged sole of her pretty foot as she used it to masturbate him. She thought of the way the strings of his sperm had curled, squirting from the anguished tip of his penis to soil his royal clothing. Victoria's pretty, full lips parted and her cheeks flushed with the memory. She ran the fingertips of one gloved hand through her hair, while with the other she cradled the glass slipper that sparkled in the moonlight falling though the carriage window at her side. She drew her pretty little silken feet up to place them in the deeply plush seat across from her own. A sudden wicked urge came over her. She raised her skirts to let the wind caress her slit. The youthful blood was fired in her veins; her games with Prince Steven had not gone on long enough to bring about her own satisfaction. Her velvet-gloved fingertips descended to her unhooded clitoris as she giggled and gave herself to her own pleasure.

Rachel was utterly mystified as to why the palace bells had stopped ringing the midnight hour with the eighth tolling. As the lights of Calauverge came into sight—glittering down in a steep, lovely valley—the ninth toll sounded high in the palace tower far behind.

Rachel's whip swept out across the backs of Lucas and Elvert in her desperation to reach the house on Fountain Square before the magic of the Goddess should be undone.

The tenth toll sounded as the carriage rounded the last sharp curve on two wheels before descending into Calauverge. The eleventh toll coincided with the rumble of the carriage's heavy jewelled wheels across the carved wooden span that led into the center of the capital.

Rachel mercilessly whipped Lucas and Elvert, as they ran all out, their sides now heaving in exhaustion, their mouths dribbling streaks of foam, their eyes wild in the haste of their animal urgency.

It was well that all those of Calauverge not at the palace for the ball were fast asleep in the houses about Fountain Square. The carriage careened about the fountain court and was rumbling along the garden wall of Victoria's house, heading for the gap created by the Goddess, when the twelfth toll sounded.

The next moments seemed somehow frozen and slowed down, as if time itself was distorted by the wavering power of the Goddess' enchantment. The engraved scenes of maidens interlocked with centaurs, fawns and nymphs on the side panels of the carriage seemed to come alive for a brief moment. The carvings entwined and began thrusting in a convoluted and animated orgy of licentious abandon. Two nymphs held down a fawn and began masturbating it, while a lovely maiden embraced another as both rode an erect centaur.

Victoria sat up in excitement and alarm as she felt the magic unravel. Rachel sensed it too and braced herself. Lucas and Elvert were still running, absorbed in their animal haste. The carriage guards—having been Circe's slaves—knew what was to come and braced themselves as well.

A sparkle of rainbowed fairy light played about the sides and top of the carriage as the magic of the Goddess' enchantment began to end. The bridles and traces no longer fit the once-equine forms of Lucas' and Elvert's bodies as they began to change back into men before Rachel's very eyes. The carriage then abruptly disappeared in a flashing thunderclap of sound.

Rachel and Victoria, once again clad in but the simple clothing they had worn early in the evening, fell into the street, along with the two once-again naked slaves who had been carriage guards. Miraculously, they and the footman—who was now as old as before—landed unhurt on the pavement. The slaves and the old pensioner came to earth and slid farther than Rachel and Victoria. Lucas and Elvert kept rolling, driven on by their own forward momentum until they collapsed in a tangle, on the narrow strip of lawn that ran between the garden wall and the street. A rumble sounded and the gap in the garden wall was instantly closed by the same waning power of the Goddess that kept them all from being hurt with the disappearance of the carriage. The carriage had not actually disappeared, but had rather turned back into the sperm of the giant whom Circe had masturbated in front of Rachel and Victoria.

They both now lay wantonly in the thick puddles, giggling and exclaiming in disgust and amusement, their skirts riding nearly up to their bared hips, exposing their legs and feet to the still-warm puddles of thick fertility.

Victoria bemoaned the loss of her ballgown, so prettily crafted of creme satin and pink velvet, but remembered to safely clutch her own remaining glass slipper in her hand. At least that was an unchanged relic of the Goddess' fairy transformations!

Scintillations of light played about Circe's slaves, and they stood as if obeying a summons. In a flash they were gone as well. More radiant light played about the puddles of sperm in which Victoria and Rachel lay, and they were gone a moment later in a blaze of jewelled light. The aftereffects of the Goddess' enchantment lingered in the air, however.

There in the street off Fountain Square, outside the privacy of the garden wall, Rachel and Victoria pounced on the old pensioner and embraced him. Tears of joy streamed down his face. Rachel held him to her breasts.

"Why are you weeping, old friend?" she asked, her voice soft in her concern.

"To be young, but once again, for but one evening—has got to be the sweetest gift that could ever be bestowed on one as old and tired as I!" the old man husked.

"We can make you feel your youth in another way too, dear friend!" Victoria purred, while she and Rachel set about unfastening the garments from below his waist so they could access his genitals.

There on the street, both young women knelt beside the old pensioner and began to tenderly masturbate him. Rachel kneaded and cradled his scrotum while Victoria worked his prick up and down in her soft, goading hand.

Lucas and Elvert crept to where Victoria and Rachel both knelt on all fours over the gasping, trembling pensioner. They were naked and their penises throbbed with hot arousal. Both young women sensed their presence and pulled up their plain skirts to the small of their backs with their free hands. Lucas squatted behind Rachel, and as she gasped her permission, he slid the turgid girth of his sex organ up into the clenching embrace of her tight, youthful bottom. Elvert knelt behind Victoria's lovely bared bottom and applied kisses to the pouting circlet of her anus and to the peachlike bulge of her downy mount. Soon his penis was firmly nestled in the tight velvet grip of Victoria's moistened slit, as he moved his hips to and fro, gasping in his lust.

The pensioner squirmed in helpless delight as he looked up into the flushed and passionate faces of his two lewd masturbatrices as they knelt over him, bent to their task, while their own bodies were pleasured by the young panting men who deeply penetrated them from behind. Some secret well of reserve in the old pensioner made him hold back, not wanting to shame himself and give in to the warm young hands that teased the rigid shaft of his twitching, empurpled penis.

Cinderella

Victoria bent low, her breasts sweetly bared to his famished lips. "There, there!" the lovely young beauty cooed, somehow almost protectively, as her hand flogged his rigid penis. "Just let it happen. Surrender to us and let your seed squirt out into our hands. Let us relieve your passion!"

As the sperm oozed from the pensioner's penis to bathe the hands of the pretty women who knelt writhing lewdly over him, Lord San Sebastian regained consciousness and found himself of full size and lying across the bare lap of a sleeping Sonia. The hand of a likewise sleeping Maria del Castillo still gripped his flaccid and exhausted sex organ.

Lord San Sebastian had heard no commotion in the street below the windows of the chamber in which Sonia and Maria del Castillo had amused themselves with him. Yet now something—he knew not what—had awakened him. Sonia and Maria had mercilessly used him and emptied his balls time and time again, nearly suffocating him beneath the carnal curves of their bare bottoms and clefts. He knew the childlike helplessness of a pet or plaything as he squirmed in the hands of the giggling women. His body, made tiny and helpless by the cruel, laughing Goddess, proved no match for the strength of the maids. He was still not certain his memories had not been caused by some strange hallucination, and he wanted out of the house of Fountain Square at once.

He removed Maria del Castillo's hand from his genitals and got to his feet, his legs trembling in his exhaustion. He silently cursed, remembering that his clothes were in the training-room–level several stories below. He would have to creep through the house, hoping no servants were awake to see the shame of his nakedness.

As he quietly shut the door behind him and stole into the hall, Sonia and Maria del Castillo rolled into each other's arms, and went on sleeping in a naked tangle.

Lord San Sebastian tiptoed through halls and passages and crept down flights of stairs, everywhere stepping over the sleeping and exhausted forms of servants and maids, many still tangled together as if in the last throes of their orgy of passion before sleep overtook them. To his profound relief, Lord San Sebastian was able to reach the training-room–level below the kitchens, regain the security of his clothes, and leave the house without being seen. He adored the hooded beauty who time and time again had proved so expert in toying with him. Yet delight at her hands was not worth the risk of meeting the laughing Goddess again!

The page lay sprawled in an upstairs corridor below a draperied window that overlooked the top of the garden wall. After he had been used by the Goddess, her maids, and the naked slave, he was thrust out of his chamber and left to the mercy of his fellow servants and the maids who had always resented his preferential treatment by Regine. For hours he was bullied, mostly by the pretty maids, and subjected to unimaginable indignities and humiliations. The maids and servants had organized a contest to see who could cane him best, and his upper thighs and buttocks were covered with rows of thin, searing welts. Now, however, he slept, at peace and exhausted, breathing deeply.

If anyone had been standing at the window, above where the page lay sleeping, he would have seen the last rays of the setting moon illuminate the return of Victoria and her three friends as they climbed over the garden wall. Lucas boosted Victoria to the top of the wall, his hand cupped under the warm bare pout of her slit as she pulled herself up and turned about to sit on the wall above him. Victoria and Rachel were both giggling as Elvert lifted Rachel up. She quivered in a response of delight as his hands cupped the globes of her bare bottom and boosted her to the top of the wall to sit beside Victoria. Rachel and Victoria knelt on the top of the wall, holding each other steady about the waist, and proffered their free hands to Lucas and Elvert. The two young men could not but appreciate the exposed dangle of the young women's breasts as they grasped the soft hands of their friends and clambered atop the wall.

The foursome laughed as they leaped down onto the soft garden lawn and embraced in a series of lingering kisses before entering the doors of the house.

The old pensioner wended his way home through the silent streets of Calauverge, his heart light. He felt glad and free, and his steps were as easy as those of a young man one-third his age. The memories of Rachel's and Victoria's laughing faces, their breasts, their hands on his penis, not to mention the wild ride down from the royal palace, stirred and invigorated his blood.

CHAPTER TWENTY-FOUR

High above Calauverge, in his royal bedchamber, Prince Steven Targete knelt by his great canopied bed.

The huge room was decorated in dark panelling and plush velvet. The ornate lamp burned low, its scented flame casting fanciful shadows about the room. Fantastic figures loomed and moved, brief shapes cast by the dancing light. The statuette of a lithe nymph that occupied the center of his mantelpiece turned itself into a mythic goddess, promising at once power and pleasure—but the prince was oblivious. Beyond the inlaid cherry panels of his door, a clock chimed the wee morning hour, and the occasional muted tread of trained servants slipped past unnoticed.

The prince reclined on the Turkoman carpet that floored his room. His back rested, arched over the intricately embroidered covering of his plush bed. His heavy shoulders and broad chest were clad in a ruffled shirt with expansive sleeves, below which he was naked. His great truncheonlike penis loomed hotly erect between his splayed thighs. His large scrotum hung low to rest weightily on the fine gold-threaded carpet.

The prince looked dreamily on the precious little object that he held in his hands. Hands that had carelessly thrust a dueling rapier through a dying adversary gently cradled the high-heeled glass dancing slipper. As he turned it ever so gently in his grasp, its dainty sculpted facets caught the lamplight and sent it out in softly rainbowed arcs to play about his muscular thighs and the floor.

He let his head fall back as he thought of her once again. The Princesse de la Masquerade's voice and form were imprinted forever in the mind and sensibilities of Prince Steven. Alone in his room, the anguish of his longing for her possessed his very soul. The lovely face and the soft laughter of the Princesse de la Masquerade filled his mind and obsessed his being.

The prince knelt upright beside his bed. Ever so gently he worked his penis down into the toe of the dainty glass dancing slipper. He began to move his hips as his erection made love to the pretty little shoe in which it was imprisoned.

He would turn his kingdom upside down to find the masked beauty. Tomorrow he would gather a regiment of royal dragoons and commission them with a Targete document bearing the seal of his signet ring to find her. Prince Steven rested his right hand on the coverlet of his bed as his left held the heel of the luscious little glass slipper. His buttocks flexed and perspiration appeared on his fevered brow as he thrust his penis to and fro in the dainty little point-toed shoe of his masked, laughing mistress. For a brief and delicious moment his penis was sweetly ensconced in the tight pointed toe of the shoe, where her toes had so recently nestled. It twitched there exquisitely, until his pumping motions slid it away, toward the shoe's heel, before he made himself thrust forward once again. The Princesse de la Masquerade loomed in the prince's active mind almost as a goddess, a figure to be worshipped, a laughing tease to grovel before, naked and bursting with adoration.

He gasped as his tempo increased. As his penis repeatedly slid forward to twitch and jolt in the daintily pointed toe of the fairy shoe, Prince Steven could not shake the notion that he was making love to the masked princess herself. Somehow the shoe was part of her and he made love to it reverently. His mind reeled, recalling the vision of her prettily arched feet, the coy impudence of her silk-stockinged toes, the rounded sensual curve of her pretty heels and the maddening shape of her calves and ankles.

In Prince Steven's vision, the masked beauty sat watching him as he made love to her shoe with the twitching adoration of his imprisoned penis. She sat laughing, her skirts up to her hips, revealing the curves of her bottom and the sweet beckoning pout of her bare slit. His penis churned and jolted as he gritted his teeth, poised and trembling, every muscle taut as his crisis overtook him. He rammed his penis forward, one last time, until its tip was stopped by the sweetly compressing point of the toe of the jewelled little shoe. He groaned, a low wrenching cry as—with every muscle tensed to an agony of longing and release—he ejaculated his fertile tribute into the little shoe that held him prisoner.

His eyes had twitched shut in the throes of his ecstasy, so Prince Steven was very shocked indeed to hear soft, feminine laughter in his room. He opened his eyes and started, visibly shaken though his orgasm continued unabated, the little shoe dancing and twitching to the jolts of his climaxing penis upon which it rode. A naked woman lay on his bed facing him. She had lovely golden hair and she was laughing at him as she cupped her chin in her hands, seeming to curiously study him even in her amusement.

The prince's gaze travelled down across her bare buttocks to the curve of her trim calves. The Goddess lay with her knees bent and her ankles crossed and her feet raised up behind her. The prince savored the beauty of her ankles and noticed that her shoes were of gleaming black onyx and jet, and had heels so wickedly high he had never seen the like of them, not even in the most jaded and outrageous examples of court fashion. Between his legs, his penis continued to jump and spurt in an agonizing and continuing paroxysm of unbearable delight.

The Goddess raised her perfect eyebrows ever so slightly. Her lips formed into a soft, luscious pout that conveyed both amusement and exaggerated sympathy.

"Oh you poor boy!" the Goddess cooed. Her voice silken, soft and smooth as velvet. "You seem to be undergoing a perfectly delightful torment! Perhaps I can help relieve you," she added sweetly, almost as an afterthought. "No, I shall let nature run its course after all. See that your body pays both your masked princess and me a generous tribute!" she purred, lapsing once again into her soft and maddening laughter.

The prince sensed that the Goddess prolonged his climax by some art or enchantment, yet he was utterly helpless to gainsay her. He trembled, pleading for the unbearable and still-peaking pleasure to end before it was the death of him. The Goddess simply laughed into his straining, anguished face, savoring every pang and twitch of his sexual torment. The glass slipper fell from his penis, though his organ continued pumping strings of sperm that splashed about its high heel and instep. The prince's eyes clenched shut and he reeled forward gasping and fainting before the Goddess. As his mind spun within the delirium of his pleasure she sat up and cradled his head upon the lovely curves of her bare thighs. He fainted with her words, "You must find your princess! There's no time to waste!" ringing in his ears.

CHAPTER TWENTY-FIVE

But a fortnight after the royal ball, the whole kingdom was still fairly buzzing with talk of the unknown Princesse de la Masquerade, who above all others, had enamored—some would say even enslaved—Prince Steven Targete.

Those who lived adjacent to the Madeira vineyards of Challon and Pompere still talked about the fairy coach that sped down from the palace in a streak of flame, drawn by two gigantic horses who snorted fire—and then the entire vehicle vanished in a flash of sparks never to be seen again. All the nobility still talked of the strange lewdness that swept the guests of the royal ball, and of Prince Steven's search for his mysterious princess. Indeed, it was said that King Philip had especially empowered a royal vice-chamberlain under Lord Rodney Fallone, one Lord Basil Foxton, to bear the glass slipper that the Princesse de la Masquerade left behind about the kingdom in a ceaseless search for her.

Lord Foxton was accompanied by a mounted regiment of royal dragoons bearing the standard of the house of Targete. The crescent moon cast its beams through the open window of the high council chamber in the royal palace. King Philip Targete, his son Prince Steven, Lord Rodney Fallone and Lord Basil Foxton sat at the great oval surface of a polished table deep in thought.

Lord Basil Foxton was animated, hunching forward in his high-backed chair, his broad shoulders tight as though he required a physical release from his tension. His square-jawed face and black hair, swept into a tail that hung at the rear of his high collar, gave him a look that was rather untamed. It was true that the hearts of many otherwise spoiled and bored young women beat rapidly when they found themselves in his presence. His fingers drummed the table, the engraved crest of his ring catching the dim lamplight, creating the illusion of movement among the elaborate gold griffins of his signet.

"And I tell you that the glass slipper fits them all!" Lord Basil Foxton said with resignation in his voice. "It fits them all, my lords! It may be that the Princesse de la Masquerade's feet are the tiniest of all, but it is also true that the lovely young contessas and marquises of our kingdom have dainty feet, and they are not all of the same size. Yet the slipper seems to, perhaps by some device of magic or enchantment, expand or contract, ever so slightly, to form to the feet of whatever pretty maiden tries it on!"

King Philip Targete looked from Lord Foxton, to his chamberlain Lord Rodney, and thence to his son Prince Steven, before turning his gaze back again to Lord Foxton. He sighed deeply, "What hope then can there be! It seems that our only way of finding her was by seeing whose lovely foot would fit the glass slipper. And now we have no chance at all!"

Lord Rodney spoke quietly. "Tell us Lord Basil, the slipper had another strange effect on the young women who tried it on, did it not?"

Lord Basil Foxton was an accomplished courtier and in his own way jaded, and given to vice, but he blushed nonetheless. Lord Rodney urged him to continue. Lord Foxton cleared his throat and did so. "I must be blunt, my lords. The glass slipper makes the young beauties who slip it on their feet fairly mad with passion. They flaunt their most deep-seated lusts and cravings. The captain of dragoons and I first noticed this when at the Chateau Piron, the summer home of Godilieva Prumm. First she had her maidens try the shoe on. She had to summon several up from the cellars where she said they were beating naked servants. I knelt at their feet and removed the shoe from its cushioned case. As soon as I slipped it on their feet they began writhing, gasping and caressing each other. When Godilieva's turn came, she went mad with a passion for me!"

Lord Foxton stopped briefly to collect his thoughts, and then he continued, "As soon as the jewelled shoe was on her foot, she lunged forward from her chair and into my arms. I jumped in surprise, reeling backward, and hit my head on the carved leg of a harpsichord. When I came to myself, she had torn aside my clothes and was impaled on my penis, writhing and squirming her hips most deliciously! And she was laughing! I must confess the sensations were so compelling that I ejaculated, before the stunned captain of dragoons could help drag her from my person. When the shoe was removed she became herself again, seeming to have no memory of our carnal engagement. She even expressed surprise at the dishevelled appearance of our clothing!"

Lord Foxton went on to tell more of how the young

maidens who had tried on the glass slipper became wild with their basest passion, in front of Lord Foxton, the dragoons and their own assembled households. Some ran to their footmen, trying desperately to consummate their passions before the dragoons could pull them away. Others had simply raised their skirts and masturbated, sighing and softly moaning in their delight. Still others had even begged their own maids to lick them!

Prince Steven was sitting quietly, lost in thought. At last he slammed his big fist down on the table and stood up with such force that his chair crashed backward behind him to the carpeted floor.

"I have it! The glass slipper did not cause my masked princess to lose control!"

Prince Steven paused, remembering their games together above the moonlit garden.

"She was always in control and knew every nuance of what she was doing! When we find the young woman who is unchanged when the glass slipper is placed upon her foot, then we shall have my masked princess!"

Prince Steven turned his gaze to Lord Foxton and spoke thoughtfully: "Lord Basil, did the glass slipper sparkle on the foot of any of the young maidens who tried it on?"

Lord Foxton thought for a moment.

"No, my liege. It is a lovely, jewelled shoe—but it does not sparkle!"

Triumph colored Prince Steven's face.

"We have another sign by which we shall know our masked princess! The fairy shoe sparkled when enfolding her pretty little foot!"

Chapter Twenty-Six

Three days later, the regiment of Royal dragoons who bore the glass slipper arrived at the house on Fountain Square.

Lord Basil, despite his size and strength, had been injured in a scuffle with several impassioned young maidens before the dragoons accompanying him leapt forward to break up the fray. Lord Basil's place was taken by a more junior member of Lord Rodney Fallone's staff, a young vicomte named Augus Valprom.

Augus Valprom knelt on the floor, while a royal dragoon stood beside him holding the cushioned case containing the glass slipper. Ana sat in the chair before him, her skirts drawn lewdly up to mid-thigh. She surveyed Marcella and her mother questioningly and then stifled a wicked giggle. Her eyes gloated over the kneeling form of the suddenly blushing Vicomte Valprom. His white riding pants did very little, in their tightness, to conceal the shape and size of his very erect male organ.

Augus Valprom had had a very long day indeed. The luscious bare and stockinged toes of dozens of laughing maidens had teased him beyond endurance. Long ago, his pretty, stern young stepmother had often forced him to kneel and kiss her lovely feet; he had ever since shared the same obsession as Prince Steven.

The Marquise of Rousillion had mercilessly teased him, sensing his weakness. She had raised her wickedly pointed, silk-stockinged toes to his face and asked him to kiss them with a low mocking giggle. Lord Augus had nearly soiled himself in his excitement.

Regine smiled like a cat and an understanding of Augus Valprom's weakness added a sweetly venomous tone to her voice.

"I am sorry if our presence but interrupts your private pleasures, though I feel you should continue, rather than keep us waiting while you worshipfully gaze at Ana's feet and legs."

Ana tiptoed her pretty bare feet on the carpeted floor directly in front of where Vicomte Valprom knelt. She laughed openly at him. The poor fellow bent to his duty, his erection still tented between his legs, his face flushed in the deep crimson signature of his embarrassment.

Marcella had already tried on the lovely little sculpted glass slipper, as had Dona Alicia, Maria, and Sonia.

Regine had sent the latter two upstairs to deal with Victoria, to bind her, and see that she did not cry out or come down. Rachel stood by Regine miserably awaiting her own turn. Regine had no idea of the identity of the Princesse de la Masquerade but she did not want to allow her lovely stepdaughter even a brief exposure to scrutiny from the royal palace. Regine was only too aware of Victoria's breathtaking beauty and begrudged her any opportunity for recognition.

Rachel's heart still thudded with the sickening certainty that Regine meant every cruel detail of the threat she held over Rachel's head, if she were but to mention the existence of Victoria. Augus Valprom's trembling hands slipped the glass slipper gently on Ana's coyly arched bare foot. He studied the slipper carefully and detected not the faintest sparkle.

"Just what are you looking for, my lord?" Regine asked, her mocking, insinuating tone still failing to cloak her curiosity.

"I have sworn to my royal master not to divulge the signs by which we shall know the Princesse de la Masquerade when her foot is graced by her glass slipper!" the vicomte said abruptly.

Ana began to breathe rapidly and her cheeks flushed with highlights of color. She squirmed in her chair, raising her delicately shod foot high in the air. She gasped, in apparent and lewd ecstasy, and drew the hem of her dress up nearly to her hips. She began then to touch the slit of her own sex, apparently unaware of the presence of Regine, Rachel, Marcella, Dona Alicia Antigua, Vicomte Augus Valprom and a dozen high-booted, wooden-faced dragoons.

She raised her hands imploringly to Dona Alicia Antigua, who had been first to try on the glass slipper.

"Embrace me! Hold me to your breasts!" Ana giggled almost drunkenly.

Dona Alicia looked to Regine, her face set in an expression of dismay and embarrassment.

"I have seen enough: this is not the Princesse de la Masquerade," Augus Valprom declared as two dragoons stepped forward to hold Ana still while he removed the slipper.

"No! Don't remove it! It is mine! I have never felt anything so delicious! I spent as soon as it was placed on my foot!"

When the glass slipper was removed from her foot

and again cradled in the vicomte's hand, Ana came to herself and pulled her skirts down with a start. She flushed and turned questioning eyes to Regine and Dona Alicia Antigua.

"It had no effect on me! Did it? Tell me I did not squirm and gyrate like Marcella!"

As Rachel took Ana's place in the chair before which knelt the young and handsome Vicomte Valprom, Victoria was in a very compromising position indeed three floors above.

Regine had cunningly devised a method to keep her out of sight and out of mind. Victoria lay bound fast with soft kidskin straps, naked, and upon her stomach. She lay squirming in her bonds, upon a heavily built leather-cushioned table.

The table was so fashioned as to keep her almost kneeling, her pretty bare bottom raised in the air, and the small of her back hollowed most sweetly.

Behind her, Elvert sat, also bound fast, upon a similarly equipped stool. His penis had been handled and caressed by Sonia and Maria del Castillo, both of whom now stood nearby, directing what was to follow with eager cruelty.

Both maids were clad in simple black dresses of a plain severity. Both wore their hair up in a severe style, by Regine's own design. Both pretty young maids wore gloves that clad their arms from fingertip to elbow.

Elvert was naked as well, and acutely conscious of his vulnerability. His penis twitched between his legs, maddened by the lewd pulls and caresses the maids had given him.

Sonia knelt giggling and turned a crank. The bench upon which Victoria lay bound and the stool where Elvert sat, also immobilized, were both part of the same complex apparatus. As Sonia turned the crank, Victoria gasped because her legs were slowly spread yet further, exposing the pink pout of her bare slit. Elvert averted his gaze. Maria del Castillo knelt, also laughing softly, and turned another crank in the side of the apparatus. The base of Elvert's stool slid forward silently along an oiled, recessed groove. The result was that Elvert's erect penis soon encountered Victoria's bare bottom.

Victoria tried to squirm away from the anal penetration. Elvert, too, tried manfully to twist his hips and spare the virtue of his lovely, gasping companion. Maria and Sonia would brook no refusal. By tightening straps and bindings here and there, and by operating a series of small concealed levers, they succeeded in aligning the private parts of both their prisoners perfectly. Both maids giggled as they together turned a small brass wheel. Their gloating eyes watched as Elvert's erection slowly penetrated the tight, denying clench of Victoria's cringing anal circlet.

Elvert gulped, contorting, trying desperately to pull back, but couldn't. Victoria looked back over her shoulder, eyes wide with consternation.

"Don't, Elvert! Don't you dare!" she cried, her eyes narrowing as she gave him a vicious look.

"I am trying, Victoria! I cannot help it. Oh please you must believe me ... uh!"

Elvert's syllables terminated in an unconscious groan of unwanted pleasure. The dainty, gloved hands of the smirking maids kept turning the wheel. Inch by inch, the excited girth of his erect penis slid into the dilated pink tightness of Victoria's bare bottom. Elvert bravely grit his teeth, refusing to begin the pumping motion that the maids obviously wanted of him.

Maria del Castillo laughed, "Regine has seen to it that the apparatus has been modified, since you were last placed on it with that hopelessly bungling upstairs maid for Marcella's birthday. We can do your motion for you now, silly boy!"

With that, both laughing maids began to jig the brass wheel, ever so slightly, to and fro. The result was that Elvert's penis slid back and forth in Victoria's exquisitely tight bare bottom. Neither victim needed to deliberately participate in any way.

The machine was an invention of Regine's friend Godilieva, who thought it to be an amusing conversation piece that would perhaps prove useful in breeding servants.

Victoria gasped with the feel of this invasion, even as she threatened Elvert with certain doom if he did not withdraw. This the poor fellow was quite unable to do, and as the sensations of pleasure mastered him, he gave vent to his own moans and cries of delight.

Even as Victoria and Elvert suffered through the tormenting mix of sensations their forced coupling aroused in them, Rachel unwittingly became their savior. She was completely cowed by Regine's threats and despite her love and loyalty to Victoria, she had determined to give nothing away. Regine however, had not reckoned on the enchanted power of the glass slipper.

When the Vicomte Augus Valprom placed the dainty crystal and glass shoe upon her foot, Rachel lost all inhibition. She squirmed and writhed, raising her leg as Ana had, to enjoy the play of light on the glass facets of the heel and sole. A moment later she was gasping for her friend Victoria, for whom the raven-haired beauty had always had a secret passion. Rachel had torn aside her threadbare bodice and rubbed her erecting nipples, as her face flushed in her delirium.

"Oh Victoria! Oh Victoria!" she moaned continuously as her loins flamed with sapphic passion. In her beleaguered mind, the sweet young beauty knelt again, by Regine's command, licking Victoria's genitals.

Augus Valprom noted that there was no trace of sparkle, but leaned forward, his face a mask of concentration. His eyes lingered on the sweet exposure of the arch of Rachel's foot, due to the fashionable low cut of the glass slipper. His thoughts, however, were locked and focused upon her mention of another—this Victoria.

According to Regine, all the maidens of household, servant and guest alike, had been given their chance to try the fairy shoe on their feet. Augus Valprom knew, by Rachel's gasping words, that Regine was concealing another.

The orders of his royal master were most explicit. He removed the shoe from Rachel's foot. Rachel's eyes lost their cloudy and glazed look at once.

"There is another!" Augus Valprom demanded. "Is she in the house?" His burning eyes were fixed on Rachel. "Well, speak! Is she in the house?"

Rachel's fearful silence and her pleading glances toward Regine spoke volumes. Then Vicomte Augus Valprom stood up, towering over Regine and Marcella.

"So I have played the fool and been your witless clod!"

He turned to the now-scowling dragoons. "Search the house! Every nook and every room! There is another. Do not be too careful; break what you must."

Regine's eyes darkened with hatred and anger, but she was silent.

Rachel spoke, her voice trembling, and the dragoons paused.

"It may be unseemly the way you shall find her my lord," she said, her voice husky with pleading. Braving Regine's malice, she continued, her words pouring from her lips. "She shall be queen! She was the Princesse de la Masquerade! She has the other slipper! It would not be proper for the royal guard to find her indisposed or in disarray. Let me summon Lucas and we will bring her down directly."

At Rachel's words both Marcella and Regine assumed

expressions poignant with stunned disbelief. Ana became livid with fury and she lunged at Rachel, her lovely face contorted in hate. Two dragoons stepped forward and dragged her from the room.

Augus Valprom spoke: "Very well! It seems this Victoria has at least one loyal friend after all. You may bring her, but do not delay. My dragoons will turn this house upside down if necessary!"

Rachel found Lucas, and they breathlessly ran up the carpeted steps together. Well they knew the sort of degradation they would see when they entered Regine's upstairs chamber of amusements.

By now Elvert was nearing the end of his tether. The cruel maids still ceaselessly jigged the brass wheel, imparting the forced pumping motion to their coupling. Victoria squirmed, her hair wild and fallen in her eyes, her face passionate in her helpless pleasure. Elvert looked as though he was being slowly tortured. He was tormented by guilt for each and every twitch and throb of his penis in Victoria's bottom. Even as his penis lurched, alarmingly close to ejaculating its load of sperm deep into Victoria's sweetly compelling anus, he groaned and gritted his desperate apologies. Victoria knew his helplessness, but in her own desperation, she threatened and berated him for his wickedness.

The door to the room burst open and Rachel rushed inside with Lucas fairly upon her heels.

Before Maria del Castillo or Sonia could begin to protest, Rachel hissed, "The vicomte knows of Victoria, so now there is no reason to resist us! Leave us at once or this room will soon fill with royal dragoons who will take brutal exception to your obstinance!"

The two black-clad maids were convinced by Rachel's fearless tone. If she were suddenly unafraid of Regine, then their words must be truth. Both maids walked from the room, their faces assuming expressions

Cinderella

of innocent affront, though their eyes lingered lewdly for a moment on the naked helpless coupling of their victims.

Lucas' eyes followed their departure with a glaring, icy gaze of contempt.

Rachel turned her attention to Victoria at once and reached out to stroke her face, "Oh, I am so sorry, Victoria! If only I had courage to speak out before. But Regine threatened me with the most frightful consequences. Things that I could not bear!"

Victoria's eyes spoke volumes in her love and gratitude to Rachel, then suddenly widened in consternation. Elvert sagged forward behind Victoria, his trembling lips venting a low groan of defeat.

"Rachel, quick!" Victoria cried out in desperation. "He is spending! He cannot help it! Spin the brass wheel at once, to the right! To the right!"

Rachel gasped, and instantaneously obeyed. She grasped the wheel in her hands and spun it furiously, drawing Elvert's twitching penis from Victoria's bottom. Victoria twisted about, trying in her desperation to speed the withdrawal lest she be lewdly soiled.

That very motion proved too compelling for Elvert to bear. His penis lurched and twitched, flexing the tight circlet of Victoria's pink anus one last time as it plopped free. As Rachel finished turning the brass wheel to draw them apart yet more, Elvert's sex organ spasmed and squirted a long string of seed across the lovely flexing cheeks of Victoria's bare bottom. Victoria squealed in vexation at the hot liquid sensation of Elvert's tribute.

Rachel acted quickly. She bent forward and took tight purchase on Elvert's exploding penis. She gripped it in her fist and pointed it away from Victoria's bare bottom. The succeeding bursts of Elvert's helpless passion curled in thick strings from the tip of his prick to splash onto the lower rails and tracks of the apparatus below

Victoria's bench. Rachel held Elvert's penis, her cheeks flushing bright crimson, until his orgasm was finally over.

Victoria watched also, peering backward over her shoulder, her sweetly beautiful face showing an expressive mixture of fascination and distaste. Lucas watched in stunned disbelief.

After Elvert's orgasm ended, both Rachel and Lucas helped their companions extricate themselves from the tight bonds that confined them to the bench and to the stool. Rachel dabbed away the splashes of Elvert's passion that glistened across Victoria's bare bottom.

Elvert cleaned and dressed himself once Lucas had freed him. Rachel sent Lucas to Victoria's chamber at the back of the house to retrieve the other glass slipper that Victoria had kept since the night of the ball. Victoria told him where it was carefully hidden. It was not long before the four friends, now presentable and set aright, descended the steps that led down to the room where the Vicomte Valprom and his dragoons waited.

Victoria was in the lead. None could guess from her regal bearing and composure the indignities to which she and Elvert had just been subjected. She walked barefoot, in her simple household dress, but her demeanor and comportment bespoke royalty and flawless, youthful beauty. The Vicomte Augus Valprom stood, an expression of wonder lighting his face, as he beheld Victoria as she entered the room. Her dainty hands carefully cradled the exact mate of the glass slipper that he held in his own hands.

"She cannot be the one! It is simply impossible!" Marcella cried, desperate in her wavering assurance.

"Simply absurd," Regine spat, before she and Marcella were forcibly removed from the room by the same dragoons that had taken Ana out. Rachel stood with Lucas and Elvert. They smiled their loyalty and friendship. Dona Alicia Antigua stood stock still, her features conveying disbelief and wonder. Victoria sat in the chair before the Vicomte Valprom and delicately raised her skirts to her knees. She gracefully extended her lovely little point-toed feet and the vicomte slipped on first one beautiful little shoe, and then the other. All in the room gasped out in mutual wonder then. The fairy shoes sparkled with a rainbowed brilliance, which, though subtle, scintillated and played about the carpeted floor at Victoria's feet.

The vicomte, with a titanic effort, tore his glance from the most sweetly compelling feet he had ever seen and raised it to Victoria's face. She gazed down at him like a breathless young queen. She was in absolute control, and showed no sign of the lewd sensual madness that had swept over the others.

Victoria's lips were prettily parted and her smile conveyed both grandeur and feminine innocence. The twelve tall dragoons knelt as one, first removing their plumed caps, their heads bowed in solemn respect, though their eyes were captured by the exquisite beauty of Victoria's legs and feet.

Victoria's three friends knelt also, their faces alight with pride and adoration. The Vicomte Valprom prostrated himself on the floor at Victoria's feet. His penis lurched in tribute to her charms, dangerously close to emission.

"My queen!" was all he said.

Victoria graciously raised her pretty high-heeled foot to the lips of the Vicomte Augus Valprom. "Then as token of your fealty and devotion, you may kiss the toe of my shoe!" she cooed, her voice as soft as satin.

As Augus Valprom bent to do just that, his penis jolted against the tight fabric of his riding pants, and with a low cry of mingled adoration and shame, he ejaculated. Victoria looked down upon him, her lips pursed in amusement, her eyes wide with sympathetic innocence.

CHAPTER TWENTY-SEVEN

A fortnight later, the bells of wedding jubilee tolled from the palace towers high above Calauverge.

White pennants streamed in the fragrant breeze of a midsummer's morning from every embrasure and battlement. The streets of Calauverge were decorated with bright ribbons, flowers, and awnings in celebration of the joyous occasion.

In keeping with the traditions of the land, when Prince Steven Targete married Victoria, the Princesse de la Masquerade, he would become king and his lovely bride would be queen. King Philip would remain a sovereign-advisor, content to help his son steer the ship of state rather than direct its course himself. Ambassadors and dignitaries from all the royal houses of Europe, along with the families of the most noble lords, descended upon the island kingdom in honor of the occasion. The names of the royal wedding guests covered an ornate vellum scroll that flowed with intricate script to an unrolled length of nearly three hundred feet. Royal heralds, trumpeters, and musicians filled the palace and the city. Regiments of royal guards and cavalrymen were equipped in white livery for the occasion.

The celebration would be complimented by the finest grape harvest yet on record in all the island kingdom. Older fruits of the Madeira vineyards of Challon and Pompere awaited the joyous day, deep in cool mold-hung cellars, safe in oaken and cherry casks.

Whole caravans of freight wagons rumbled through the streets of Calauverge and travelled up the high road to the royal palace. Each wagon was laden down with gifts for the royal couple. Fine laces, ornate gold and ruby-crusted jewelled eggs from the court of Catherine the Great, intricate sets of fine silver, three hundred white horses, and many other presents beside, graced the long colonnade of gifts just below the royal ballroom.

Rachel was Victoria's maid of honor; Lucas and Elvert also received high places in the wedding party. Victoria impressed the entire court with her flawlessly regal and graceful bearing. The strangest gift of all was a pretty young maiden, bearing a black onyx signet, who arrived for Victoria's service. Her name was Saniea, and she was sent from the Goddess herself as a token of good will. She and Victoria formed a fast and deep friendship almost at once.

Rachel was at first a trifle resentful, but she and Saniea soon built their own close relationship and became companions in their own right.

The royal wedding was held in the high chapel of the inner palace, a great vaulted room, alive with the floral brilliance of a thousand stained glass windows. Victoria's gown was a high-collared, bodiced contrivance of sheer gossamer and lace, mixed with floral motifs worked in satin. Her breasts nearly spilled from its low *décolletage*.

Cinderella

Silken hose caressed Victoria's lovely legs and her pretty little feet were tiptoed in dainty white shoes, with pink velvet bows and quite scandalously high heels.

The guest list included the Vicomte Cevenne, the comte de Languedoc, and the Baron Roth-Haupfelds. Each simply kissed Victoria's proffered lace-gloved hand. Their worshipful eyes conveyed no hint of their knowledge of her previous life. They adored her absolutely and their lips were silent of their past connection.

Lord San Sebastian was also included in the throng of five thousand invited guests. He too kissed Victoria's hand, though he looked up into her warm, smiling face with more than a little relief that her Goddess-replacement—who he felt had nearly killed him—had returned from whence she came.

The bells in the towers of the high chapel joined those of the royal parliament tower in proclaiming the culmination of the wedding-coronation, and the flower-strewn courtyard filled with festive peals of celebration.

Prince Steven Targete and Victoria, the Princesse de la Masquerade, walked from chapel to audience hall to mount their shared throne.

In that very moment the influence of the Goddess extended through Victoria over the island kingdom. The old pensioner was abed, sick and very frail, when suddenly his daughter's taut face relaxed a trifle. A wild scent seemed to fill his room, and when his daughter looked upon him, she found he had changed! A smiling young man got up from the bed, golden-haired, with muscles rippling. He laughed, picking her up bodily and danced with her about the room.

"Victoria is queen," her roared in glee. "Victoria is queen and I shall be the captain of her guard!"

He looked down tenderly into the eyes of his daughter who had unselfishly cared for him for so long.

"And you!" he said softly. "I can promise you that

your poverty is ended! Your children will never again know hunger!"

Calauverge went fairly mad with revelry and celebrations that lasted for a fortnight after the wedding-coronation. The parades and wild dancing lasted day and night, with scant pause for sleep. Fireworks were launched from the palace battlements to explode in ornate patterns over Calauverge far below.

CHAPTER TWENTY-EIGHT

The night following the end of the wedding celebration, Victoria was informed that the Vicomte Cevenne wished to see her on a matter of state urgency.

She received him in her informal audience room, while being tended by several of her personal maids. He entered, obviously very fearful, and scanned the room before moving quickly to bow at Victoria's feet and kiss her hand.

The palace maids ignored his entry, concentrating rather on placing Victoria's hair in a high and formal swirl. Their lovely young queen was readying herself to attend a small, informal party held in celebration of her perpetual banishment of Regine and her daughters. Victoria's sources told her that Regine's sister owned a small chateau deep in the Loire Valley and made her living disciplining certain masochistic members of France's nobility.

The vicomte spoke quickly, his voice thick with worry and fear, "There is a conspiracy to unseat the Targete family from the throne. The lives of your royal consort, his younger brother and even King Philip are in danger and have been for some time!" He turned imploring eyes to Victoria. "You must believe me for now your own life is in jeopardy as well!"

Victoria was silent for a time, and then had her maids summon Saniea. While Saniea listened intently, Victoria questioned the Vicomte Cevenne.

"Who is involved in the conspiracy and when do they plan to move against us to seize the throne?"

"Lord Carlyle and the Marquise de Besançon are central players in the plot. There are others but I do not know who they are. I fear the conspiracy is quite extensive. As for their timetable, I am not sure. Until now I thought that they were not ready to move, but now I think the coup to be imminent—though I am not certain."

"Why have you not warned the house of Targete before?" Victoria asked, her eyes searching the vicomte's face. Saniea sat studying him also. Her pretty lips pursed thoughtfully, her long dark hair framing her sweetly youthful face.

"The de Besançons dispatched two female assassins to kill me and, when they failed, they tried to kill my wife and very nearly succeeded in killing one of my household servants. I sent a courier to warn King Philip, but never heard from him again, I fear that the assassins may have killed him. At the royal ball I set out for the king's gallery but I knew I was being watched. I think perhaps two pretty young women in gold colored gowns were the assassins but I am not certain. At any rate they were ceaselessly hanging about the door to the stairs of the royal gallery and I felt they were waiting for me to leave the safety of the crowd. The only time they left the doors to the gallery steps was to take Prince Rupert to one of the drawing rooms. I feared they were going to slit his throat, but as I listened at the door I heard no commotion. Who knows how they may have toyed with him? When next I looked up into the royal gallery I saw the Marquise de Besançon sitting with the king. They were conversing like old friends and I despaired of being believed. I have been in hiding with my family and preparing to send another courier with a message. When, however, you married Prince Steven, I decided I must risk all and tell you everything I know of the plot."

Victoria reached down to gently ruffle the vicomte's hair as he still remained kneeling before her. She smiled and thanked him, though there was a hint of doubt in her demeanor.

Saniea spoke. "He speaks the truth my lady. The Marquis and Marquise de Besançon, Lord Carlyle and Lady Jane Broughton, the Contessa of Albion and her consort are all involved in the conspiracy."

"The regiment of the palace guard called the Royal Watch is also involved, as is the Baron of Telfleur. The female members of the conspiring families have been sent to the continent until the coup is successful, all except Justine de Besançon who, though cruel and pleasure-loving, has no part or knowledge of the treason. In fact, the Goddess wishes her to enter into your circle of confidantes, Victoria."

"Very well," Victoria said, a malicious smile upon her lips. "Summon to me the captains of all palace guard regiments save for the Royal Watch. I shall issue arrest warrants for all the conspirators this very night. There is no need to alarm King Philip with this dreadful news until the crisis is past. Prince Steven is fast asleep and so is the king. I shall act decisively and act tonight. This will be my present to the house of Targete. I shall assume my full powers as co-regent and diffuse the crisis at once."

That very night, troops of the royal guard, along with mounted dragoon regiments, descended on the Chateau Furnald, home of the de Besançons; the Chateau Ceriffe, home of the Baron Telfleur; and Deianeira, home of Lord Carlyle and Lady Jane Broughton. All the conspirators were arrested and placed in the royal dungeons beneath the palace. After a brief skirmish, all the troops of the Royal Watch regiment of the palace guard joined them there.

CHAPTER TWENTY-NINE

News of the plot's overthrow spread throughout the kingdom like wildfire.

Victoria was held in awe by her subjects and immediately placed on a high pedestal. Prince Steven and the king declared that the week of the plot's overthrow should be one of annual celebration throughout the kingdom, extending the revels which would occur on the dates of the wedding coronation.

One of Victoria's glass slippers was set upon a marble pedestal in Market Square and guarded by a brigade of dragoons day and night. Victoria summoned the captain of her personal bodyguard, who was also a lieutenant of the royal dragoons. She instructed him to carefully search the palace to see if there might be any hidden devices of injury or assassination secreted by the plotters.

The captain of her personal bodyguard and his inspectors found an ornate sculpture given by the

Marquise de Besançon to King Philip but a month before. It was a beautifully crafted bronze of Aphrodite cradling a naked Cupid across her lap. Upon closer scrutiny, the inspectors found the Cupid's arms were movable and that the tiny bow was workable and strung with a minute, though razor-sharp, arrow. The device was set by means of a partial clock mechanism to fire the poison-tipped arrow directly at King Philip's dressing chair. The murderous little sculpture was rendered harmless at once, and it was not long before a well-respected valet of King Philip's joined his comrades in rebellion in the deep dungeons below the palace. The discovery of the assassination machine at the initiative of Prince Steven's lovely young bride Victoria made the entire kingdom adore and respect her all the more.

Godilieva Prumm held a great ball in Victoria's honor at her estate, the Chateau Piron.

Like all of Godilieva's functions, the occasion bespoke wild excess. Wicked costumes were provided for all the young women of Victoria's court and the guests. The brevity and price of the fashionable little gowns stunned even the most jaded courtesans. Godilieva provided shoes as well, with heels so high as to render walking impossible. Indeed, the feet of every pretty guest were posed in outrageous tiptoe by the design of the shoes. Their consorts carried them up the broad marble steps to the long, pillared ballroom of the Chateau Piron. In honor of Victoria, all the female guests wore ornate masks, to go with their lovely— though wicked—shoes.

The guests were served by naked servants who found themselves mercilessly teased and handled, sometimes to ejaculation, by the haughty, masked young women to whom they catered. Victoria led the throng of guests in toasting her loyal friends Rachel, Elvert, and Lucas.

Cinderella

Godilieva's wild party lasted nearly two days. Godilieva, ever an orchestrator of spectacle, had her servants put on a show for her assembled guests. A gigantic naked male servant, who was equipped between his legs like a studding bull, was ridden about the room by the maids of Chateau Piron.

While the male and female guests watched wide-eyed, the huge naked servant was spanked, subjected to every humiliation, and then finally masturbated before the crowd as a tribute to the Goddess.

Victoria requested and received permission of the house of Targete to subject to conspirators to public ridicule. They were borne ignobly to Market Square in cage wagons and removed, bound fast and naked, before a laughing crowd. Some were placed in genitalia pillories and whipped by nearly naked, masked women until their buttocks were striped and heavily welted. The crowds cheered the whipmistresses on and the blows fell mercilessly.

Other conspirators were bound in hanging cages, so placed that women could masturbate them with long, looped sticks from passing carriages that stopped in the square simply for that purpose.

Victoria had placed Mademoiselle Seline d'Elbernne, the royal dressage trainer, in charge of the total degradation of the conspirators and she delighted in the smallest detail.

Finally all conspirators were forced to kneel in a circle about the marble pedestal where Victoria's glass dancing slipper glittered in the sunlight. They were whipped by pretty young women in riding boots and plumed caps, while being forced with threats of emasculation to masturbate in tribute of the pretty little shoe and the masked princess. As their sperm spurted from their loins to splash the base and column of the pedestal, the conspirators were told to gaze upon the symbol of their utter defeat. They hung their heads in shame as they took their hands from their shrivelling and shrinking organs while the crowd laughed at their humiliation.

CHAPTER THIRTY

The full moon shed its beams of light over Calauverge and the palace crag above, on the last night of the high celebration.

In his palace chamber, Prince Rupert lay naked upon his bed, his bare buttocks clenching as Godilieva Prumm stood over him and beat him soundly with a thick leather strap. Saniea had told Victoria of his penchant for spying on the royal dressage trainer and masturbating. Victoria had laughed at the tale but seen to it that Prince Rupert received a suitable punishment as well.

Prince Rupert's head rested in the lap of his idol, Mademoiselle Seline d'Elbernne herself, who stroked his perspiring brow and told him to lay still or Godilieva would begin all over. Seline, like Godilieva, was naked save for a short black rubber apron and dainty high-heeled dancing shoes. Seline had worked on Prince Rupert first, slowly spanking and masturbating him until he sobbed with pain and frustration.

Prince Rupert's arms were bound to his sides and a pink ribbon was tied about the shaft of his agonizingly erect penis. Already the poor boy was utterly enslaved by his two disciplinarians and hopelessly twisted about their little fingers.

At last Godilieva finished her measured count and both women rolled their royal prisoner over on the counterpane of his bed, giggling at his twitching and erect penis as it bobbed into view. They then proceeded to nearly suffocate him beneath their bare bottoms, taking turns forcing him to impart the intimate delights of oral pleasure upon their most private recesses. His penis was tickled and stroked, but always abandoned just short of relief.

In a large tower room, whose windows overlooked an intricate walled formal garden, King Philip Targete lay gasping. He reclined upon his bed, lying upon his back. His nightclothes had been tucked up about his hips and stomach, leaving him in the ever so undignified position of being naked from the waist down. His face was flush with the deep crimson hue of total and absolute embarrassment. He looked like he was quite unable to gulp enough air into his lungs and, indeed, nearly had the appearance of someone being slowly strangled.

Giselle and Justine de Besançon knelt prettily upon his bed, one on each side of his spread and trembling legs. Both haughty young women wore expressions of proper innocence as they took turns ever so slowly masturbating their king.

Both Justine and Giselle wore high-collared gowns that were almost staid in their styling. Their breasts were completely covered, and, though their kneeling positions revealed a good portion of their pretty thighs, their dresses were otherwise fashioned to cater toward discretion. They had removed their pretty little high-heeled dancing shoes before kneeling up upon the bed to masturbate the king, so both were quite comfortable.

King Philip appeared to be anything but comfortable, however, and he was certainly not relaxed. Giselle and Justine de Besançon had been masturbating him gently for nearly two hours and neither showed any willingness to let him spurt his relief into their shaming, maddening hands. King Philip was drenched in sweat and his lower lip trembled spasmodically. His eyes were clenched tightly shut as his body pleaded eloquently for release by its twitches and contortions. He looked like a man experiencing the horrors of low interrogation by torturers with all the leisure in the world to apply the utmost pain.

Giselle fisted his big, drooling sex organ, pulling the loose skin up and down the thick shaft with an expression of superiority and mild distaste upon her lovely features. She looked down at her gasping victim with an air that bespoke disapproval and censure, as if she despised his weakness in finding himself helpless to escape the merciless torment of her hands.

Justine's eyes were glued to the motions of Giselle's hands, as they slowly abused and tormented the king's big, flopping sex organ.

The head of the king's penis was crimson and gasping clear droplets of his excitement. The drops oozed and dribbled down upon the little beringed fingers of his cruel masturbatrix.

Justine giggled.

"It's my turn to masturbate him for a while, Giselle; you've been working him for twenty minutes and it's high time I tried my hand again."

Giselle's glistening hands reluctantly abandoned the big, twitching toy that sprang up from a forest of hair on the king's lower belly.

Every vein stood out in swollen, bloated relief down the length of the king's tormented penis. Neither young woman bothered to use any sort of lubrication, so the king's penis was more than a little red and chafed where their insistent hands had coaxed and teased it over and over again.

Giselle maliciously grasped the large heavy sac of the king's scrotum and squeezed it in her tightly clenching fist to express her displeasure with Justine's insistence for a turn.

The king gritted his teeth and arched his back high enough above his bedclothes so that his tormentors giggled to view his clenching buttocks.

Giselle maintained her grip upon his testicles but eased up on it a bit while Justine smirked and extended her pretty hand to recapture the big pulsing sex organ and begin its slow abuse all over again. She pumped his penis firmly, her face alive with knowing delight, savoring every exquisite agony she forced the king to undergo.

Giselle released King Philip's scrotum so she could watch it slap and dangle unprotected against the crack of his bare bottom.

Justine masturbated the king with a lewd little twist of her wrist at the completion of every stroke, and did it almost roughly.

Giselle watched fascinated, her nose wrinkling a trifle.

"It's disgusting when you masturbate him like that, Justine! It makes him enjoy it too much."

Justine laughed, a low, sweet, gloating sound, and changed the tempo of her strokes. She used shorter, more teasing strokes for a time, though she applied them just as firmly. Then she changed her method altogether. She released the king's penis and the young women giggled as they watched it quiver and twitch as if still undergoing its goading abuse from their soft hands. Then Justine extended her left hand and grasped King Philip's penis just below the head, using only her thumb and forefinger. She stroked him ever so gently while using the thumb and index finger of her right hand to squeeze and tease the king's left testicle, sliding it about in the soft wrinkled sac that hung helpless between his legs.

Giselle thoughtlessly wiped her own glistening hands on the king's taut thigh and awaited her own turn with a self-satisfied smile.

The king had become a mindless, yearning thing, appearing for the moment scarcely human at all. He writhed and squirmed, tensing and contorting every muscle and feature in the throes of the slow torturous delight his two sadistic subjects were inflicting upon him.

As Justine continued the stroking, King Philip began sobbing and giving vent to a low series of incomprehensible whimpers. Indeed, he hardly knew who or where he was. He was maddened, enslaved, and reduced to a simple, yearning, infantile need by the slow masturbation. He was a pathetic thing, his very being and existence centered in what their knowing hands did between his legs.

Across the walled formal garden from King Philip's tower room, Prince Steven Targete was also experiencing his own brand of torment. His chamber was located in a wing of the palace opposite that of his father. Prince Steven knelt naked upon his marriage bed, his big royal sex organ rigidly erect and twitching the fever of his arousal against his stomach. Victoria lay before him. She was naked and the sweetly lewd curves of her body bespoke her attitude of catlike relaxation. Her nakedness offered him sweet consolation. Her bottom and slit were lushly exposed as she lay wantonly before him, her legs apart and knees bent.

Victoria's hair was up in a regal swirl and there was a

wicked flush to her cheeks as her eyes caressed her royal consort's penis. The prince's eyes were locked upon Victoria's dainty little feet. Victoria wore her glass slippers, and the prince was enthralled at the exquisitely high crystal heels, and the low jewelled sides that have flirty exposure to his dainty bride's high arches. The little magic shoes were also cut low at the toe, low enough for the pretty little clefts between Victoria's toes to beckon him—as the cleavage between a woman's breasts would lure so many others.

Rachel knelt upon the bed beside Prince Steven. She smiled as she reached through between his legs from behind, under his buttocks, and suavely handled and squeezed his scrotum. Saniea stood at the bedside, one knee bent and resting on the coverlet, her other foot tiptoed upon the carpeted floor.

Both Rachel and Saniea wore pink and white hourglass corsets, from whose tops their pretty breasts spilled free. Neither young woman needed their corsets for any purpose other than to further enslave the fetshistic sensibilities of Prince Steven.

Saniea casually rested one of her hands on Prince Steven's bare bottom, stroking it nonchalantly, almost as if he were but her toy or plaything.

Rachel bent forward, the erecting pink nipples of her breasts prominent in their dangling as she did so. She released Prince Steven's testicles and, still reaching from under and behind, she captured his big sex organ in her brazen little fist. While Victoria watched, smiling, Rachel began to slowly fist Prince Steven's penis, allowing its turgid girth to slide to and fro in her maddening palm.

Prince Steven groaned and begged Victoria to let him enter her. Victoria giggled and stretched, noting her consort's helpless gaze fall upon the large, conical nipples of her pert breasts.

"I will soothe you with my body, and allow you to

plunge your fevered organ into the warmth and sweetness of my slit," she cooed, her voice silken with pity and understanding. "But first I would ask my royal liege to grant me the tiniest and perhaps most insignificant boon ever bestowed."

"Anything!" Prince Steven groaned as Rachel's pumping fist maintained the peak of his sexual excitement. "Anything at all! For the love of God, Victoria, anything!"

Victoria squirmed and sat up, leaning back, balancing her upper body with her palms flat on the coverlet behind her. She arched her back, emphasizing her breasts and causing her slit to pout open deliciously just a bit in the process, exposing the pink flower of her sex and the swollen morsel of her clitoris.

"Then, sweet Steven," she purred. "Put the determination of the conspirators' fate in my hands. I wish absolute say in what punishments and degradations may befall them."

"Yes Victoria! This I grant you—their fate is in your hands. Utterly. Please, Victoria! Show some mercy! Now at least may I enter you?"

Victoria replied with but a gesture to her maids. As his smiling bride reclined again in lewd comfort before him, legs spread, knees bent and feet raised, Saniea pushed Prince Steven's buttocks forward. Rachel steered his penis toward Victoria's pink slit with one hand, while the other used his testicles as a bridle to also direct the forward motion of his hips. In a moment, Prince Steven Targete's penis felt the soft, pink heat of Victoria's sex close around it as it slid, ever so slowly and inch by inch into the luscious depths of her cleft. He gritted his teeth, the heavy muscles of his arms and shoulders knotting visibly at the sensation. She was tight! She gripped him in the velvet and sweetly tormenting embrace of her intimacy.

Rachel and Saniea giggled. Victoria sighed with pleasure, her cheeks reddening further as her lips prettily parted. Rachel renewed her grip on Prince Steven's testicles and Saniea began to pass her hand invasively into the crack between the cheeks of his bottom. For the first time the prince felt himself so hard that his rigidness caused him actual pain. He was erect beyond belief: His very soul seemed concentrated in the rigid flesh with which he impaled his sweetly naked bride.

Prince Steven hung his head and jerked his hips as he felt Saniea suddenly push an unlubricated finger into his anus. His haggard eyes focused enough, as he looked down at their coupling, to get the distinct impression that Victoria was devouring him, and that her prettily pink and swollen outer lips were sucking at him, trying to coax the precious manhood from his loins. He raised his eyes again to her flawless feet, tiptoed and revealed in the delicate embrace of her wickedly high-heeled fairy shoes that sparkled and shone.

With the assistance of the lewd goading hands of Victoria's maidens, Saniea and Rachel, Prince Steven began thrusting to and fro, grunting in his animal pleasure as his big truncheon-like organ slid into the clinging depths of his lovely, squirming consort.

He could sense the eagerness of a huge load of sperm, churning and building in the silly, dangling sac between his legs. Rachel enjoyed slapping and pinching it as she drove him to ever greater feats of lovemaking. His prostate was prodded and stimulated most wickedly by Saniea's lewdly wiggling finger. It dilated the tight, cringing clench of his anus.

The prince was panting, slack-jawed and haggard in the urgency of his arousal. Suddenly Victoria squirmed away and his penis slopped from her cleft. He tried to follow her retreat with his hips but the hands of her maidens prevented him. He trembled in the urgency of his despair.

"I request but one more sign of your royal favor, my prince," Victoria cooed, giggling at his anguish. "May I be allowed to do anything I wish to the conspirators? Really anything at all? May I have them executed in the most excruciating and slow torment if I desire?" she breathed, the lips of her slit oozing the moisture of their combined excitement.

The prince's reply was but a barely audible groan of acquiescence.

A moment later he was again thrusting in the sweet depths of his enslaving bride, while her maidens gripped his testicles and violated his anus with their fingers. His eyes locked on Victoria's pretty, tiptoed little feet in the enticing clasp of their fairy shoes, and, with a cry of delight so potent it was akin to agony, he ejaculated into her. Victoria lay savoring every hot, fertile spurt of her royal consort's orgasm. She milked him dry with a wiggling motion of her bare hips, and as she did, she laughed, a low yet sweet sound.

A soft sound of triumph.

Orgasms are healthy.

(and they feel really good, too.)

a public service message brought to you by

Good Vibrations
Promoting sexual health & pleasure since 1977

quality erotic toys and videos: call for a FREE catalog!
1-800-BUY-VIBE • goodvibes.com

Skin-tight shiny leather

the click of high heels on the dungeon floor, the swish of the whip, women in uniform, submission and domination

If you love these things, as we do, you may like to know that they are covered with style and intelligence by the world's leading fetish magazine,

SKIN TWO

Produced in London to the highest standards, SKIN TWO features the world's best writers and photographers in the BDSM subject area

Available from the best fetish stores worldwide, SKIN TWO can also be ordered directly from the publishers, on the web or by phone

We also make top quality fetish clothing and run the world's top international fetish event

Check us out today at **www.skintwo.com**

From the USA, phone us in London on

011 44 20 7735 7195

mastering mary sue $7.95
mary love   ISBN 0-9716384-7-0

Mary Sue is a rich nymphomaniac whose husband is determined to pervert her, declare her mentally incompetent, and gain control of her fortune. He brings her to a castle in Europe, where, to Mary Sue's delight, they have stumbled on an unimaginably depraved sex cult!t

judith boston $7.95
titian beresford   ISBN 0-9716384-6-2

A new, unexpurgated edition! Naughty Edward's compulsive carnal experiments never go unpunished by the severe Judith Boston. Edward would be lucky to get the stodgy companion he thinks his parents have hired for him. Instead, an exquisite woman arrives at his door, and from the top of her tightly bound bun to the tips of her impossibly high heels, Judith Boston is in complete control.

the limousine $7.95
n.t. morley   ISBN 0-937609-26-9

Luscious Brenda was enthralled with her roommate Kristi's illicit sex life: a never-ending parade of men who satisfied Kristi's desire to be dominated. While barely admitting she shared these desires, Brenda issued herself the ultimate challenge – a trip into total submission, beginning in the long, white limousine where Kristi first met the Master. Following in the footsteps of her lascivious roommate, Brenda embarks on the erotic journey of her life.

the parlour $7.95
n.t. morley   ISBN 0-9716384-3-8

"The Parlour is a hot new take on a classic fantasy-or two! For those with dreams of service to a sexy, powerful couple, look no further.

—Carol Queen

"A beautifully dark and wonderfully erotic tale, The Parlour succeeds admirably at what so many erotic novels can only try to be: a story of sex and power to the Nth degree.

—M. Christian

provincetown summer $7.95
lindsay welsh   ISBN 0-9716384-2-X

From the casual encounters of women on the prowl to the enduring erotic bonds between old lovers, these women will set your senses on fire!

Pure lesbian libido explodes in this book of short stories written by and about the sisters of Sappho. This completely original collection is devoted exclusively to white-hot desire between women. In the title story, a writer shares a passionate but impossible love with an artist in a sleepy seaside town. From the casual encounters of women on the prowl to the enduring erotic bond between old lovers, the women of Provincetown Summer will set your senses on fire!

the virgin $7.95
alison tyler   ISBN 0-9716384-4

Does he satisfy you? Is something missing? Maybe you don't need a man at all — maybe you need me. I know I need you.

Veronica answers a personal ad in the "Women Seeking Women" category — and discovers a whole sensual world she never knew existed! And she never dreamed she'd be prized as a virgin all over again, by someone who would deflower her with a passion no man could ever show...

love's illusion $7.95
anonymous   ISBN 0-9716384-9-7

Elizabeth Renard yearned for the body of rich and successful Dan Harrington. Then she discovered Harrington's secret weakness: a need to be humiliated....her slave, and together they commence a journey into depravity that leaves nothing to the imagination--nothing!

man with a maid $7.95
anonymous   ISBN 0-937609-25-0

The ultimate epic of sexual domination. In the "snuggery", a padded soundproofed room equipped with wall pulleys, a strap down table, and a chair with hand and leg shackles. The untiring pervert, Jack, bends beautiful Alice to his will. She corrupts her maid and her best friend into lesbianism, then the three girls lure a voluptuous mother and her demure daughter into the snuggery for a forcible seduction and orgy. Perhaps, the all-time hottest book!

ORDERING IS EASY

orders can be placed by calling our toll-free number
PHONE: 800.729.6423/FAX: 310.532.7001/E.MAIL: magic-carpet-books.com
or mail this coupon to:
Magic Carpet Books
15608 South New Century Drive
Gardena, CA 90248

QTY.	TITLE	NO.	PRICE

We never sell, give or trade any of our customer's names

SUBTOTAL	
POSTAGE + HANDLING	
TOTAL	

In the U.S., please add $1.50 for the first book and 75¢ for each additional book;
in Canada, add $2.00 for the first book and $1.25 for each additional book.
Foreign countries: add $4.00 for the first book and $2.00 for each additional book.
Sorry, no C.O.D. orders.
Please make all checks payable to Magic Carpet Books
Payable in U.S. Currency only. CA state residents add 8.25% sales tax.
Please allow 4-6 weeks for delivery.

Name: _____

Address: _____

City: _____ State _____ Zip _____

Telephone: [   ] _____

E.mail: _____

Payment: ☐ check ☐ money order ☐ visa ☐ mc ☐ amex ☐ discover ☐ diners club

Card No: _____